"Why did you leave me standing at your door that night?"

His voice was husky at her ear, his breath warm at her neck. "You know the night I mean."

Her chest tightened beneath his scrutiny. She moved over to the medicine bag lying beside her on the grass, hastening to tidy her bottles. "Now I know you're feeling better," she said, trying to sound casual. "But next time I'll give you laudanum instead of morphine."

He reached out and touched the back of her hair, weaving his fingers between the black strands and her spine, sending waves of pleasure tumbling across her skin. "Why did you flee? Don't you want to answer the question?"

"No," she whispered, completely still beneath his stroke.

"Then how about this one—if you were going to run away, why did you tempt me? Why, Amanda, did you bother to kiss me back?"

Praise for KATE BRIDGES's book

The Doctor's Homecoming
"Dual romances, disarming characters
and a lush landscape make first-time author Bridges's
late-19th-century romance a delightful read."
—*Publishers Weekly*

"The great Montana setting and high Western action
combine for a top-notch romantic ending."
—*Romantic Times*

"Kate Bridges has penned an entertaining,
heartwarming story that will live in your heart
long after you turn the last page."
—Romance Reviews Today (romrevtoday.com)

Luke's Runaway Bride
"Bridges is comfortable in her western setting, and her
characters' humorous sparring makes this boisterous mix
of romance and skullduggery an engrossing read."
—*Publishers Weekly*

THE
Midwife's
Secret

KATE BRIDGES

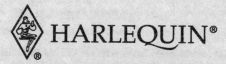

HARLEQUIN®

TORONTO • NEW YORK • LONDON
AMSTERDAM • PARIS • SYDNEY • HAMBURG
STOCKHOLM • ATHENS • TOKYO • MILAN • MADRID
PRAGUE • WARSAW • BUDAPEST • AUCKLAND

ISBN 0-373-29244-9

THE MIDWIFE'S SECRET

Copyright © 2003 by Katherine Haupt

This edition published by arrangement with Harlequin Books S.A.

Visit us at www.eHarlequin.com

Printed in U.S.A.

Available from Harlequin Historicals and
KATE BRIDGES

The Doctor's Homecoming #597
Luke's Runaway Bride #626
The Midwife's Secret #644

Please address questions and book requests to:
Harlequin Reader Service
U.S.: 3010 Walden Ave., P.O. Box 1325, Buffalo, NY 14269
Canadian: P.O. Box 609, Fort Erie, Ont. L2A 5X3

Dedicated to all the loving mothers I met
while working in the Neonatal Intensive care.
My heart goes out to each of you.

Chapter One

May 1888, Town of Banff
Rocky Mountains Park, District of Alberta

It had been eighteen long months since she'd felt aware of a man's gaze.

The man she was here to meet, Tom Murdock, stalked into the sawmill at precisely ten-fifteen and slammed the papers he was carrying onto the corner desk. With a groan of frustration, he glanced up through the cloud of sawdust to the back, noticed Amanda Ryan walking toward him, and caught and held her eye.

A sprinkle of nerves took root in her stomach. Raindrops trickled down her bonnet. Horses clomped in the mud outside.

"That's him, that's the boss," said the thin Scotsman leading her, but Amanda had already deduced it from Murdock's confident glare.

With a quick, sharp breath, he released her from his scrutiny and shouted orders to his men, straining to be heard above the buzzing band saw and clatter of boards. Dressed as if he'd just come from outdoors, he tossed away his cowboy hat, yanked off his long leather duster, then shook the rain from its massive sleeves. He wore miner's pants, indigo Levi's with orange stitching that melted into muscular thighs, and black pointed boots with shiny silver toes. Of strapping height, with powerful hands and a dark profile, he looked more like a leader of a cattle drive than mill owner and log builder. He radiated masculinity. And anger. And she'd come at a bad time.

"Right this way, ma'am." Dressed in baggy overalls, the Scotsman squeezed between two worktables and ignored the other men's inquisitive glances. "Watch your head."

Amanda veered beneath the water pails hoisted from the ceiling—a first line of defense in case of fire. The scent of pine and sawdust tickled her nostrils. Ignoring her queasy stomach, she pressed her oilskin slicker to her green twill skirt and wove from the side door from where she'd entered, to the front where Tom Murdock stood. Who could be upset here, surrounded by the beauty of ice-capped mountains, springtime air and acres of trees? And where was his partner, Mr. Finnigan? The older, stockier man she'd met in Calgary town, eighty miles east, who'd smiled readily and invited her to come? Should she leave and come back later?

"Watch your step over that log."

Passing over it, she smiled gently at the bearded, friendly faces. Many of these men had wives and children. Some of their wives had yet to become mothers, and hopefully Amanda would grow to be their friend, even deliver their babies.

Of course she shouldn't leave. She'd come a long way to hire Tom Murdock, and a long way to build her dream. Just because he was in a surly mood didn't mean she had to be.

While the sun broke through the clouds, streaming

through the high windows, highlighting his black hair and clean-shaven jaw, a big, wet, white husky dog barreled around his desk.

"Wolf," he shouted, pointing to the door. "Get out of here. You're soaking wet."

His laced, black leather vest fell open, revealing a row of shiny buttons down a crisp blue shirt. His rigid face softened into handsome planes and deep dimples. He was a pleasure to look at, but that's not why she'd come. Good looks were not something you could respect, like being a hard worker, or a good husband, or a kind man.

The Scotsman leading her stepped aside. "Tom, this lady says she wants to speak to you. Mrs. Amanda Ryan."

Mr. Murdock regarded her for a moment. Heat emanated from his muscular body, as well as the scent of shaving lotion. A current of curiosity passed between them.

Amanda peeled off her worn leather gloves, tugging a bit harder over the finger with the hole, and held out her hand. Tilting her face at him, she sent him an exploratory smile. "How do you do, Mr. Murdock?"

Her knitted scarf dipped around her throat. Green. His eyes were green, but he didn't smile back.

"Mrs. Ryan. Call me Tom." As he nodded, a strand of black hair slid down his forehead. Leaning closer with extended palm, he glanced down at her ringless fingers.

Self-conscious, she gulped. She'd finally removed it six months ago and could no longer hide behind it when a man looked her up and down. But, selling her ring had funded a dozen bottles of medicinal tonics, one crate of silk sutures and a brand-spanking-new fetal stethoscope.

When his long, calloused fingers laced into hers, his grasp was firm and warm. It maddened her the way her pulse began to rush.

"I'm in a bit of a jam and don't have much time," he

said. "If you've come about the woodstove, I can have i delivered in the morning. Works fine, never gave me trou ble."

She glanced to where he motioned. Surrounded by a stone floor that would deaden any stray sparks, a shiny cast-iron stove crackled with fire. Beside it sat an empty smaller stove, the one to which he pointed. She took a step closer, enjoying the warmth on her frozen toes. It'd taken such a long time for her to stoke the fire in the shack thi morning due to the damp wood, and longer still to get i rolling to this wonderful blaze. She hoped her grandmothe was still enjoying its heat.

"I'm not here about the stove."

When she turned around again, he was seated and rum maging through his desk. "Well, whatever it is, my fore man will handle it. I'm expected somewhere in twenty minutes. Patrick, come here a moment," he shouted to the far side of the mill, at one of the men hammering a cabinet then reached back into his top drawer. "What on earth is this?" He pulled out a gray envelope, tore open the lette and began to read.

While keeping her waiting! Perhaps she should take he business elsewhere and forget about his excellent recom mendations. How could he let her sit at his heels while he read his correspondence?

He winced, then paled. A flash of vulnerability ripple across his face.

Was he in some sort of trouble? She didn't know much about him. Mr. Finnigan had mentioned he was unmarried that the sawmill was a Murdock family business and tha Finnigan himself was simply an investor. She moaned with sympathy. You never knew what someone else's pain fel like until you walked in their shoes. The neighborly thing to do would be to help instead of to criticize.

Stepping closer, she squeezed the frayed ribbon of her purse. "What is it? Is it...bad news?"

He jerked out of his concentration. A wave of redness washed his face. "Nothing." He folded the sheet and jammed it into his denim pocket.

Before she had a moment to think about that, a flash of white fur caught the corner of her eye. She looked up as the dog raced toward her. He shook himself, spraying water in a six foot diameter.

Amanda yelped, then laughed, cupping a hand over her face.

Disarmed, Tom leaped from his chair, encircling her waist, tugging her out of the spray and standing in the line of fire himself. "Wolf!" When the dog stopped, Tom peered down at her. "Sorry, he's gotten you all wet."

She managed an awkward smile, well aware of his hard fingers pressing through her clothing. How long had it been since a man had touched her?

"Luckily, I've got my rain slicker on," she murmured, inches from his face.

At least the dog had penetrated Tom's veneer. Transformed him, really. Creases appeared at the corners of his warm eyes. A boyish smile touched his mouth and those deep dimples reappeared. The scent of his shaving lotion met her nostrils again. It was something she missed, sharing those intimacies with a man, waking up together, watching him shave.

Uncomfortable with the awkward silence and his touch, she wriggled free and removed her plaid bonnet. She wasn't ready for any man to touch her, no matter how much she wished she were. He cleared his throat with an anxious cough, but his eyes followed the movement of her hand as she patted the damp bun beneath her mended kerchief. When he glanced at her plain clothing, she moist-

ened her dry lips. How long had it been since she'd dressed
to impress anyone?

The moment dispelled at the sound of the dog chewing.
Tom's tall dark figure sprang toward a stack of lumber
where the dog crouched, chewing on something brown.
"Hey, dammit, give me back my glove."

The husky wanted to play. Tom charged around her, his
broad shoulders leaning behind the desk, but the dog escaped with a glove between his teeth. The two were amus-
ing, and the beautiful animal reminded her of her own two
lovable mutts, Missy and Ranger, which she'd lost when
she'd lost her husband, William. She missed the dogs.

"I'll get the glove," hollered Patrick as he whizzed by.

With a look of exasperation, Tom shoved a hand through
his wavy black hair, turned back to her and caught her soft
laughter.

"My dog's well trained, don't you think? Took me
nearly a year to get him to this level of obedience."

"You've done a marvelous job."

Tom's subtle grin played with her pulse. Friendliness
flickered in his eyes, and he seemed ten years younger.
Mid-thirties? This time, he really looked at her, her simple
country bonnet, her kerchief, her high-laced, worn-out
leather boots with the temporary insole covering the hole
she hoped he couldn't see. Heat seeped into her cheeks as
she glanced away. But the boots *had* lasted one more winter, and the cold weather *was* almost over for the year.
Speaking of which, her toes had warmed up, but were
thawing and tingling with pain.

She moved her slender body away from the fire. Perhaps
she should ask for his partner. "I've…I've come to see
Mr. Finnigan."

Tom shifted. A thundercloud appeared on his face again.
"Finnigan? What business do you have with him?"

The harsh tone of his voice sent a shiver through her spine. How could a man turn abruptly from one mood to the next?

"I'm new to town, and you're a builder, aren't you? And you do supply lumber? That's what Mr. Finnigan told me."

As she stared into Tom's intimidating features, the firm line of his lips, the challenge in his eyes, her body vibrated with determination. She already knew he supplied the cheapest lumber in town, seeing that he owned the only sawmill.

"Zeb Finnigan hasn't been in town for five days. How did you happen to meet him if he wasn't here?"

"We met in Calgary last month, at the Cattlemen's dinner. My...my husband used to be a member."

"Used to?"

She gulped. "He's gone now. I'm...I'm widowed."

The harsh line of his black brows softened, but the caution in his voice remained. "I'm sorry."

She pressed her lips closed and glanced down at the floor, away from his appraising stare. She hadn't meant to...tell a *fib*. It just came out. In truth, she hadn't known for sure what she'd say when someone asked about her former husband, and yet here it was. She'd fibbed. And why?

Because looking up at Tom Murdock, she didn't feel like fessing up to her failures. She didn't feel like having him look at her with sorrow, the way everyone always did. She'd finished with her mourning, and her anger at her former husband, and was ready to start anew. She was eager to resume the skills her late grandfather—one of the hardest working doctors in Calgary—had taught her. Midwifery skills to help the women who sought her help, and medical knowledge to tend to children and their ailments.

Realizing her fib wouldn't hold for long, for as soon as Mr. Finnigan arrived, he was a man who knew the truth about her husband, she felt herself flush. She'd fibbed and hadn't done it well.

Amanda straightened her spine. It was no one's business but hers. "I've bought some property and I'd like to build a log cabin. Something simple, with a couple of spare rooms in the back." She'd already allotted every nickel of her small inheritance to put toward her practice and the children.

"I think I've heard of you," he said, recognition shimmering in his bright eyes. He sat on the edge of his desk. The wood creaked beneath his muscled weight. "You're new to town, just been here since yesterday, right? Are you that woman I spotted at the mercantile yesterday afternoon, who rides that—"

"What difference does that make?"

"No difference." His grin was charming. The row of strong, white teeth wasn't quite centered, so his smile seemed especially intriguing. "We're friendly folks in Banff. We've never seen anything like it before, that's all."

She pressed her fingers into her skirt, clasping her bonnet, surprised again by his unpredictability.

He stood and grabbed his duster. "Sorry about... Let's start again. Forgive me, I really do have an appointment. Patrick will be back in a minute to take the information from you, and I'll take it from there. What property did you buy?" He tugged on his cowboy hat. Now he was even taller.

Tension left her muscles. She fell into step with his long stride as he walked to the door. "That pretty square along the mountain, on the end of Hillside Road."

He stopped in surprise. *"What?"*

When she stopped beside him, her dangling purse slammed against her slicker. She answered cheerfully, "Mr. Finnigan sold me that shack on the five-acre square—"

"On the right or left side of the road?"

"The left."

His voice lowered to a deadly calm, his face grew solemn. "The one with the huge spruce? Lot D ninety-five?"

What was wrong with him? She swallowed past the dryness in her throat. "Yes. And the tall pines. You know it?"

Bracing himself, he stepped back and stared at her. "What the hell is going on here? Finnigan sold you *my* property?"

Her heart began to thump. She answered in a rush of words. "Well...it might have belonged to you and Mr. Finnigan at one time, maybe as partners here at the sawmill, but didn't he tell you? He sold it."

Tom blinked, then grinned slowly. "This is a joke, right? Dammit, my whole morning's been one whole joke, hasn't it? Finnigan's been known to pull my leg, he's a real practical joker around here—"

"I don't know what you're talking about, but he sold me that property."

He paused, then clenched his jaw. A moment passed. "I don't believe you." His menacing stance caused her stomach to quiver. "You might be part of this whole thing." His eyes narrowed. "Lady, just who the hell are you?"

A warning voice whispered at the back of her mind, but she ignored it. She lifted her chin a notch and matched his icy gaze with one of her own. "I told you who I am. And I don't like the way you're talking to—"

"Do you have a deed?"

"Of course I do."

"Let me see it."

She fumbled in her purse. "It's right here." It was right here, but she was darn well keeping it to herself. There was a problem here. A *big* problem.

Out of the corner of her eye, she pretended to reach into her bag, but she judged the distance to the door. Three feet. What would he do if she refused? He wouldn't try anything physical in front of witnesses. And if he did, she'd kick him as hard as she could. Her heart drummed. She dug her heels into the floor and met his eyes without flinching. "On second thought, I think I'd better wait for Mr. Finnigan. I'd rather deal with him."

In a flutter of arms and legs, she sprang to the door for freedom. Neighborly or not, she didn't like Tom Murdock.

"Get off me, Wolf," Tom shouted.

Wolf clamped his teeth on the edge of the note, trying to pull it out of Tom's pocket, but Tom grabbed it back. He stepped around the playful dog and tore after Amanda Ryan. He couldn't let her escape without seeing the deed. Where'd she go?

He glanced down the street past a horse and buggy, past the tinsmith's, the apothecary's, the boot-maker's and finally past his brother's office with the freshly painted sign: Dr. Quaid Murdock. Tom wheeled around to scour the other side of town. Soaring through the pine trees of the Rocky Mountains like a massive fairy-tale castle, the new Banff Springs Hotel glistened in the spreading sunlight. The largest and most expensive hotel in the world was a month away from opening. No sign of—

What was that? Around the corner, the edge of a petticoat and hem. He raced toward it, turning into the lumberyard.

The rush of waterfalls over the man-made dam echoed

in the sunny air. The park teemed with wild animals. A dozen bighorn sheep grazed the slopes, and red squirrels raced down the aspens. He glimpsed her near the back of the building, sliding onto her bicycle. She'd left it leaning underneath the side door canopy, which had protected it from the light rain.

He stomped toward her in the mud. A stack of quarter-sawn lumber loomed at his shoulders. In drier conditions, they wouldn't be alone. A dozen of his men would be splitting logs and unloading wagons.

"Stop right there." His voice thundered across the fifty feet separating them.

Her eyes blazed into his as she worked harder to speed up, trying to tie her bonnet while grabbing the handles at the same time.

"Leave me alone," she shouted, leaning into the wind. "Or, I'll…I'll call the Mounties."

He swore under his breath. The Mounties, federal agents appointed to keep law and order in the West. He planned on seeing them himself. Hell, he'd already set up an appointment with his Mountie friend, and she was making him late.

Was she working with Finnigan? Did the two of them plan to build a log cabin on the property together, maybe sell it for a larger sum? Or was Finnigan working alone, and an even bigger bastard than Tom had first imagined?

Things had been going pretty well up until nine o'clock this morning.

Then at the bank, when the bank's president, Mr. Thimbleton, swore up and down that there was no more money in the sawmill account, Tom had seen firsthand what Finnigan had done. Cleared it out. The whole fourteen thousand, seven hundred and thirty-three dollars. An all-time high due to final payment they'd received Friday for construction on the Banff Springs Hotel. More money than Tom had ever seen.

Finnigan had planned it well. Hadn't even bothered to leave Tom the payroll for this coming week. Never mind Tom's other bills—the sawmill's mortgage, payment for his youngest brother's law school tuition, payment on his middle brother's medical supplies for his new office. Finnigan hadn't even left enough to cover Tom's gift to his pa, the new team of horses.

Tom kicked the dirt. *Dammit.*

He'd written a bank draft Saturday, but it hadn't cleared the account before Finnigan had, which meant Tom'd have to give the horses back. Who could rob an old man in Pa's condition? And Tom had worked for weeks to select those horses, gentle mares that wouldn't spook Pa, but strong enough to till soil and pull stumps, if that's what Pa chose to do with them.

Amanda mounted what looked to be a cracked leather seat. She headed toward him, veering to his left. The solid rubber tires dug a good one-and-a-half-inch groove into the soft mud. It'd be easier to ride on the pebbly street, or the side of the road where new grass was growing. But first, she'd damn well had to pass by him, and he wouldn't let her get away before she talked.

"You're going to ride that thing in the rain?"

"It's no longer raining."

He pulled in a deep breath of cool mountain air and blocked her path. As he moved, the note in his pocket slipped out, but he shoved it back in. He braced his hands on either side of his hips to confront her.

Her blue eyes flickered. With a look of defiance, she rose off the seat, her skirt catching in the cracked leather and pedaled faster toward him. "Get out of my way or I'll run you down!"

When he caught the flash of terror in her eyes, he realized with a thud she was physically afraid of him. Afraid of him? With a shudder of guilt, he stepped out of her path to show her he meant no harm.

"I'd never lay a hand on a woman. You have nothing to fear from me." He lowered the harsh tone of his voice. "I just need to get the facts straight." Was it possible she'd bought the land from Finnigan, fair and square? "Don't you want to get them straightened out, too?"

She gulped and slowed down. He placed a firm hand on her bicycle handles to help balance her stop. The wire basket hooked to the front shifted with a sack of packages.

Dismounting, she planted a firm foot on both sides of her bicycle. Taller than most women, she reached to his jaw. She was thin, with a pale complexion, square cheekbones, wiry black hair and long feet, but something about her…

She dressed in baggy clothing, as if to hide her figure. Under normal circumstances, he found that more alluring in a woman than tight blouses and low-cut necklines. It always made him imagine the curves she might be hiding. But these weren't normal circumstances.

"Cripes, this is heavy." He glanced down at the metal frame, the chain-and-sprocket-driving rear wheel, the almost equal-size rubber tires. Was that why she was so thin? Because the bicycle was heavy and hard to ride?

The bars felt cool beneath his heated grip. "How did you get that property?"

"I bought it."

"From Finnigan?"

"That's right."

"When?"

"Last month in Calgary."

He scowled. When he got his hands around Finnigan's

throat... *Hell.* Looking into the clear eyes of Amanda Ryan, he vowed he wouldn't lose his piece of property. That land alone was worth more than his little cabin behind the sawmill.

Her jaw stiffened. "I thought you had an appointment."

"It can wait." Her gave her body a gaze from head to toe.

She stepped back, flushing. "What do you want from me?"

"Some answers. Have you ever met Finnigan before?"

"No."

"Are you living up in the shack now?"

Wisps of black hair framed her creamy skin. "Yes."

"Yesterday, I spotted you with an older woman. Who's she?"

"My grandmother."

The animation of her face held him rooted. "Just the two of you staying up there?"

She spoke with a composed, regal quality, in direct contrast to her words. "And my *shotgun.*"

He laughed at the contradiction. "Pardon me, I wouldn't want to come between you and your shotgun." He paused. "How can you afford to live alone?"

If she was offended by the comment, she didn't show it. "I'm a midwife and make my own way. That's why I want the log cabin built, to set up a practice."

A midwife? Well, that seemed like a fairly honorable way to make a living. You couldn't fake being a midwife. He shoved a large hand into his Levi's pocket. On the other hand, there'd been a quack or two who'd passed through here before, pretending to be doctors when they weren't, taking money from people and selling medicinal tonics that were nothing more than pure alcohol.

She folded her arms across her chest. Her slicker ballooned beneath her. Her throat looked warm and satiny at the opening of her collar, but he *wasn't* noticing.

"Now," she said, "let me ask you some questions."

He pulled back and let go of her bars. "Go ahead."

"Finnigan sold me this land without your knowledge?"

He clenched his jaw. "Seems so."

"Was it your land, or the sawmill's?"

He propped a hand on his hip. She asked good questions. "The sawmill's," he said with irritation.

"He's your partner. Does he have signing privileges?"

Yes. Goddammit, yes. Tom avoided an answer. "That seems to be the question, doesn't it?"

Staring into a stranger's eyes, he couldn't bear to admit his stupidity in trusting Finnigan. Tom had given away a full partnership two years ago for a huge five-thousand-dollar investment. But the money was used for the sawmill's expansion, which Tom needed to offset the costs of putting his brothers through medical and law schools.

Her bonnet dipped. "Well, it seems simple enough to solve. I've got my receipts from Mr. Finnigan. I paid my money, and as his partner, you got your half. But let's ask him. You said he's been out of town for five days. When do you expect him back?"

Tom laughed without humor. "Three days ago."

Her shoulders sagged. "Oh."

Shaking his head in disappointment, he deliberately kept his voice low and friendly, hoping she'd abide him. "Please, may I see your deed?"

Her lips tugged. She hesitated for a moment. Sliding one leg over the seat and bars, she carefully extracted the caught fabric of her skirt. The bicycle was well worn, a touch rusty in spots, but recently polished and oiled. As the rest of what she was wearing, it was second or third hand. Was that a split skirt she had on?

He'd never seen one before and couldn't help but stare at the way the green fabric shifted around her slender-ankled boots, one of which was unlaced. And staring at a woman's boots and ankles…it was a racy thing for him to do. No, Banff hadn't seen anyone like her before.

Her mended clothing bespoke of poor times. How could she afford his five acres and the cost of building a log cabin? Had her husband left her that much money? If he had, why hadn't she bought herself some decent clothing? Or a horse?

Or was this simply an act? Was she a cohort of Finnigan's? Pretending to be poor, but secretly accumulating a fortune.

He leaned closer and surprised himself with the next question. "Why don't you still wear your wedding ring?" It was out before he could stop it. But now that he'd asked, he was glad he had. Maybe her astonishment would cause her to blurt a clue. "I mean, most widows do."

Her cheeks deepened to a brilliant red, the same hue that adorned maple trees in the autumn. "I sold it. To pay for medical supplies."

It was his turn to feel embarrassed. He shuffled in his boots. "I'm sorry. That question was uncalled for."

She merely stared. Her eyes were the most striking thing about her. She had deep black hair, but blue eyes. Not brown as you might expect would go with black hair, but tender blue.

She unfolded a yellowish piece of paper from a similar-colored envelope. "Can I trust you to show you this?"

Could *she* trust *him?* He shook his head in disgust at the question and slipped it and the envelope from her fingers.

Looking it over, he let a long sigh escape. It looked legitimate. Signed and dated in Calgary. The barristers and solicitors seal. Finnigan's signature. Because they lived in

Canada's national park, no one in Banff actually owned the land, just the buildings, but they might as well have. The grid sections were leased from the federal government for forty-two years, renewable in perpetuity. According to this deed, she'd bought his building and the rights to his property. But who could really tell?

"Thank you, I'll return it when I've had it verified."

"What?" She leaped into the air, trying to swipe it from him. *"Give that back."*

He pulled away and bumped shoulders with her, surprised at the jolt that shot through him. "I will, after I've had a chance to show it to someone."

"I didn't *give* it to you. I allowed you to look at it."

"Under the circumstances, I think I have every right to keep it for a couple of days."

Stepping closer until she was only inches from his face, she tossed back her head and glared at him. "If you tear it up…" Her blue eyes sparked against her fair skin. "Well, it won't make any difference if you tear it up."

He stiffened at the challenge. She grabbed for it one more time, somehow lost her balance, went careening over him and the bicycle, and he followed her into the mud.

"Oh, blazes," she muttered, one knee and one gloved hand sunk three inches deep.

Tom's rear end felt cold and wet, sitting in the muck, but he grappled to rise and to help her. "Are you all right?"

She got up first, hoisting her sopping skirts, disentangling them from the bicycle chain.

"Just fine." Her boot had slipped off and she held her stockinged foot in the air. He hastily glanced away, aware of the impropriety. When she replaced her boot, she gave him a scowl that sent a shudder through his limbs.

Luckily, the deed was safe between his fingers. However, the note from his denim pocket had dropped into the mud beside her foot, face up, fully displayed for her to read. He leaped for it, but not before she gave it an innocent glance.

Embarrassed that she might read the two sentences, he snatched it from her view. It had nothing to do with Finnigan or the sawmill. It was private business between himself and Clarissa Ashford. One he hadn't even had a chance to fully digest himself. He groaned.

Amanda glanced from his face to the pocket where he tucked the note. Her cheeks heightened with color. "When you're done with my deed, you know where to find me."

She braced the handle of her bicycle, replaced her fallen packages—including a big turnip—and with barely a glance to him, tore off down the main street of town, through the people and horses on Banff Avenue.

Well, he hadn't made a friend out of her. But that wasn't the point, was it?

Two women, bundled in spring cloaks, gaped in amazement as Amanda passed. Children pointed to her bicycle. Keeping her head held high with dignity, she rode across the steel bridge. She turned up Hillside Road where the forest was so thick that trees didn't have room to grow wide, so they grew tall instead to reach the sun.

When he glanced down at the deed again, he braced himself. It was like a bad dream. Was he this close to losing everything he owned? And Clarissa, too?

And now, not only was he missing fourteen thousand dollars, but he had a sopping backside, as well. If Amanda hadn't fallen over... He glanced down at the mud. What was that peeking out of the wet earth? He picked up a piece of crudely cut leather. The shape of five toes were firmly grooved. A makeshift insole.

He gazed toward the massive mountains, searching for

her, but found an empty trail. The rain had washed the snow from the lower slopes and the southern ones were covered with yellow sun lilies. When he thought again of her glancing at Clarissa's blasted note, heat pounded through his muscles. How much had Mrs. Ryan read?

And why would he care what a stranger thought?

Chapter Two

What was she supposed to do about Tom Murdock?

Amanda's breathing grew labored as she pedaled uphill. The sound of wheels swooshing through grass echoed off the mountains. Imagine! He'd ripped her deed right out of her hands. Landsake's, it wouldn't help him. Yesterday on her arrival, she'd visited the land registry and *her* name was written in the ledger.

She thought of his note and bristled. Normally she'd never read another person's mail, but it'd fallen right beneath her nose. She didn't recall it word for word, but it went something like: "Dear Tom, I've decided to spend the summer with my family in Calgary. I'm taking this evening's train. Yours, Clarissa."

It was written on pretty stationery with fancy handwriting, and he'd turned tomato red when he'd looked at it. Nothing would cause a man to turn that red unless Clarissa was a woman he was involved with. Well, they didn't seem particularly close, as it was only signed *Yours,* not *Affectionately Yours* or *With Love.*

Hard to imagine that coldhearted man passionately involved with any woman. William had been in the beginning, but it hadn't lasted. They were in love, she'd thought.

Happily married homesteaders on their ranch just west of Calgary, trying hard to make ends meet and planning for a large family. Maybe if he'd paced his feelings, his love for her would've endured. The way a man's love was supposed to endure when he said his vows. In sickness and in health.

She'd heard William had remarried quickly; that his new wife was already in her eighth month. Amanda had silently forgiven him two months ago, when she'd decided to move from her family's home in Calgary to Banff and not let her anger eat her alive. There were more important things she could do, helping other women through the same horrible loss. If she could ease their burden, then she figured what had happened to her would somehow all make sense.

Dismounting her bicycle, she peered through the faraway pines and glimpsed her dilapidated shack, its chimney smoke rising above it, a welcome sight after her rough morning.

''Howdy, Missus Amanda!''

Laughter from the six smallest O'Hara children next door reached her. They froze beside their log cabin as soon as they caught sight of her. You'd think she were from another star, how awed they were by her bicycle. Pigs grunted in their fieldstone pen and chickens clucked in scattered directions. The children's dirty, smudged noses and exuberant waving brought a gush of warm, wonderful feelings. She waved back.

She was almost healed, she recognized with pleasure. That sudden stab of pain when she glanced at boisterous children was almost gone. And yet…other times, in her deepest thoughts, mostly during nighttime when she yearned for sleep but it wouldn't come, those same questions assailed her.

Did it make her less of a woman because she could no

longer bear any more children herself? Did it make her less of a woman because the one sweet baby she'd had, had come into the world stillborn?

Of course it didn't, she knew in her logical mind. But sometimes, in her illogical heart, she floundered. What kind of woman did it make her, when her husband had left her, divorced her, because of her inabilities?

Exhaling softly, she turned onto the dirt path, leaned the bicycle against the big spruce, then removed her store-bought items. She hadn't held her baby and that was her greatest loss.

Eighteen months ago, the people helping in the delivery, including her loving grandpa, thought it would be kindest to protect Amanda from that anguish. Placenta previa, they'd declared. Her placenta had partially covered her cervix. During delivery, Amanda had lost her baby as well as her uterus. Later, she'd learned that the little infant girl had taken two small gasps, then was gone. Amanda hadn't even seen her face.

What had she looked like? What would seven and a half pounds feel like to cradle in one's arms? Amanda had never paid deliberate attention before, holding other people's babies, but it wasn't anything she'd take lightly anymore. She hiked the muddy turnip into her arms. Would seven and a half pounds feel like this?

The rhythm of her breathing faltered. Too light.

She hoisted the sack of flour into her arms. Like this? Her throat ached. A touch too heavy. And Ten Pounds was clearly stamped on the burlap.

"Amanda, is that you?"

Amanda cleared her throat. "Yes, Grandma." Composing herself, she stepped into the clearing and bid good morning.

Dressed in dark clothing, in mourning for her husband

for another two months, Grandma flung a gray braid over her dumpling figure and smiled. She'd taken a chair into the sunshine and was working on her rag rug, an idea she had to earn them extra money. A fire blazed beside her— and the shotgun that protected them from marauding wolves and black bears.

Amanda couldn't bear to mention bad news. She would use her last three hundred dollars to build the cabin, despite Tom Murdock. William had left her with nothing. He'd taken the ranch, the cattle, the quarter section land, even her two dogs. And because he was an old friend of both law practices in Calgary, legally she hadn't stood a chance.

She also had her grandmother to support, despite the small inheritance Grandma, and the rest of the family, had received after Grandpa's fatal stroke. For the past five years while Grandpa had trained Amanda in his home, she and her grandma had spent most of their days in the pleasure of each other's company. Now the two women preferred to live together. Besides, Amanda's mother and father were busy tending to the rest of the family—Amanda's brother, and sister, and all their new babies—to tend to Grandma, so it'd worked out for the best.

"Howdy, honey. Did you meet Mr. Finnigan?"

Amanda slid her packages to the ground. "He's out of town. I met his partner, Mr. Murdock."

"Did he quote you a fair price?" Grandma's plump nose spread wider as she smiled, and Amanda realized how lucky she was, still to have her grandmother, to have this land, to have the sun shining on her face.

Amanda would shoulder the burden of Tom Murdock alone. "Mr. Murdock is busy with other projects, but there are two other builders in town. I'll visit them this afternoon."

* * *

Two nights later Graham Robarts burst into the sawmill startling Tom.

"What the heck are you doin' workin' so late?" asked Graham. "It's after ten o'clock." Short and blond, dressed in a fringed deerskin coat, he cast long shadows on the wall as he passed by the scattered kerosene lamps. Although a constable in the North West Mounted Police, he came dressed in civilian clothes as Tom had requested. I would arouse fewer questions.

Squatting beside the kitchen cupboard he was building, Tom tapped the cornice moulding into place. "If I get these cupboards finished by the end of this week instead of next, I'll *almost* be able to make payroll."

"Are these for the big hotel?"

"Yeah." Finer furniture had been ordered from Quebec and Europe for the hotel's public spaces—reproductions of English masters—but Tom was contracted for the everyday furniture for the kitchens, cleaning areas and staff quarters.

"Can't you get your men to help you?"

Tom towered over his friend. "That would compound my problem. I'd have to pay them extra for their time. I I work alone, I can speed the payments coming in."

"You can't work both mornin' and night. And when' the last time you ate anything?"

Tom blinked his tired eyes. "If I don't make payroll my men will lose their jobs. Eleven out of fourteen have wives and children to support. You know Donald O'Hara On top of his eight, he just told me he's got another one on the way."

The friendly wrinkles at Graham's eyes faded with concern. He was a good man, Tom thought, a childhood friend who'd grown up with him back east, halfway across the continent in the big city of Toronto. Where Tom and his father had practiced carpentry, Graham and his were in the police force.

"All right," said Tom. "Give me the bad news. What did you find out about that Ryan woman?"

"It's clear to me that the deed is binding."

The words caused Tom's body to sink. He picked up a piece of sanding paper and began rubbing. Deep in his heart, he knew that already. He'd known it two days ago when he'd checked the land registry, and then again when he'd reread the article of signing privileges in his partnership agreement with Finnigan.

"I'll do everything I can to find Finnigan," Graham vowed.

Clenching his jaw, Tom dug the sandpaper deeper into the wood. "The sawmill was nearly paid off. Tourists about to arrive, Banff about to expand. Lots of business for everyone." *And me, about to get married to a woman I loved.*

"Let me open an official file, Tom. Press the charges. We'll get Finnigan."

Tom sighed. Opening an official file meant opening his wounds to the world.

When he shrugged, Graham removed his jacket, picked up a rag cloth and tin of linseed oil, then began varnishing one of a dozen clock shelves. "How's Clarissa? How's she takin' this?"

Tom scowled. "She's not around. She left."

Graham squinted. "Aw, hell, I'm sorry."

Yeah, so was Tom. He thought Clarissa Ashford would be his wife. Originally from Ottawa, she'd moved with her folks to Calgary when they'd opened their jewelry store. When they'd visited Banff last summer, she bumped into Tom at Ruby's Dining and Boarding House, and extended her visit. She was a woman who laughed readily, enjoyed

an intelligent conversation and was eager to start a family
Tom's family. Maybe a son or two Tom could pass th
sawmill down to, or a daughter Tom could teach how t
ride, or how to appreciate a fine piece of furniture. Hell
had he lost that dream, too?

Clarissa had accused him of working too hard, of ig
noring her. She thought he spent too much time worryin
about his brothers and father, and not enough about *them*
He ran a hand through his sleek hair and wondered. Wa
she right?

If he didn't change his ways, she'd threatened, she'
leave and head back to Calgary. At first she said sh
wanted to help Tom and Finnigan expand their business
And how many times had she told them, with that teasin
smile of hers, she couldn't decide which one of them wa
smarter....

Hold on a minute. Tom's gut squeezed. She wouldn'
have... She couldn't have been part of Finnigan's leaving

Tom's palms began to slide with sweat. "If you ope
an official file, how confidential can you keep it?"

"Just between me and the sergeant, if that's what yo
want." Graham studied his friend. "Why don't you as
for Quaid's help?"

"My brother would just hit the roof. You know how
everyone panics in my family. Soon as there's a possibilit
of something going wrong, they panic. They panicke
about Pa, didn't they?"

When they'd decided to move West three years ago t
start the sawmill, Pa was as energetic and quick-minded a
a twenty-year-old. But very soon, he began the forgettin
spells, and it was Tom who'd taken over the business, wh
looked out for Pa. The rest of the family wanted him t
live with someone—a nurse or guardian—while they con

pleted their studies, but Tom insisted on Pa's freedom. Pa wasn't an invalid.

Even so, Tom didn't blame his family. They were scared. They loved their father and wanted the best for him. But it all washed to the same thing. Tom's family and his men all depended on Tom. Yesterday he'd carefully raked through the bills, looking for ones he could hold off paying. Gabe's Toronto law tuition could wait until the end of August. For Quaid's medical instruments, Tom would try for a credit note from the bank. As for Pa's horses... well, shoot.

"What are you going to do about Miss Ryan?" asked Graham.

"I'll go back and talk to her." He prickled with the thought of having to go back to beg for work. "If she hires me, I'll insist on a down payment. That'll make the rest of payroll for the week."

"What can I do?"

"Use your leads to find Finnigan." Tom glanced up from screwing hinges. He had to be careful how he worded his next request, for there were some things he couldn't share with Graham. "Find out if Clarissa's all right, back with her folks. Then check on Amanda Ryan's background. I've got this feeling...Mrs. Ryan's hiding something."

"They're blackfly bites, and all over his arms. No wonder Willy's scratching," Amanda said, helping the four-year-old boy off the worn, wooden chair. "Ellie, rub this calamine lotion on it twice a day, and bring your boy back in two days."

Morning sunshine poured through the shack's open door, around the six children, the damp, dirt floor, the tiny alcove of Amanda's narrow bed, then Grandma's in the other corner. The rain had left three days ago. The crisp mountain air smelled of budding trees.

Ellie O'Hara squinted at the homemade canning jar full of calamine. Her curly red hair streamed down her shoulders. She patted her four-month-pregnant belly in a loving, absent way that reminded Amanda how she'd once done that herself. Amanda swallowed and glanced away, but was very happy to help.

She'd taken a quick liking to her neighbor, who'd moved from Ireland ten years ago but still spoke with her beautiful brogue. "Aye, I was worried it might be measles."

"Thank goodness it's not, not in your condition. You've got to take care of yourself, too. Please go to the apothecary's and get those grains of iron. That's why you've been tired lately. Ask your older boys—Pierce, especially—to lift the heavy things. The smaller children will help you, too, won't you?"

A chorus of yeses and laughter filled the cabin. Amanda swooped them all outdoors, a mix of pigtails, freckles and scruffy woolen clothing.

"Hello!" A man's voice boomed through the tall spruces, startling everyone.

She quaked with apprehension when she saw Tom Murdock, sitting high in the saddle of his chestnut mare. He tipped his cowboy hat. When his questioning eyes sought Amanda's, she tingled with warning. Placing a hand on little Katie's shoulders, Amanda adjusted her kerchief over her long loose hair, then tugged her apron. Why did he always make her feel self-conscious of what she was wearing? And why was he here? To return her deed, she hoped, and not to argue further.

Ellie, with her petite figure and narrow face, stepped

toward him. "Mr. Murdock, how lovely to see you this mornin'."

"Ma'am," he replied, sliding out of his saddle.

His gaze searched the shack, glossing over the new curtain on the only window, the freshly scrubbed but weathered pine planks, and no doubt noticing the missing winter mud, and the missing cobwebs dangling from the half-rotten shingles.

"I'd like to thank you, Mr. Murdock," said Ellie in her brogue, "for givin' the extra work to Donald. Especially now."

Amanda recalled her husband worked at the sawmill.

"You're most welcome. How are you feeling?"

"Fine, thank you." Ellie flushed at his attentive gaze. "Come along, children, it's time to gather eggs." She stepped close to Amanda and whispered, "Are you sure six eggs is enough payment?"

"That'll be fine," Amanda said softly. "I haven't eaten eggs for almost two weeks and I miss them."

Ellie broke into a bright smile. Amanda was tempted to beg her to stay, to protect Amanda from being alone with Tom, but she knew she was being ridiculous. She battled with her fears and prayed Grandma would soon return from her ride.

When the O'Haras left, Tom looked up at the blue sky and removed his hat. His long hair was a rich, raven black. His clean-shaven jaw gleamed bronze in the sun.

"Good morning," he said again, intimately, addressing only her this time. A corner of his handsome mouth tugged up, almost apologetic.

She swallowed. "Good morning. What brings you here?"

"I've got something of yours to return." The muscles in his shoulders played beneath his shirt as he slid out a square yellow envelope from his leather vest. He offered it to her.

"My deed?"

"That's right."

She took it, being very careful not to stand too close. "Thank you." Flustered, she slid it into her skirt pocket, then tucked her baggy blouse into her narrow waistline. His eyes slowly followed the movements over her body.

When he didn't say anything more, she pulled in a brisk breath and steadied her nerves. "Well, I best be getting back to my duties. There's a young couple in town I met yesterday. They're expecting their first, and I promised I'd stop by." *Later this afternoon,* but he didn't need to know that.

"That would be the tinsmith's daughter, Fannie."

"That's right. Good day." She turned and walked away.

He sidestepped her and barred her path. Lord, the man was big. He peered at the shack, as if he were searching for something to prolong the conversation. "It's still lopsided and won't hold out for another year, but it must have taken you hours to scrub it down."

She followed his gaze. "It did." Thinking of the yellow envelope she'd just stuffed into her pocket, Amanda blurted, "I assume you verified my deed?"

His green eyes lit with amber. His profile exuded power. "Yeah."

She was curious to know what had happened to Mr. Finnigan, but feared mentioning his name might put her own property in jeopardy again, so she let the topic pass.

Her fingers trembled into her apron. "Well, then, I suppose there's nothing else to say. Thanks for dropping it by." She turned to go. Tom's warm hand grabbed her shoulder and spun her back, gently, sending her stomach twisting in a thousand directions. She blinked up at his handsome face, the dashing age lines around his eyes and mouth.

His gaze trailed over her forehead, down her lips and back into her eyes. "You know," he said with a soft voice, "you've got the saddest eyes I've ever seen."

Stumbling out of his grasp, she stammered, "What do you— How could you—"

Quickly stepping away, he played with the brim of his hat. "I'm sorry, it just struck me."

His comment left her speechless. What a thing to say! She wasn't sad, she tried her best to be cheerful.

He cleared his throat while she caught her breath, then he scratched the back of his neck. "We got off on the wrong foot, and I'm here to apologize. You're not making this easy." He stared off at the mountains. "I was thinking," he continued, "if you're still aiming to build your log cabin, I'd like to make a bid."

Her guard was stronger now. "Why?"

"What sort of question is that? I'm a builder and that's what I do."

She stood her ground. "Why do you want to build *my* cabin? I'm sure there's other work out there. For that fancy hotel, I imagine. And the others that are going up."

"I've got a large crew, and I'd like to keep them working." His tone was firm but civil. "Most of the large construction is over, and there'll be a lull in the summer."

"I just heard Ellie thank you for giving her husband *extra* work."

"He needs it." His dark brows arched with a challenge.

"No thank you, I don't think we could work together." In several long strides she wove her way into the forest, toward the river to haul some water. She had to do *something* with the extra energy he evoked in her, which he seemed to evoke every time they met. Grabbing the water yoke that lay along the path, she slid the smooth wooden handle across her shoulder blades, allowing the buckets to dangle from the ropes on either end.

"Would you stop running away from me," he said, following her, causing her to catch her breath again. "Don't you want to hear my bid?"

"There are two other builders in town, and they've already given me their quotes."

He ducked a tree. "Let's start over. I didn't mean to get mad at you in the mill. You happened to walk in while I was getting bad news."

From Clarissa? she wondered. No, it had started before he'd opened the note from Clarissa.

They reached the bank of the Bow River and stopped for a moment. She slid her yoke and buckets to the ground. The sound of surging water, three hundred feet wide, gushed around them. Cut logs thudded against each other, floating downriver from the lumbering camps, making their journey to Calgary.

When she glanced upriver, she spotted the huge brick-and-limestone facade of the new hotel. Only three short days ago, she was thrilled to have moved to Banff.

The town itself was less than five years old, the population under a thousand. In posters across the prairies, the Canadian Pacific Railway promised that a tourist industry would follow the building of their Banff Springs Hotel. They claimed it would make their railroad self-supporting, give the tourists all the excitement of the wild West without the pesky discomforts and create a spectacular opportunity for anyone wanting to be part of it.

She still wanted to be a part of it. What else would give her life meaning, but to open a midwifery practice and to put to good use the excellent training and experience she had?

"Let's see, how big do you want your log cabin?" he asked. "Twenty-four by twenty-four? One big room with a stone fireplace?"

Was there any harm in getting his bid? She didn't have to take it, and maybe then the man would leave. "I'd like to have two spare bedrooms attached, so that would make the overall building twenty by thirty."

"Two spare rooms? For a future family, I suppose."

The comment caught her by surprise.

"I mean," he explained softly, "if you do remarry, and you might, you might need the spare rooms."

"I'll be using them to take in homeless children."

The lines around his eyes deepened with respect. "I see. Unfortunately, Banff does get a few orphans. Mostly because of accidents. Sometimes an avalanche. Or consumption. Or a fire." He stepped back and seemed to soak her in. "How many windows are there to cut?"

"Four."

"Porch?"

"I'd like one around the front."

"Well, that's an easy estimate. I'd say it'd cost you roughly two hundred and twenty dollars."

With an exclamation of surprise, she dropped into the soft grass of the riverbank.

"I know I'm under the other two bids. I always am. I can cut and saw lumber cheaper than anyone else in town."

He was a lot under. Sixty dollars under. A world of difference.

"I paid Mr. Finnigan five hundred dollars for this piece—"

"*What?* You paid him five hundred for what?"

"For the shack, and the right to the property."

That, for some reason, seemed to knock the wind out of

him. He sank into the grass beside her. He really was surprised by Mr. Finnigan's sale, wasn't he? Well, it didn't matter. The money had still gone into their joint sawmill coffers. And Amanda was sure five hundred dollars didn't make much of a dent in the thousands of dollars of construction he saw in a year.

Standing up, he shoved his hat back onto his head. As she deliberated what to do, Tom dunked the buckets into the river and hoisted them to his shoulders. He did it with such ease, she wondered what it'd be like to have a man to help her here with the harder, backbreaking work. To spend the evenings together, to call on neighbors, to keep her body warm at night. But then, the last thing she wanted was another man. Some men couldn't be counted on when a woman really needed them, and she had no desire to find out what kind of man Tom Murdock was.

When she bounded into the clearing, Grandma, in her split skirt, turned down the path on the bicycle. "Honey, I'm back." Spotting Tom, she added, "I didn't know we had company."

"Howdy, ma'am. My name's Tom Murdock."

A smooth rider, Grandma gave a little gasp of delight as she dismounted. They gathered around the pounded earth by the logs where they usually lit the fire. With hesitation, Amanda introduced them. "This is my grandmother, Clementine Stewart."

"Pleased to meet you," said Grandma, patting her thick gray braids. "But I thought you were too busy to come around."

"I had a slight change of plans." He smiled graciously as they shook hands, then glanced at Grandma's dark clothing.

Grandma explained. "My husband passed away ten months ago. He was the dear fella who trained Amanda here. My poor, dear Scott, he taught this little lady everything she knows about medicine.''

Grandma rambled on, much to Amanda's dismay. Grandma loved to visit, and if you didn't watch, she'd spill every secret they had. ''He was a doctor, servin' the poorer folks in town, never insistin' on payment, but those who could paid mostly with goods. Matter of fact, one of his customers gave him this here bicycle. What was his name? Mr. Withers, that's right. He had gall bladder problems.''

With a twinkle in his eye, Tom leaned close to Grandma. ''He didn't get it from the bicycle, did he?''

''Heavens, no!'' Grandma shrieked with laughter. It had been a while since she'd had visitors, thought Amanda, and she should be around more people, if this is how much enjoyment she was getting out of Tom's visit.

''My sympathies on your husband, ma'am,'' he acknowledged to Grandma, then turned solemnly to face Amanda. ''I don't mean any disrespect, but you said you were widowed, as well. How long ago did your husband pass away?''

Grandma fell into a coughing spell at Amanda's obvious lie.

Amanda's heart lurched. The women stared at each other. They signaled wildly behind Tom's back; Grandma urging her to tell the truth, Amanda adamantly refusing.

''Yes, dear,'' Grandma said between coughs, ''go on, tell us.''

Amanda clutched her apron. She already knew Grandma's thoughts on this. That Amanda shouldn't hide anything from her past. That she should stand up to everyone who asked. *Nothin' to be ashamed of.* ''It's difficult for me to talk about, if you don't mind.''

Glancing toward his mare that was ripping grass by the

tree where he'd tied it, Tom tilted his dark head. "I understand."

"What exactly is so difficult?" Grandma raised her wide gray eyebrows and spoke innocently. "Tell the man what he asked."

Tom cleared his throat. He looked uncomfortable, getting trapped between the two women. "I don't mean to intrude."

Amanda pursed her lips at Grandma. "It's difficult to talk about the painful things in my past."

"Well, sometimes, they get less difficult the more you talk about them. Amazin' things can happen. Sometimes, you can start talking about your widowed past, and before you finish the sentence and you've got it all off your chest, you feel like you're not widowed at all."

Grandma eyed her. Amanda eyed her back. It was her concern alone. A blunt man such as Tom Murdock wouldn't understand.

Tom turned to Grandma. "Is that how you feel, ma'am, about being widowed?"

Grandma sputtered. "No."

Rubbing his smooth jaw, Tom looked more perplexed. "Well, I best be going."

He was probably leaving, thought Amanda with a twinge of embarrassment, because he thought they were talking in circles. Which they were. Something she and Grandma were good at.

Amanda followed as he walked to his mare.

"Do we have a deal then?" he asked, unhitching the reins from the branch.

"How soon could you start?"

"How does tomorrow morning suit you?"

"How quickly could you get it done?"

"Six weeks."

"It's a deal on two conditions."

Tom groaned. "Go on."

"Number one. I get the agreement in writing, and receipts for each deposit."

"A handshake's not good enough, I see."

"Number two. For every day earlier that you finish before the six weeks is up, could you take off fifty cents?"

His eyes narrowed. "What do you mean?"

"I mean, I'd like to help with the work. The other two builders agreed, and for each day of labor, I'd be getting paid fifty cents a day. But only if it saves you time, so you're able to speed along to your next job."

"How much time could that amount to? You could help with clearing brush, but the other work is too heavy. You might save me two days, so you'd earn…maybe one dollar?" He gazed over the shack. "If you really need—" He caught himself before he finished the insulting comment. "All right. I'll need a starting deposit of ten percent in the morning. See you bright and early."

She pulled in a deep sigh of satisfaction. "See you."

He reached for his saddle horn, about to swing up, but stopped himself. He turned around. "The other two builders didn't really agree to your help, did they?"

A nervous smile fluttered over her lips. "Not exactly."

His lips curled as if on the edge of laughter. "Didn't think so."

As she turned to leave, he tapped her shoulder, reminding her again how long it'd been since she'd been touched by a man.

"If you don't mind," he said, "*I* still go by a handshake."

With a rapid thud of her pulse, she pressed her hot, wet palm into his slick, hard grip, trembling at the thought of what tomorrow would bring. What on earth was she agreeing to, with this forceful man?

Chapter Three

W hy did Amanda Ryan keep cropping into his mind?
The next morning, Tom stood shaving above the washstand, twisting his jaw into the air to scrape beneath it, and
while he should've been planning ahead to the day's work,
he thought of Amanda's strength instead. Moving to Banff
without a man, caring for her grandmother, hauling her
well-worn treasures into the tumbling shack. Not four days
in town and she'd already tended to her first two patients,
Ellie O'Hara, and the tinsmith's daughter.

In the barn, while he watered and fed his work horses,
he thought of her independence. The sheer physical stam-
ina it required to pedal a bicycle uphill when he was certain
no other woman in town even owned a split skirt. Hell, no
other woman in town lived alone in the countryside without a man to help her.

And while the early morning sunrise reflected into the
sawmill and he listed instructions to his foreman, he
thought of her again. He looked beyond her drab clothing,
the hidden pile of thick hair, the pale, indoor complexion,
and wondered how long ago she'd lost her husband. How
had she lost him? Who had been the messenger who'd

come to tell her he'd died? Had she wept for days? In whose arms had she sought comfort?

Questions he shouldn't have been asking of a widow he'd only met.

He should have been thinking about his mortgage payments and his problems with Finnigan and Clarissa. He'd just lost Clarissa and he should've been thinking more of her. But then, what else was there to think about? Graham was checking on her in Calgary, and there was nothing Tom could do but wait to hear.

In the meantime, he had a cabin to build.

When he pulled up to Amanda's shack in his horse and wagon, Wolf wagging his bushy white tail and Donald O'Hara sitting beside him ready to help, she was tossing a shovel of dirt onto the fire. Her hesitant smile brought color to her face and a youthfulness to her appearance.

She was ready to get started on the hard work, plowing ahead with her life, with or without her husband. It filled Tom with a healthy dose of respect.

"Top 'o the mornin' to ya, ma'am," said Donald, jumping off the wagon into the spring dew.

"Good morning," she shouted as Tom hopped off. Wolf bounded through the trees, barking at a groundhog. There were plenty of mountain animals for him to chase, and he gloried in it.

At the sound of their voices, a flock of swallows—hundreds of them—rose from the trees, sailed into the air, stretched their pointed wings and in unison, tilted their bodies into the wind. A magnificent sight.

With a gloved hand, he readjusted his hat and glanced back at the other two. Donald was busy unloading pick axes and shovels. Amanda was cupping a hand over her eyes, gasping in delight at the birds. She looked like a washer woman, bundled in a long wool skirt, with gray collar peeking out of a checkered flannel shirt—obviously a man's.

Her late husband's? Her late grandfather's? Something about her expression held Tom's attention. Her oval face was pale but proud, her nose straight, her curved, parted lips turned upward. When she turned back and caught his eye, he noticed again the sky-blue clarity of her eyes, and the sadness trapped there. What was she so sad about?

Why should it interest him so much? He averted his gaze and got to work. It was getting warm and he removed his tan suede coat. The sheepskin collar and lining might be necessary during the nightly freezes and morning chill, but not in the soaring sixties and low seventies of the day.

"I'd like it built right over here." She indicated the top of the property, at the edge of the one-hundred-foot clearing. Jagged mountains framed her intriguing silhouette.

He sauntered to where she stood and braced his hands on his hips. "It's a good location. Rain will drain down to the river, so the cabin floor will remain dry. It's close to the road for safety and convenience. And if we clear the six trees to the Bow River, you'll have an unobstructed view of the water."

He almost groaned as he said it, knowing at one time he and his father had planned a similar location. Pa no longer remembered. And as for Tom, well, he'd buy himself another pretty—*prettier*—piece of property.

Amanda gave such a huge sigh of contentment, his eyes followed the movement of her breathing down to her chest. A nicely rounded swell that she was hiding beneath shapeless clothing. He muttered to himself and glanced away.

After smearing the stinky concoction Amanda had given them on their skin for protection against the blackflies, Tom grabbed the two-man saw.

"Let's start with the big cedar." He indicated to Donald.

Although Donald was a good ten inches shorter, he was a muscular man who walked with a spring in his step and who easily took direction.

Amanda pulled on her leather gloves and Tom moaned. So she was serious about helping. Glancing up, he caught Grandma exiting the shack, dressed in a workman's shirt tucked over her dark dress. A quake of alarm bounced through him. Both of them planned on helping? It wasn't women's work, not even for younger Amanda, but certainly not a woman as old as Grandma.

Donald stopped. "Sweet Jesus O'Grady," he muttered. "You're hirin' women now, are ya?"

"It's not my idea," Tom declared.

"And a good mornin' to you, too," bellowed Grandma in good humor. "You can both close your mouths now."

How old must she be? Tom wondered.

"Sixty-two, since you're lookin' at me like that. But I'm not a weak old woman. I was splittin' logs and cordin' wood long before you arrived in your mama's cabbage patch."

"Don't worry about us." Amanda brought out her own shovel. "We'll clear the raspberry bushes and the juniper shrubs. We promise we'll stay out of your hair." She lifted her chin and met his gaze.

Was he supposed to allow *women* to help him? He was ashamed to see them work so hard. They should be sitting out in the sun and knitting, or mending clothing. But as much as he ached to have the final word and say no, a deal was a deal.

So while the men cleared the clump of green cedars, the women transplanted raspberry bushes to the far side of the shack. Amanda seemed to take pleasure in the company of Wolf, scratching behind his furry pointed ears and patting his luxurious double coat.

"Why, you've got two different colored eyes," Tom heard her murmur to the dog. "One blue, one brown."

Near lunchtime, Grandma waddled off to the privy. Amanda slid off her gloves and wiped the perspiration from her forehead. "It's time for lunch. I've got some stew."

Just then, Ellie strolled around the corner with a picnic basket, obviously thinking of lunch, too. "The children have eaten and the three oldest girls are hangin' the laundry. I thought we might go fer a picnic by the river."

Tom stumbled forward. For cryin' out loud, this wasn't a social call. This was difficult work, and if he accepted one invitation, the woman might appear every day. "I don't think so. I brought an apple and a slice of ham, and I'll enjoy sitting under that tree. Alone. You go ahead with Donald."

Amanda wrung her hands into her shirt and tried to slide out of the invitation, too.

Ellie insisted. "I'm not taking no fer an answer. I've been cookin' fer the last hour. Fresh bread. Fried-egg sandwiches and pickled peppers." Spotting Amanda's grandmother as she came out of the privy, she called out "You'll join us, won't you, Miss Clementine?"

Miss Clementine waved them off with a plump arm, like a queen waving from a balcony. "Go on without me. I'll have my tea and toast sitting on a chair, thank you."

It seemed there was no way out. But tomorrow, he vowed as he trudged through the aspens to the river, he'd come more prepared to say no. Around women, you always had to stay on your toes. How much time would this take?

Amanda found a seat on the other side of Ellie, by a large boulder heating in the sun. In the distance, the Banff Springs Hotel towered over the pines. While the women discussed babies and delivery, the men grunted a few words at each other about the snow melt. Tom was eating as fast as he could.

Amanda ate only half of his quantity. Her delicate lashes flashed over high cheekbones as she sipped cold tea. When Donald and Ellie nuzzled closer together, discussing something intimate, the silence between Amanda and Tom grew uncomfortable.

How did he get trapped in this awkward situation?

Finally, staring up the mountainside at the turrets and balconies of the big hotel, Amanda broke it. "Imagine being so wealthy you could afford to travel simply for the pleasure."

Tom leaned back on the hard log, his long legs crossed in front of him. "I can't imagine it myself. Starting at three dollars and fifty cents a room."

Amanda choked on her drink. "*Every* night?"

"Ridiculous what tourists will pay, isn't it?"

"Who are they, the people who come here?"

"Wealthy from the east. Some from the States. Most from England and the rest of Europe. Last year, we got almost three thousand visitors. This year, we expect five thousand. During the next three weeks, guests will be trickling into the big hotel. Hundreds of them, eventually, to fill the two hundred and fifty rooms. Some of the other boarding houses are full already. New restaurants are being built."

He gazed at the huge monument, designed after a Scottish baronial castle. "They're folks who want to dip their bodies in hot springs and explore uncharted mountains. Mountaineers, they call them in Switzerland. Only five miles on either side of this railroad has been surveyed, the rest is waiting for human contact. Have you ever been on top of a mountain?"

Their breathing came in unison. "No."

"You should. It's pretty." He couldn't miss the feminine, musky smell of her. "Have you ever tried the hot springs?"

She lowered her tin cup. "No," she whispered. "It appears I haven't done much."

"The Cave and Basin have cabins set up, one for men and one for women." He studied her. Clarissa had done it all—hiking, soaking in the hot springs, packing trails, fishing, hunting, ice-boat sailing in the winter. What would it be like to take Amanda to the springs? He was certain she'd be shy to remove her clothing, even if she were only surrounded by other women. Unlike Clarissa. "Did you know they accidentally built the hotel backward?"

She bit her lip. "Now you're teasing."

"Aye, it's true," Ellie piped in.

"Apparently," said Tom, "someone misinterpreted the blueprints."

"Blueprints?" Amanda asked.

"The drawing plans."

"Oh." As she turned to face him, her waist twisted, accentuating the outline of her breasts beneath the cloth. "But weren't you involved in its building?"

He pulled up to a sitting position and tried to find something else to look at, rather than her unexpected contours. He spotted an elk lapping at the river's edge. When he indicated the elk to her, she smiled, unaware of her allure.

"I supplied the lumber and one crew of finishing carpenters, but they hired their own framers. The front of the building is where the back should be, and the back is where the front should be. The kitchen staff got the best view of the river valley, so they're not complaining. Luckily, the view is beautiful no matter what direction you turn the hotel."

Donald plucked the checkered cloths from their laps and

packed them. "I hear now they're havin' their troubles with burstin' water pipes. Too much water pressure."

"Even after piping the water sixty-nine hundred feet," Tom said, "it still comes out strong. A hot one hundred and ten degrees. Amazing."

"Tell us what it looks like on the inside," said Donald. "Has the fancy furniture arrived fer it yet?"

Tom nodded. "Yeah, last week. In the ballroom, they've got mahogany dining chairs with ball and claw feet, look just like authentic Chippendale. Smooth as silk. As you enter the lobby, they've got tables with inlaid patterns of satinwood. Tapered legs and shield-back chairs to match, replicas of Hepplewhite."

When they'd finished eating, Amanda wiped crumbs off her skirt. Was it his imagination, or was she squirming away from him? Tom wondered as they headed back.

As soon as she spotted them, Grandma tore off on her bicycle to visit the neighbors rather than help in the afternoon. Tom breathed a huge sigh of relief, but Donald frowned in disapproval.

He leaned in close to Tom's ear. "Folks are sayin' they're a wee bit strange, ridin' around on that thing."

Tom kept chopping his cedar. "It's their choice to do as they please. Timmm...bbber." He watched the tree crash, being very careful of Amanda's whereabouts. He'd been aware of her whereabouts the whole day. He didn't want any injuries on his hands, he told himself.

But every time he looked her way or stepped closer to offer his help in dragging branches, she'd ignored him. Ignored *him!* He wasn't used to being ignored.

In the late afternoon, loading up their supplies, Amanda removed her gloves and ran a hand over her mass of thick hair, tendrils that had escaped in the wind. She'd been bitten by blackflies, Tom noticed, along her slender neck and in the hollow of her throat. Even the tops of her hands. He shook his head. Her lotion must have rubbed off. If he'd noticed earlier, he would have sent her to sit in the shack.

Donald took the shovel from Amanda. "Why do you ride a bicycle and not a horse?"

She clapped the dust from her gloves. "The cost of oats for a bicycle is remarkably low."

Tom laughed, but Donald wasn't so sure.

Keeping his gaze on Amanda, Tom replied thoughtfully. "And you don't have to water it, or shoe it, or ever file its teeth. Or worry that the wild hay you're feeding it is lacking nourishment because there was too much summer rain."

She made a quick, involuntary appraisal of his face. Her eyes softened. "That's right."

Yeah, she was a damn fascinating woman.

"I'll need a well dug," she said to Tom as they were leaving. "Can you set up a spring room in the cabin?"

"I could. I'll bring my father before the week is up. He's good at finding water. We'll locate the well, then build the house around that. You should go in now, put something on those bites." The last part came out more tenderly than he'd wanted.

She swallowed and nodded gently. Donald disappeared down the path that led to his home. Tom walked in the opposite direction to his wagon.

While the horse pulled out and clomped down the path, something made Tom turn to stare at the cabin window. She was watching him. A lantern glowed behind her, playing softly against her cheeks. When she pulled the curtain closed, his body sank with an unexpected feeling of...what?

Disappointment. He turned around and settled into the stiff wooden seat. So what if he was a little lonesome.

He certainly knew the cause. It had nothing to do with Amanda. With a weary sigh, he thought about what he'd lost with Clarissa.

During breakfast, Amanda found herself peeking down the path for signs of Donald and Tom more frequently than necessary. Their fourth day together, and they'd gotten into a rhythm.

"Is *he* here yet?" her grandma asked over porridge, scrutinizing Amanda.

"No sign of *them.*" Amanda knew what her Grandma was up to. What she'd been up to for the past year, trying to attach Amanda to every available, half-decent man who came calling.

"I'm just eager for the company of friends, Grandma. Good hard work, clear mountain air and sunshine is what both of us need after the year we've been through."

"Why don't you tell people the truth—"

"I think I hear a horse." Amanda bolted out the door, happy to escape the unwanted questions.

Donald hadn't arrived yet on foot, but Tom and Wolf were rolling in.

Tom's breath could be seen in the chill air as he leaped off the wagon. Looking up as she approached, he swung his lean body over the back boards and in one fluid motion, lifted the heavy axes. The warmth of his smile echoed in his husky voice. "How's everyone this morning?"

She stooped to pet Wolf's head. "Very well."

With powerful arms, Tom unhitched his horse. His shoulders filled the corners of his suede coat. He glanced at the stack of wood by the shack door. "I see you got someone to help you chop those branches we cut yesterday. That's a neat little pile of firewood.''

When she didn't meet his gaze, he glanced down at her, then at her fidgeting hands. Why hadn't she put on gloves before she'd come outside? She hid her arms behind her back.

With a calculating eye, he took a long step forward and slid out her hands, holding them in his. His head dipped so close to hers, she could barely think of anything else. He stared at her blisters. ''Don't tell me you chopped the firewood on your own? By *yourself?*''

She gulped hard. ''Who else is there?''

The question brought a twinge of compassion to his features.

After a moment of stumped silence, he nodded quietly, turned slowly, and began sorting through his tools. ''We should be finished clearing the trees today. Tomorrow, I'll bring the mules to dig the stumps.''

''When do you think your pa will be coming?''

''I asked him to come this morning. He lives just up the road and around the corner.''

Amanda glanced through the trees. A red wool coat and a white horse flashed through the leaves. ''Is that him now?''

Tom swung around. ''Pa?''

Wearing an old straw hat, a lumbering old man slid off his horse onto the road, but didn't head down her path.

She could see the resemblance. But where Tom was a thick, solid oak tree, his father was a fragile bending willow. Still, the handsome resemblance of dark features, square chin, and sauntering gait was striking.

''Pa!'' Tom shouted. His voice grew edgy and she wondered why. ''Over here!''

Old Mr. Murdock petted the husky dog circling around his work boots. "Wolf? Is that you?"

Tom smiled in relief and with Amanda a few steps behind, bounded to his father. "Mornin', Pa. Did you bring your divining rods?"

Mr. Murdock gazed at him with a blank expression.

Tom's tender smile faded. A rush of color infused his neck. He lowered his voice, but the wind had stilled and Amanda could hear. Tom's normally confident voice quivered as he bent to his father's level. "It's me. It's Tom."

"Tom who?"

Tom swallowed. "Your son. Remember? The oldest one. You've got Gabe and Quaid, too."

Amanda's heart spiraled. Father didn't recognize son? He recognized the dog but not Tom? Oh...she slumped against the wagon boards and closed her eyes for a moment. She could barely watch the heartache in Tom's face as he tried to explain his existence to his father.

Tom's voice fell to a whisper. "*Tom...* I own the sawmill," he explained, raw with emotion. "Remember? You taught me how to chop my first tree. We built this shack together three years ago, remember?"

Dazed, Mr. Murdock glanced to the shack and back, then to Amanda. Donald was strolling down the trail with Ellie and four children in tow, Willy with his scabbed-over blackfly bites, all approaching closer. Tom glanced frantically to them then back to his father, then back to them. He froze as Amanda watched.

Trying to spare Tom the anguish of Donald and Ellie's witnessing the situation, Amanda sprang forward. "Mr. Murdock, it's a pleasure to meet you."

She shook Mr. Murdock's hand, clasping her warmth over the wrinkles, desperately searching for words to help orient the man. "Tom told me you live up the road. That makes us neighbors. He said you're good at finding water, and that's great because I need a well dug, you see.''

Mr. Murdock gazed to the partially cleared area and something twinkled in his eyes. ''Digging a well, that's what I've come for. Tom,'' he said with recognition, ''come help me get the stuff off my horse. Sorry, I, uh, the dog…the dog caught me off guard.''

While the old man straightened, Tom's watery eyes turned to Amanda. She pretended she hadn't seen what had happened, but by the grateful look in Tom's eyes, he knew the truth.

''Ellie, Donald, howdy,'' Amanda said, giving Tom time to recover. She crouched to the children's eye level. ''Willy, how are those blackfly bites? Is the calamine helping? I've got some of my own to show you.''

As they exchanged pleasantries, Donald hollered to Mr. Murdock, ''Mornin', John!''

John Murdock waved back.

What must it be like to have a father who didn't recognize you? Poor Tom. A parent's decline was a big heartache to endure alone. Did he have any other family members who could help him through it?

Was his father suffering from early dementia? Tom's brother Quaid was a doctor, and surely John Murdock was getting the best care possible.

While the others went to work, Amanda made the gentleman sit with her and have coffee. When he got up to do his work, he held his wooden sticks parallel to the ground and slowly walked the site, waiting for them to twitch when they passed over underground water. Amanda wasn't sure how the set-up worked, but folks swore by it.

Grandma looked up from hauling branches, eyeing John Murdock with something on her mind. ''You don't happen to need a rag rug, do you? A pretty one for your cabin floor?''

Mr. Murdock put down his sticks. "I might. The floor's awfully cold this time of year."

"Well, I've got one for sale. Real cushiony. I made it myself from some of my prettiest scraps."

The elderly man laughed, rich and warm, endearing him to Amanda. "Bring it out. Let's see it." He removed his straw hat, revealing a receding hairline, and squinted in the sunshine. "Just don't make me lose my shirt on the price."

Grandma chuckled. "Ten cents is what it costs."

Amanda watched Tom noticing the exchange. Although he'd avoided glancing Amanda's way while they worked, his rigid shoulders relaxed and the tenseness to his jaw dissolved. She wasn't sure why he wasn't looking her way, but it was just as well. She didn't need any more complication in her life than she had already.

When the day was over, Ellie dropped by with the children to retrieve her husband. They offered to walk Mr. Murdock and his horse home. Grandma wanted to join them, eager to see how Mr. Murdock's new rag rug would look in his house, so they all set out together.

Amanda gave Tom a curt nod. "Thank you for your hard work. Your father found two well locations for me to choose from, and I think we're making good time." She gazed up at the cloudy sky. "Hopefully, we won't get any rain to slow us down."

The red setting sun grazed the snowy mountain peaks, casting shadows on the rocky cliffs, and deepening the green timberline of pine trees.

The rays also shimmered off Tom's dark hair. She thought he'd be quick to leave. But instead of harnessing his draft horse, he adjusted his leather gloves and picked up the ax.

"What are you doing?"

"You need someone to chop this wood."

Stepping closer, she removed her apron. "Please don't do that. You've worked hard all day."

"So have you."

"Please don't make me say it." Her voice lowered to a breeze. "I can't *afford* to have you chop my wood."

"There's no charge."

He was already chopping. With quiet dignity, she accepted his kind offer. She admired the gesture. Not many men had offered to do something like this for her. None at all, in the past eighteen months.

They worked side by side for an hour in the setting sun, she stacking wood, he pounding away. She grew warmer, feeling his proximity, every muscle that moved with every strike.

The air seemed hot and heavy. What was this thing between them? This ripe awareness that swelled and rolled, seeming as though it would burst?

When they finished, he turned to look at her. Drops of moisture clung to his temples. His eyes glowed with life. She found herself extremely conscious of his sensuality. Nervous under his gaze, she went to take the ax, but she shouldn't have stepped so close. Beneath their work gloves, their fingers pressed together. She heard his sharp intake of breath. He slid out of his gloves.

She set the ax along the shack wall, but he bent closer and grasped her hand. With one erotically smooth motion, he peeled off her one glove, then the other. Standing alone with this potent man, surrounded by the scent of damp ferns and his clean sweat, she felt as if with this one intimate gesture he was peeling off her clothing. She could barely breathe. At his feathery touch, she trembled right down to her toes.

"You've got such beautiful hands," he murmured. "Yet they work too hard."

Stroking his way over the tiny little calluses, he rubbed and kneaded and massaged. Everything about him felt hot. His hands, his breath, his touch. Long, loose strokes as if he were stroking her entire body. No man had caressed her like this. Never. Not her hand, nowhere on her body.

It made a woman yearn for his exploration. Imagining him dipping down her bare shoulders, over her languid arms, gently exploring her soft breasts and down her belly. And lower....

She closed her eyes and gasped when she felt his kiss along the back of her palm. Sweet, tender lips grazing her flesh, the heat of his mouth kissing along the openings. Her nipples went hard. If she let him go any further, she'd be sorry....

This was mad.

She knew what it was. It was a thank-you for today, for coming to his father's aid. She could never let it be more. She'd given everything she had to William, her heart, her body, her beloved baby, and she had nothing left to offer. Not to a potent man like Tom Murdock.

And what about his other woman?

As silently as it started, it ended. Without looking at him, she withdrew her hand. "You've got Clarissa to think about." Escaping into the dark shack, Amanda pressed the door closed behind her. Getting caught up with a man was just too wretchedly painful.

She was right, he had Clarissa to think about.

Tom swore softly under his breath as he found his way from his cabin door to the sawmill. The full moon glinted over his shoulder. With a jangle of keys, he unlocked the side door and entered. He struck a match and lit the largest lantern.

What in heaven's name had happened back there at the shack? Why had he completely lost himself in Amanda? Every time he looked into her heavy, blue eyes, he had to stifle his urge to touch her.

She didn't have a father to watch out for her, no brother to ward off Tom's advances. She had only herself to protect, and it wasn't fair to take advantage of a lone woman if he wasn't free to take it further. Was he free? Where did he stand with Clarissa? Where did he *want* to stand with Clarissa?

He dipped his brush in a pail of white paint, then swept it over a three-legged stool, more furniture designated for the big hotel.

"You in here, Tom?" Graham's voice shattered the silence. "I've got some news for you."

Tom rose. "What is it?"

Boots thudded across the floor. The fringes dangling from Graham's coat swayed as he walked. "A warrant's been put out for Finnigan's arrest. Robbery, fraud and larceny. I've wired the information across the country. The last sighting of him was in the coal mines just east of here. He's disappeared, but we'll flush him out."

Tom pulled in a long breath.

"I've had to ask some questions around town for Finnigan's last whereabouts, but I don't think anyone's suspicious."

"Good."

"About Clarissa…"

"She's not in Calgary, is she?"

Graham shook his head. "Can't seem to locate her. She never showed up there. Bought a train ticket but never used it."

Tom snorted in disgust. He started painting again, coating the stool's legs.

Graham pulled out a chair, sat and scratched his curly blond sideburn. "Why aren't you surprised?"

Tom's spirits sank. "What would you say if I told you I think they disappeared together?"

"Aw, hell."

Betrayed. Tom swallowed past the hard lump in his throat. What was worse? Losing his business to Finnigan? Or losing his woman to the man? Tom had been betrayed by two of the people he trusted most.

Clarissa wasn't the dignified woman he thought she was. How could he have been involved with a woman who tore off with his partner?

Amanda wasn't like her. She was as far removed from the word conniving as one could get. Amanda didn't have the easy life that Clarissa had. Amanda was a tender, widowed woman trying to survive on her own. She didn't have anything to do with Finnigan's scam, either, because he'd overcharged her.

Amanda was an honest woman, and right about now, he held the virtue of honesty highest on his list.

"About Amanda Ryan."

"Yeah?" Tom held his breath.

"I did some checking. You were right. She's got a hell of a secret. She's not widowed. The woman's divorced."

Chapter Four

*D*ivorced. Tom scowled as he hitched the mules to the stump-puller on Amanda's property the next morning. She hadn't been waiting for him as she usually was—which made him happy—but stepped out of the shack and into the thick forest thirty minutes after he, Donald and Pa arrived.

They'd all lied to him. Finnigan, Clarissa, then her.

"Nice day, isn't it?" Amanda's welcoming smile and pretense of a blush sickened him. A shaft of light struck her high cheekbones beneath the bonnet. Wasn't she an innocent? A naive divorcée, blushing at the man who'd brazenly kissed her hand the day before. Damn her anyway, for getting to him.

His muscles clenched. "Good for working," he muttered.

He turned his back, not caring how rude he was, and secured one of two wooden columns to the mule's harness. The contraption looked like an inverted V over the stump. With a long, sauntering stride, pulling his hat closer to his brow to shade himself from the sun, he left her standing there and joined Donald by the other mule. The animals would walk the columns in a circle, turning the screw and chains attached to the stump, thereby pulling out the root. Tom would finish his work as quickly as he could, and in five weeks time he'd say good riddance to Mrs. Amanda Ryan.

Amanda had looked into his eyes and stole his affections—*stole*—under false pretenses of him feeling sorry for a widow. And her grandma wasn't any better. How the two of them must have laughed that day when he'd first met Miss Clementine and they'd discussed widowhood. He'd made a fool of himself for falling for Amanda's fabrications.

Persistent, dressed in her old flannel, Amanda slid her slender figure next to his broad one, dressed in denim. The demure smile he'd found so endearing yesterday looked like one of deceit today. What did the woman want from him? A friendly conversation? More kisses? Although she'd pulled back yesterday, maybe she'd changed her mind and thought he'd make a good catch. Maybe he'd be able to support her down the road!

"What happened to your two big draft horses?" she asked in a friendly tone that he found irritating.

"I sold them," he snapped. "I can rent Donald's mules any time I need them."

He'd sold them so that Pa could keep his gentle mares. Tom's secret credit note at the bank had gotten Quaid his new shipment of instruments, but Tom hadn't wanted to borrow too much. Fortunately, he still had his three best horses, and when he dug out of this financial mess, he'd be able to buy the others back.

He felt a movement beside his boot and looked down. Wolf was digging a deep hole.

"Stop that," Tom reprimanded. "If someone falls in that hole, they could twist their ankle. Go chase a squirrel." After a friendly pat on the head, the dog bounced away, but Amanda frowned at his gruffness. When he ignored her, she left. Good. He gently slapped the rear of one of the mules to start it walking in a circle, then adjusted his big leather work gloves.

He admitted, being divorced wasn't a thing most people would brag about, but why hide who you are?

He knew of only three people who'd ever been divorced; none in this town. One older gent back in Toronto who was an alcoholic, one young miner in the Rockies whose poor wife couldn't take any more beatings, and a tourist passing through last summer whose wife had caught him with his third mistress.

It was common knowledge that more women were divorced in the West than the East. Women were scarcer here, so if their husbands mistreated them in any way, they divorced, taking their children and quickly remarrying—to one of many men in the West grateful for the company and partnership of a woman. But that's not what had happened to Amanda.

From what Graham had said, it was Amanda's husband who'd divorced *her*. Graham hadn't uncovered the circumstances, and Tom had stopped Amanda's investigation. No sense asking Graham to uncover more about a woman Tom didn't care for. Besides, it was bordering on prying, and *he* still had *his* code of honor.

While Donald tended to the mules and gave them water, Tom cleared brush beside his father, who was creating a garden for the women. Pa was in a jovial mood this morning, causing Tom to brighten.

"Sure is nice today," Pa said. "The blackflies are gone and the sun is warm."

Squinting in the warm rays, Tom gazed up at the hills. The landscape quivered in the wind, with a dozen hues of green. The soft yellow-green of fresh grass, the brilliant green of unfolding maple leaves, and the blue-green growth of spruce needles. Blue jays and cardinals rustled through the woods, and insects hummed above his head. The earthy scent was intoxicating.

Tom blurted affectionately, ''Pa, why don't you come live with me?''

The old man took off his straw hat and fanned the air. ''Go on now. Come live with you and Clarissa? You know me and her don't see eye to eye. Why, she'd have my things packed and bundled by the door before I got back from the privy.''

Lifting his shovel, Tom flipped a furrow of dirt. The hard muscles of his biceps tightened. ''Clarissa's not going to be around.''

''Whaddya mean?''

''She's gone to visit family for the summer.''

''For good?''

''For the summer.''

''What does that mean? Are you two over?''

Tom stopped digging to catch his breath. ''Yeah, I guess we are.'' Saying it out loud made it seem final. It was final.

Pa kept shoveling, surprising Tom with his endurance. ''I'm not helpless, no matter what your brothers think. I'll live alone until I can no longer put my pants on by myself.''

Tom sighed. When the mules finished uprooting the first stump, Tom and Donald hitched them to the second. It was hard, physical work, and Tom was reminded of Clarissa's asking, *Why don't you become the doctor or lawyer? Why do you do it all for your brothers? Why do you choose such difficult labor?*

Because I feel like a trapped rabbit inside the walls of any office. I like fresh air and miles of wilderness, he'd told her, but obviously, she hadn't been impressed.

Tom stepped beside his father. "How are your new horses doing?"

"They're magnificent." Pa beamed, making all of Tom's perseverance worthwhile.

"Glad you like 'em."

"Now, I think I've got some black licorice gum to deliver," Pa said, gazing at Miss Clementine by the outdoor fire. He rooted for something in the top pocket of his red jacket. "Her favorite."

With caution, Tom gazed at the two ladies, who were boiling a kettle of potatoes over an open flame. Realizing he ought to warn his pa about the type of women they were, Tom decided he would mention it when the two men were alone.

Toward noon, Tom refused Amanda's offer of lunch and tea for the third time.

"What is it?" she finally asked. She'd removed her bonnet. Her mended kerchief held back some of her wavy black hair, but the rest tumbled over her shoulders. "If it's about last evening, I'm sorry I pulled away from you…but you have…and I'm not interested…"

He grumbled. She wasn't interested? Well, he wasn't interested, either, to be hoodwinked and bamboozled by another conniving woman. *Conniving,* he repeated in his mind as he gazed into her fraudulent blue eyes. Cold, heartless, lying.

In the background, he heard Wolf bark, then Pa and Miss Clementine laugh. "For your information," Tom said, "not that it's any of your concern, Clarissa is not a big part of my life. And I've got a lot of work to do today." He gave her a dismissive nod, hoping she'd walk away.

"Let me help—"

"No." He straightened his shoulders and finally confronted her.

Her lips tightened. Her brows arched. "I knew it was a mistake to hire you."

"How dare you say that."

She placed her hands on her rounded hips and glared at him. "Then what is it? What am I supposed to think as you continue to play games and not accept my tea…and not accept my help…and not even look in my direction? Why are you so hostile? Because yesterday I didn't accept your advances? Haven't you ever been turned down before?"

Tom balked. "Is that what you think it's about?"

"I know that a successful man like you, who has a booming business and the respect of the town, isn't used to be given a no—"

"Stop before you regret it—"

"Why, every woman in town must be flattered beyond belief when you look in her direction—"

Tom cut her off with an iron grip on her arm, being careful not to hurt her. The heat of her flesh seeped into his fingers. Fury laced his words. "Would you like me more if you thought my life were difficult?"

Their eyes locked. She opened her mouth to answer.

"Well?" He tugged her closer, an inch away from his face.

Slowly she closed her lips and took a deep breath. His question left her speechless, and trembling.

He was shaking a bit himself. Releasing her, he stepped away.

With quivering lips, she hiked her skirts to leave.

Now that she'd opened up the discussion, he couldn't stop himself from hurling a question at her stiffened back. "Why couldn't people be more honest?"

She spun around. "Pardon?"

"Why didn't you tell me you were divorced, Amanda?"

Her gaze clouded. The question seemed to weigh on her, choking her. "Well...I..."

Maybe she did have a conscience, or was she just embarrassed she'd been caught in her own lie?

She stared at his rigid stance. "That's why you're upset."

"Were you and your grandmother having a little chuckle at my expense?"

A flash of grief rippled across her face. "We weren't laughing at you."

"Why didn't you tell me the truth?"

"Because I...couldn't."

"The easily fooled jackass, Tom Murdock."

Her eyes glistened in sympathy. She shook her head. "We weren't laughing at you."

"Turns out, I've got a few jokes of my own to tell. Like this property here, for instance. Zeb Finnigan took you to town. You paid five hundred, but I would have sold it to you for a whopping three."

Another blow. She staggered. "What?"

He momentarily felt sorry for her. Was he being too hard on her? Was he taking out the rage he felt at Clarissa and Finnigan, at the only person here to take it?

"I see," she said quietly. The mules brayed behind her as the beasts continued plodding. "By the way, how did you discover I was divorced?"

Wanting to protect Graham, Tom answered, "That's not important." He swooped down to pick his shovel off the ground.

"Then how do you know you can trust your source?"

She had the nerve to try to turn the tables on him? "Because he's a Mountie." He cursed himself for letting it slip out, but he couldn't bridle his anger.

"You had Finnigan *and* me investigated." Her face was

full of strength. How quickly she'd pieced it together. "Do you think having me investigated is any more honest than me claiming I'm widowed?"

Her sudden question jarred him. His mind swirled with doubts.

"Did your…Mountie friend discover anything else?"

"Like what? The reason you divorced?" Tom shook his head. "No. That's your private business, and I don't really care."

She shuddered at his barb.

He continued recklessly. "One of the Calgary Mounties visited the Cattlemen's Association, and your name came up. Your husband had been there the day before for a meeting, boasting about his new wife and children."

Her eyes flashed. "His n-new children?"

"Twin boys. Born last week."

Amanda stumbled back and didn't speak for a long time. The tail of her flannel shirt caught the gentle breeze. "Are they healthy babies?"

Of all the things for her to say, what a strange choice. But then again, maybe it was natural because she was a midwife. "As far as I know. Your former husband was giving out cigars."

This time when her shoulders sagged, he knew his words had stung. He stepped back for a moment, trying to understand. Beneath his hat, a bead of perspiration trickled down his temple.

He hadn't meant to hurt her, but he obviously had.

Apparently he didn't know how to talk to a divorced woman. Did she still care about her husband? Her husband had divorced *her,* so maybe she still had feelings for him. But how silly of Tom to assume anything. The issues were likely complicated, each divorce different in how the folks dealt with each other.

He wavered, not knowing if he should apologize for being blunt. The woman was divorced, but if she truly meant nothing to Tom, then why had he gotten so fired up? His confusion kept him rooted, and his stubborn pride from apologizing.

"I'm glad, then," she said quietly. "William always wanted boys to take over the ranch and carry on his family name. And beautiful children coming into the world is always a blessed event."

He could see the truthfulness in her eyes this time. They were not conspiring blue eyes. They held that tenderness and depth of sorrow he couldn't fathom. No matter what the circumstances of her divorce, she was generous to put the innocent babies before her own wounds.

When she slipped into the woods, saying she had to haul water, he watched her proud, retreating form. But as soon as she thought she was out of his view, she slumped against the nearest tree, as if crumpling beneath a heavy blow. For some unknown reason, his heart trembled along with hers.

Had he done that to her?

"I've got some mighty interestin' news," Ellie said a week later when she came to retrieve Donald after his day of work. She'd brought her older boy, Pierce, to carry the crate of heavy jam preserves that she was using as payment for her care. "I heard it in the mercantile today."

Standing in the warm sunset trimming bushes, Amanda motioned to red-haired, sixteen-year-old Pierce to take the jams into the shack to Grandma, then focused on Ellie. She smoothed her fallen strands of strawberry hair into her top-knot bun, the movement causing her pregnant belly to protrude beneath her apron. The tender image brought a smile to Amanda's lips.

She and Ellie were spending lots of time together. It was

wonderful to have a friend to confide in, although Amanda hadn't yet been able to share her deepest personal problems.

Ellie watched Pierce walk to the shack. It seemed whatever she had to say, she'd say it when her son was out of earshot.

Tom and Donald glanced up from where they were hinging a cedar door onto the new root cellar, which they'd built into the side of a small hill. The clearing for the cabin had been leveled, and the six-by-six boards laid for the floor. Toward the back of the structure, where the kitchen would be, a shiny water pump handle protruded three feet above the new well. It was starting to shape up nicely, and Amanda was counting down the days when she'd no longer have to work with Tom Murdock. The sting of their last argument still burned in her cheeks.

Her divorce was still no one's business but hers.

She knew it wasn't Tom's fault that he'd been the messenger about William's new sons.

After this year's winter, the coldest blizzard they'd had in decades, she'd heard William had lost half his cattle in the freeze. Knowing how difficult that struggle must have been for his wife, Amanda was happy the young woman had healthy babies to keep her company.

But Amanda's argument with Tom just went to prove how different they were.

She watched the rich outline of his shoulders as he heaved on the door. Did he know she'd lost a baby? She doubted it. He hadn't mentioned it when they'd argued. Neither she nor William had registered the baby's birth—as most parents didn't—so the Mounties wouldn't have easily discovered it.

''What is it?'' Amanda asked after Pierce had disappeared inside. She offered her friend a chair.

Ellie preferred to stand. "Two orphans are comin' to town."

"Orphans?" Amanda felt her pulse rush in surprise.

"It's too bad your cabin's not built yet, aye, Amanda, or you could take 'em."

Amanda's mind began to race with possibilities. With hope. "Who are they?"

"Their pa was a telegrapher fer the CP Railway, and he'd been workin' up at the camp that was surveyin' the land north of here, at Lake Louise. Two years ago he and his wife drowned in a canoein' accident. One of the older women in camp has been lookin' after the children, but I hear her rheumatism's gettin' the better of her, and she can't get around anymore."

"Do they have any other family?"

"An aunt somewhere in Quebec, I hear, but the rumor is—" Ellie rushed forward and lowered her voice "—she's got a terrible marriage, with five children of 'er own. She doesn't want any more mouths to feed."

"How awful for the children."

"Yes, isn't it, though?"

With his knee-high boots caked in mud, Donald came and slung an arm around Ellie's shoulders, adjusting her blue shawl for her. It was an intimate gesture between a caring husband and his wife, and Amanda got caught up, witnessing his gentleness.

"Where are the orphans now?" Donald asked his wife.

"They're comin' in around seven or eight this evenin', on the mud wagon from Lake Louise. They'll stay with the conductor's wife overnight, then board the train for Calgary in the mornin'. One of the orphanages has agreed to take 'em."

An orphanage in Calgary? Was it Mrs. Blake's, or the one run by the church? Amanda couldn't imagine how lonely and distant it must sound to the children. They must be frightened out of their wits at being shipped out of their home. What could she do about it?

"How old are they?" Tom asked. He'd quietly joined them, standing a foot away from her. The open collar at his throat revealed a hint of the chest beneath. Tough and lean, he unnerved her.

"I don't know much more about 'em," Ellie replied. "Mr. Langston at the mercantile said they were very young, but someone else in the store thought they were older. The conductor's wife would probably know more."

What could she do? Amanda wondered again. If she could meet the children, she'd be better able to make a decision, and ask if the children even *wanted* to stay here.

"What are you thinkin', Amanda?" asked Ellie, grabbing her by the shoulders. "You couldn't possibly keep them here in the shack. There's not enough room for four people to sleep."

Could they all squeeze in? "I'd just like to meet them."

Ellie dropped her hands. Donald shifted beside his wife. "Amanda, Ellie and I have eight children of our own, and some of 'em are harder to look after than others. You've never met these children, so you don't know what they're like."

Amanda ran a hand over her soiled apron. She was dressed in work clothes, and there wasn't much time to spare if she were to meet the wagon. "There's no harm in saying hello."

Oh—she'd almost forgotten. Grandma. Amanda couldn't entertain an idea like this without asking first. The older woman was all for taking in homeless children when the cabin was completed. In fact, they'd planned it well— if Amanda were called to a delivery in the middle of the night, Grandma would be here for the children. But if, on the odd chance, these new children were to stay in the *shack* for the next four weeks—

"We have to go now," said Ellie, cutting into Amanda's thoughts. "I left the children preparin' supper, but don't dare leave 'em long. Please don't do anythin' rash."

When the three of them left, Tom stood staring at her, large hands propped on his hips. His green eyes lit with something unreadable. He was assessing her. Again.

She really didn't care what he thought of her, she told herself, or her plans for the children, but she was mighty grateful he was here at this particular moment. Surely he wouldn't refuse her request, no matter what he thought of her, being divorced.

"Tom, would you mind since there's no one else to ask on such short notice—" She moved back from him to give herself a comfortable space to breathe. "Would you mind giving me a lift to town? I prefer not to use my bicycle tonight." Because if the children returned with her, they'd have to walk and how could they lug their suitcases alongside a bicycle? She'd hitch another ride home from someone else with a wagon, but she'd get there sooner with Tom.

She glanced up at his surprised face, hoping he'd put their argument behind them. "Please."

"Children really do mean a lot to you, don't they?"

"Yes, they do. An awful lot."

His face, bronzed by the wind, was rugged and solemn. Something in his manner calmed her. "Then how can I say no?"

Her mouth curved into a soft smile. He returned her smile with one of his own, and there went that invisible pull of attraction.

"Thank you," she blurted, filling with a giddy sense of

pleasure, stumbling and racing toward the shack. "I'll tell Grandma."

"I heard every word of Ellie's explanation," bellowed the round old woman from the door. "The next time you people start talking behind the children's backs, make sure you don't talk so loud. I had to prop the door open because of the smoke—"

"The smoke?" Amanda stepped into the shack.

"I burned the flapjacks. Got distracted by one of Pierce's jokes."

"I know it's short notice, Grandma, and we weren't fig-uring on it happening so soon, but would you mind if I brought the two children back here tonight?"

Grandma gazed at her with sharp eyes, then her expres-sion softened. "I haven't seen you this flushed and excited for a year and a half. It does my old heart good. Of course you can bring them back, but only if you think it'll work out after you meet them and see who they are. Remember, they have to live with us for a while before someone adopts them, and stayin' here might not be the best thing for us or them."

Amanda hugged her plump grandmother, then glanced at the narrow cots. "I don't know how we'll all sleep in this tiny space."

"Don't you worry, I'll figure out somethin'. But you've got to change. You can't go dressed like an old farmhand. It's not proper."

"I know," said Amanda, already heading to the blue steamer trunk in the corner. She lifted the squeaky lid, searching beneath the special white angora shawl for her best suit. As a rancher's wife she hadn't needed many fancy clothes. It had been backbreaking work, tending to the cattle, and she had only one Sunday go-to-meeting suit. It didn't take her long to change. She unpinned her hair and gave it a quick brush, allowing the curls to hang loose down her back.

When she exited the shack with her everyday shawl and satchel in hand, Tom had already turned the horse and wagon around, waiting for her. He was playing fetch with Wolf. When Tom spotted her, the arm that was holding the stick froze in midair. He straightened his angular shoulders and lowered his intense gaze from her head to her toes. His obvious pleasure made her stomach flutter.

"You just want to say hello to the children, huh?" he asked in a rough voice. "You'll draw them like bees to honey."

She swallowed and nodded. She knew the creamy peach jacket clung to her slender waistline, that the peplum flared gently over her hips. The long skirt and bustle accentuated her long thighs. She chose it because she thought the children might like the cheery color.

Tom stepped forward, cupping her face in his large warm hand. What was he doing, touching her again? Her heart began to beat to the pulse at the base of his throat. "The color of your suit goes well," he murmured, "with your *sparkling* blue eyes."

"Not sad this time?"

"No," he said gently.

It must have been the thought of meeting the lonely children that did that to her.

When Tom helped her up to her seat, their warm fingers intertwined. Dressed in rough work clothes and smelling of fresh air and hard work, he was so male, his presence all-embracing.

As they rolled out, Wolf jumped into the buckboard and Grandma said goodbye.

"Is your pa feelin' okay, Tom?" Grandma hollered.

Tom looked suddenly concerned. "Yeah, I think so. Why?"

"Seems like he's been avoidin' me for the past week."

Turning red, Tom cleared his throat and resettled into the firm seat beside her. Why did Grandma's comment make him uncomfortable?

Amanda knew why. He'd probably told his father of her divorce, and the older man didn't approve of her, either.

"I'm sorry," Tom whispered with shame, and they let it rest between them. She didn't want to argue, either. Not tonight.

Dusk was falling. The woods seemed to sway with shadows, echoing with the cooing of birds, bonding her and Tom in an intimacy she tried to fight. The lull and creak of the wagon drew them closer.

"Have you found Finnigan yet?" she asked.

"Not yet."

"Did he...did he steal a lot from you?"

A muscle in his jaw tightened. "That he did."

The soft breeze toyed with her long hair. "What can I do to help you catch him?"

He stretched his long legs. "Would you speak to my friend, Graham? He's the Mountie looking after the case."

She nodded. "Sure. I can speak to him tomorrow. But I'm afraid I don't know anything more than what I've told you already."

"Anything you say about Finnigan might help Graham."

"Is overcharging for a property a crime?"

Tom shook his head. "Not that I know of."

"It should be. This cabin is all I have left. No extra money because of him."

She dipped her hand inside her jacket pocket and pulled out her scratched pocket watch. "It's close to seven. You can drop me off at the edge of town and I'll walk from there.''

He frowned. "I can't dump you and leave you all alone.''

"I'm accustomed to being on my own.''

"For the children's sake, I insist on driving you. How else would you get home?''

"I thought I'd ask someone else for a lift back.''

"Let me," he coaxed.

Was he trying to be agreeable because of how he'd spoken to her last week? Was he concerned about the children as well? "All right, then. Thank you.'' She was touched by the difference in him tonight.

Something dawned on her and she twisted in her seat to face him. "I'm sorry, Tom, I just realized you haven't eaten supper yet.''

"I'm fine.''

"But you worked hard all day. You must be starved. I had an afternoon sandwich, so didn't think of my stomach. I never thought to offer you—''

"The children are more important. I'll eat later. I'll swing by the house, though, and drop off Wolf.'' He pulled on the reins to signal the horses.

She reached out and briefly touched his sleeve. Beneath her fingertips, she felt his muscles tighten with the contact.

"Please don't,'' she urged. "Let's bring Wolf. I want the children to like me…they'll like me more if I bring a dog.''

Tom frowned at her honest admission, and she felt silly for her awkwardness.

"They'll like you,'' he said with deep sincerity. When their eyes met, her heart went out to him. "You don't have to worry about that.''

Chapter Five

They pulled into town and decided to wait in the mercantile for the time to pass. Amanda tried to contain her case of the nerves while Tom took the collar and chain he kept beneath the buckboard seat and secured Wolf to a scrub oak.

The tinsmith's daughter was leaving the store as Tom held the door open. Amanda stepped up eagerly to greet her. Fannie's freckled face glowed in the lamplight.

"Hello, Fannie," said Amanda. "How are you feeling?"

Svelte and not yet showing beneath her high-collared frock, Fannie Potter avoided looking into Amanda's eyes. "Fine, thank you. I'm glad I ran into you, though. I'm switching my care to Dr. Murdock."

Amanda withered at the news. Tom eased his broad frame next to hers, looking perplexed himself.

"You know how it is," Fannie continued. "I've known him longer than I've known you. I feel more comfortable with him." She bit her lower lip, close to tears.

More comfortable with him? Amanda tried not to show her disappointment. She placed a comforting hand on the young woman's shoulder. "It's nothing to worry about.

Heaven knows you've got enough to handle, taking care of yourself and the baby on the way. I understand your decision.''

Fannie left with an awkward glance to the floor. Was there more to it? One of the reasons Amanda had been able to afford having Tom dig the added root cellar was because she'd gotten Fannie as a patient, and others were trickling in. Last week, Amanda had made two emergency house calls. One for a girl with an aching tooth that needed yanking, and the other for an infant boy with gastroenteritis, also on the mend.

Had she done something to upset Fannie? Amanda couldn't think of anything.

While she waited to get to the crowded counter, where Emmett Langston was weighing chipped beef on his scales for three European tourists dressed in dapper clothing, she heard two young women call out to Tom behind her.

"Howdy, Tom. You going to the ball?"

"I think I have to. I'm one of the evening's speakers."

"Isn't that nice? I hear Clarissa's out of town. We'd be mighty happy to take you instead," drawled her friend.

"I'll let you know," he said, humor edging his words.

At the obvious innuendos, Amanda felt heat rush to her cheeks. Was Tom pleased with the attention?

Of course, she thought. What man wouldn't be?

She knew the ladies were speaking of the grand opening ceremonies for the Banff Springs Hotel, taking place in three weeks. The hotel would be officially opening for business in two, on the first of June, but they planned the gala ball for the Saturday a week later, after all the travelers had arrived. The whole town was bubbling with excitement at talk of a live orchestra, rich food, even fireworks. Amanda couldn't fathom spending that kind of money on a ball gown used for only one event. If she had any money to spare, she'd use it on her young patients.

Her turn came at the counter. "I need lamp oil, please."

Dressed in a white-and-black-striped shirt, and black bow tie, Mr. Langston asked, "What kind? Whale oil?"

"I tried that last week. It doesn't burn long enough."

"Fish oil? It's on sale today."

"It's too smoky."

"How about kerosene? You pay a bit extra, but it burns longest and brightest."

"That sounds just about right."

Tom dipped his mouth low to her ear and whispered, "You sound like Goldilocks, checking out her beds. Too hard, too soft, just right."

Amusement hovered at the back of her throat. He'd moved so close to her, she felt his warm breath at her temples. Their camaraderie broke the tension of the past seven days, and she felt herself warming toward him. Was it safe to be friendly?

"Here you are," Mr. Langston said, holding out the jug. "Be careful, it's heavy. Must weigh close to eight pounds."

Amanda went to reach for it, but was suddenly awash with memories. *Close to eight pounds...* She tried to steady herself, but the bottles and jars behind Mr. Langston swirled before her eyes. What would the precious weight feel like in her arms? If any of the mothers in her care ever lost their baby, Amanda would ensure they got to hold and comfort their son or daughter as their angel slipped to heaven. Who had comforted her baby girl? What kind of mother had she been?

Tom grabbed the jug. "I'll take it." He stared at her. "You look pale. Are you all right?"

She took a deep breath. Her shaky hand slipped to her

side. Here in Banff, she'd learned she wasn't the only mother who'd lost a child. Last year, rubella had taken two babies from the Smythes, and down the road, the Cavanaghs had lost a three-year-old to consumption—*tuberculosis*. People picked themselves up and carried on, and she'd carry on, too. "It's a bit crowded in here."

"Let's go outside. Do you have everything you need?"

She nodded and they left. Standing on the boardwalk in the night, she steadied her breathing, glad for the man by her side. She followed the movements of the lamplighter, making his way with his long torch, lighting the lamps one by one.

"There's the conductor's wife," Tom said, pointing across the street, in front of Ruby's Dining and Boarding House. "She must be waiting for the children."

Amanda and Tom crossed the busy road, through the buggies, oxen and tourists. Even in a crowd, Tom's presence commanded authority. He nodded at someone passing. Amanda followed his gaze, only to see two ranch hands gawking and whistling at her. She swung around, feeling herself blush.

"Mrs. Hawthorne," Tom introduced when they crossed the street, "I'd like you to meet Amanda Ryan."

"I was wondering if I might have a word with you," Amanda said to the frail, white-haired woman, "about the children."

"Yes?"

"I'm a midwife and my grandpa trained me to work with children. I understand they've been orphaned for two years. I'm considering—if they agree—to take them in, until we find a suitable adoptive family for them here in Banff. It would be so much better for them to stay in the area where they grew up."

"That's very kind of you, miss," the old woman mumbled. "But it may be a long while till someone adopts these children. Until then, they may be a bigger burden for you than you think. They'll be fine in Calgary." She gazed down Banff Avenue, but there was no sign of a stagecoach.

"Bigger burden? How do you mean?"

"The younger one, Josh, he's only four, but people say he's *slow*. He doesn't speak much. Most of it is garbled."

"Oh," said Amanda.

"How sad," said Tom, mirroring her thoughts.

"And his sister, Margaux, she's thirteen I believe, and she…well, she wears spectacles."

"Eye glasses?" Amanda asked.

The old woman nodded, as if embarrassed. "So young to be wearin' spectacles, you see, and people—potential suitors that is—worry she may go blind before her time."

"Because she wears spectacles?" Amanda nearly choked on the woman's ignorance. "Why, my grandpa wore spectacles, and his eyesight was sharper than mine. I think it's wonderful someone got her the glasses she needed. Not everyone has the good fortune to find an eye doctor—"

"I'm just tellin' you the way it is. It'll most likely be a few years for her to find a beaux. And hearin' how devoted she is to her little brother, I imagine whoever she marries will have to agree to look after the boy, as well. And then her eye problem…well, you see how it is."

Amanda longed to help the children all the more. Tom cupped his warm palm on her shoulder, and it steadied her.

The woman peered closer. "Say, you wouldn't happen to be the woman who rides that bicycle?"

"That's right," Amanda said, smiling, hoping the woman had heard she was friendly and reliable.

Mrs. Hawthorne's nose pinched. "The one who's *divorced?*"

Amanda's face heated. She looked to Tom. How had news of her divorce got out to the public?

He dropped his hand from her shoulder, but leaned closer. "I'm sorry. I don't know how that got out. I didn't mention it to anyone—" with a sigh, he looked up at the dark sky "—except my father. And I thought he knew to keep it confidential."

Amanda toyed with her fingers, unsure of how she felt. "I should have spoken up from the very beginning, like Grandma said."

Mrs. Hawthorne listened with disdain. "I'm not sure folks in town would like a divorced woman caring for the children. And shame on you, hidin' behind a veil of widowhood."

Tom's lean profile stiffened. He rallied to her defense. "Now hold on, here. Amanda did nothing to smear the honorable status of widowhood."

"*That's* why Fannie changed her mind," said Amanda.

"And a bicycle, to boot." The old woman clicked her tongue, making Amanda feel even smaller. "There's no tellin' what some women intend on doin', is there? Just comin' and goin' whenever you please. It's not natural."

"There's nothing wrong with it," Tom insisted.

Mrs. Hawthorne clutched her scarf around her wrinkled throat. "You're with her, Tom? You'll vouch for her?"

Amanda lowered her head, more determined than ever to introduce herself to the children, to give them the option of staying with whom they pleased.

She suddenly felt the earth rumble beneath her feet. Glancing down the dirt street, she spotted a team of horses thundering toward them. The rudimentary stagecoach, or mud wagon as it was called because it was designed for rough backcountry trails, was almost here.

"Yes," Tom said, springing forward. Amanda basked in the power of his voice. "I'll vouch for her."

"What have you got in the crate?" Tom asked the boy, Josh, two minutes after the mud wagon doors had opened. Tom suspected he already knew the answer because he'd glimpsed a tiny ball of orange fur through the wooden slats.

Wearing a drab, gray wool cap pulled over his unruly brown hair, gray suspenders and patched brown knickers, the four-year-old gingerly balanced the pen on his lap. He wouldn't look directly at Tom, but his solemn sister, Margaux, did. Amanda and Mrs. Hawthorne had already introduced themselves to Margaux and Josh Somerville, and were helping the slender-boned girl step down to the dimly lit, noisy boardwalk.

When Margaux's laced boots reached the planks, she bounced beside Tom, braids trailing, more energetic than she looked. A long brown dress with faded polka dots, obviously a hand-me-down belonging to a much older and bigger woman, hung off her bony shoulders.

"My brother Josh doesn't talk very much," Margaux replied cautiously, eyeing Tom through gold-wire spectacles. "He's not bein' rude, sir, he's just…not a big talker."

"That's all right." Tom grinned, trying to be friendly. "Sometimes I'm not a big talker, either."

He held out his large hand to help the boy hop out, but Josh turned to his sister instead. The two children looked as frightened as they probably felt. Tom lifted the satchel from the coach floor then eased back into his work boots and gave them the space they sought.

When the boy disembarked and stood beside the team of four horses, behind his sister's skirts, he stared at Tom. How much of the conversation did the boy understand?

The eye contact was good, Tom noticed, and there was clarity in Josh's brown gaze.

Amanda fanned a palm above the crate and smiled. "It looks like a little kitten to me. Is it yours?"

Josh didn't answer. Mrs. Hawthorne wearily shook her head.

Night lights illuminated Amanda's creamy skin. She was trying hard to put the children at ease, and her compassion was engaging. After their harsh encounter with Mrs. Hawthorne, Tom was beginning to realize why Amanda had kept her divorce to herself. Was this how all divorced women were treated?

Margaux wrapped her arm around her brother and the two of them clung together. Tom watched her pale hands tremble. "Nana gave her to us. Her cat had kittens and she wanted us to have one as a present. Said she couldn't afford anything else."

Nana must be the woman who'd cared for them in the camp. Amanda's gaze caught Tom's. By the tender expression in her eyes, he knew what she was thinking. The same thing he probably was. That he wanted to reach out and tell the youngsters that everything was going to be okay. But everything was *not* okay. They'd lost their parents two years ago, they'd just said goodbye to the woman who'd been caring for them, and were heading to an orphanage.

Even at this very minute they were facing three complete strangers. And one of them was sour-faced Mrs. Hawthorne.

The old woman cleared her grumpy throat. "You can't take a kitten with you to Calgary. Why didn't your nana think of that? The orphanage can't look after stray animals."

"Maybe they can," said Amanda. "Is it the church orphanage?"

"Yes, but it doesn't make a difference. It's not healthy for the other children. And you certainly can't keep it in my house overnight. I spent two hours this mornin' scrubbin' and waxin' my floors."

Tom wished Mrs. Hawthorne would stop complaining. He must have scowled, for both children had jumped away from the old woman and her puckered mouth, to gaze at Tom's expression.

"How long has your kitten been in there?" he asked Josh. "Would you like to let it out?"

Margaux pressed her face close to the slats and peered at the orange face. "The crate is just for carryin' her. We had her free on the ride. The driver stopped every so often to tend to her. About ten minutes ago, she drank water and ate biscuits."

"When's the last time *you* ate?" Tom asked the children.

The girl instantly sobered. "I don't remember. People keep askin', but we're not very hungry today."

Tom could understand it. Who could be hungry on the day you were being driven out of the only home you knew?

With a grumble, Amanda hiked herself to her feet, accidentally grazing Tom's arm in the process. His pulse skipped a beat.

"What's your kitten's name?" asked Amanda.

"Awggie," said Josh. His mouth twisted during the pronunciation, struggling to speak. Tom and Amanda were so surprised to hear him speak, they smiled at each other.

"The kitten's name is Awggie?" asked Tom.

"No, it's Sunset," said Margaux. "Because she's orange and red like the sunset."

"Awggie," the boy repeated, staring at the mercantile across the darkened street.

Amanda turned her head, her wavy black hair cascading like a waterfall down her back, and looked to where he was pointing. Tom followed her gaze. They stared at the laundry, then the bank, and then the log saloon.

Margaux squinted past the luggage that the stage driver began tossing down to Tom. "Usually, I can understand most of what Josh's tryin' to say, but…"

"I told you," whispered Mrs. Hawthorne, loud enough for everyone to know she had a condescending secret. "I told you what they said about him."

Mrs. Hawthorne was pressing her luck. Amanda might seem like a woman who'd back down, but from what he knew of her, she'd only take so much. She ignored the old woman's comment and kept searching. When she spotted Tom's wagon, she smiled.

"Why, you're saying 'doggie,' aren't you?" Amanda said. "Across the road, tied to the tree, he's wagging his tail at us. The big white husky. *Doggie.*"

The boy's face brightened. He dove behind his sister's dress, then slowly peered at Amanda with one chocolate-brown eye. Amanda beamed with pleasure.

Tom bent and yanked playfully on Josh's wool cap. The boy let him, without pulling away. "Do you know whose doggie that is? That's my dog. His name is Wolf. He's not a real wolf, I just liked that name. Would you like to meet him?"

The boy looked up in awe. He gave a whisper of a smile, but no verbal response. Tom could see the comprehension in the boy's eyes. Was he slow, as some had labeled him? If he wasn't, why did he talk the way he did? "Wolf's pretty friendly, but you have to watch out because he might try to lick your face."

This sent Margaux into a fit of giggles.

With a serious glance at Mrs. Hawthorne, Amanda placed an arm around the girl's shoulders and trailed her fingers along a braid. "Before we meet Wolf, can we talk for a spell? Did I tell you children that I'm a midwife?"

They shook their heads.

"That means I help deliver babies when they come into the world. And I also tend to sick children. I help them get better when they don't feel well."

"We're not sick," Margaux was quick to point out.

"I know. You look very healthy. I didn't realize you children would be so lovely. You're a very pretty girl, Margaux. I especially like your spectacles. They make you look all grown up, like a young woman."

Mrs. Hawthorne clamped her lips together. But with a squirm of delight and a blushing smile, the girl inched a little taller. And Tom silently commended Amanda.

"I live alone with my grandma, up over that hill. Right now we live in a small shack, but we're building a brand-new cabin. Mr. Murdock here is the builder. When it's all done, I'm opening a small orphanage. I'm wondering if you'd like to stay with me. Instead of going to Calgary, I mean. You could stay with me in this town, until we find someone to…"

Tom watched her struggle with the word adopt, and his admiration for her grew. As a single woman supporting herself, living in a leaky shack, she was offering what no one else in this town—single or married—would. What he himself didn't have the courage to. What she was offering was priceless.

"For how long?" Margaux asked.

"Until someone adopts you."

"Or you could come with me, as planned," interrupted Mrs. Hawthorne. "Sometimes it's better not to upset the plans that others have carefully laid out," she said pointedly to Amanda.

The children peered from Mrs. Hawthorne to Amanda. How were they supposed to choose between strangers? thought Tom.

Unfazed, Amanda brushed a hand along her skirt. "Margaux, I've got a bicycle and if you like I can teach you how to ride. Why, every girl's got to teach herself how to be independent," she said in Mrs. Hawthorne's direction.

"You've got a dog," the young girl said to Tom, then turned to Amanda, "and you've got a bicycle?" Her eyes widened momentarily, then a frown furrowed her brow. "Do you think, ma'am, we c-could try it out at your place, but if we don't like—" She halted, as if weighing her words, trying not to insult anyone. "C-can we give it a try for a week and see?"

"I think that's a very sensible solution. I'm glad you thought of it. I'll send a letter on the train tomorrow for the orphanage, explaining that you're visiting with me for a week. If you decide to make it permanent, we'll let them know then." Amanda angled her shoulders and spun toward Mrs. Hawthorne. "Would that be all right with you, ma'am?"

Mrs. Hawthorne's lips thinned. "Fine. But when I get home and tell my husband, if he disagrees with this, we'll come bangin' on your door. At least for now, I won't have to contend with a cat." She nodded goodbye, then slipped into the crowd.

Margaux gave a huge sigh of satisfaction. She squeezed her brother's shoulders again. This time, Tom noted, the girl's fragile hand didn't tremble.

Josh clung to his crate. "Sah...se," he struggled to say.

Margaux looked up at Amanda. "Josh wants to know if Sunset can stay with us."

"Of course she can," Amanda replied. Tom noticed that even though Margaux spoke for Josh, Amanda was very deliberate in responding directly to the boy. "We need a little kitten. We've got a few pesky mice around, now that the snow has melted, and I have to keep all my food and supplies in tins."

Tom lifted their two suitcases. "Come and meet my dog. I'll put your bags in the wagon, then we'll get something to eat. I don't know about you, but I'm starving. I know the owner of this dining house," he said, motioning to the glass windows behind him. "Her name's Ruby. She'll let us keep the kitten under our table, as long as you keep her in her crate."

"Sure sounds nice," said Margaux. She licked her palm then patted the hairs over her brother's ears, causing Tom to like her even more, as her brother's tender keeper. "Josh, mind your manners." She stooped down to her brother's ear and Tom heard her whisper, "I'm feelin' a bit hungry now, are you?"

Amanda must have heard, for she looked at Tom with open pleasure. His pulse quickened at the speculative glimmer in her blue eyes. Trying to ignore the strange aching in his limbs, he cleared his throat, glanced down at his own rough clothing—big mud boots and baggy work shirt—and wondered if he looked too sloppy for dining.

"You're fine," said Amanda with that shy, enticing smile, sailing by him in a wave of wonderful, feminine curves.

Chapter Six

"Where's Clarissa this evening?"

It was one of the first things Ruby Gilbert said to Tom after the stout blond-haired woman had set them up at the corner window table, said her hellos, and distributed the menus. She had preferred to take the kitten to a spare back room to let her roam, and the children had agreed.

Tom almost groaned out loud at Ruby's question, but stopped himself when he noticed Amanda watching him. A heat flared between them. Did she feel the tug, too? Did she know what it was? A passing interest? A mutual attraction? *Where could it lead them?*

"Clarissa's gone back to her family in Calgary." He unfolded his cardboard menu and read the entrées, knowing them well by heart, considering how many times he'd eaten here with his former… What exactly had Clarissa been to him? His former fiancée who hadn't known it? A familiar twinge of failure twisted in his gut.

Ruby leaned first on one foot, then the other, a habit she had, likely because her feet were sore from standing most of the day. "She'll be back for the ball, won't she?"

"Nope," said Tom, not glancing up. "What's your soup today?"

"Potato and barley. Oh, sure she will. She told me she wouldn't miss it for the world. She was so excited about that fancy dress she had made—"

"Nope," said Tom, more forcefully. "Would you children like to have a sarsaparilla?"

The distraction worked. The children glanced up from the red tablecloth, where they sat on either side of him, Amanda across the table. "What's a sarsaparilla?" Margaux asked.

"It's a special drink with soda bubbles."

Amanda requested one, too, while he asked for an ale. After they'd placed their food orders, Ruby waltzed away. "Clarissa will be back," she cooed good-naturedly, irking Tom again.

"Will she?" Amanda asked across the table. Her dark hair swung over proud shoulders, framing her oval face, trailing softly at her satiny throat, and lower still to the creamy sliver of skin above her cleavage.

His gaze was bold and honest. "If she comes back, it won't be for me."

Amanda's color heightened. She faltered in the silence, or perhaps the directness of his reply. Then the intimate moment was lost as she attended to the children's needs.

While they ate, Tom watched Amanda help the children first with their plate of potato salad and roast chicken, then her own. She patiently answered Margaux's questions about the town, about herself, about the shack, and seemed to take great pleasure in their company. She'd make a good mother herself one day, Tom thought.

Did she often think of it herself? Gazing at her tender face, listening to her soft laughter, he had no doubt that one day she'd be asked again for her hand in marriage. And judging from how many men had looked in her direction tonight, she'd have plenty of choice. Why did that make his stomach churn—

"Tom!" hollered a man at the door.

Tom looked up to see the blacksmith, Bill Seger, approaching. The hefty man nodded hello to the group, then lowered his booming voice. "I gotta ask you somethin' about the last bill you sent."

Tom preferred to discuss business during business hours. Besides, he was with company and the interruption felt rude. "Could it wait till the morning?"

Bill shoved his rectangular hands into his pockets. "All right. I'll be by around seven. I'd like to know why you and Finnigan are chargin' me more for my lumber than my neighbor."

Tom knew there was always an explanation about this sort of thing. "Sure," he said with a friendly nod. "I'll pull my receipts in the morning. Must be a different cut of lumber."

"It wasn't."

"Did he buy a larger quantity maybe, so he got a lower price?"

"It's just about dead even."

Tom ran a hand through his hair. "I'll have a careful look at it in the morning. Don't worry. If a mistake's been made, I'll rectify it."

With relief, Bill clapped him on the shoulder and shook his hand. "Good man," he said, walking away.

Someone tapped Tom on his other shoulder. When Tom whirled around, Sully Campbell, seated at the table next to theirs, was staring at him from across the bridge of his windburned nose.

"I heard that, Tom, and I'm glad Bill brought it up. Remember when my brother Slick and I came to you about buildin' the hardware store? Well, I've been scratchin' my head for a month now over all the extras you charged me. Mind if I drop by in the mornin', too?''

A month ago? Tom nodded with outward confidence, but was beginning to feel cornered. What was going on? He himself didn't keep track of the receipts, one of his men did—and occasionally, Finnigan. Mistakes were sometimes made on both sides of the journal, but never anything major. But…hell, what if…what if Finnigan…?

Across the room, elderly Mr. Thimbleton, the banker, looked up from his roast beef and gravy pie, scrutinized Tom, then slowly nodded hello.

"Is everything all right, Tom?" Amanda asked from raised lashes. Concern radiated from her face.

"Sure," he said, "everything's fine." He'd been in business for three years with never a complaint. Why should he worry now? Two people were coming by in the morning with simple questions, that's all. Two honest, hardworking people Tom knew and trusted. No problem.

But dang it, he had no money in his account for any more problems. Payroll had to be met again tomorrow.

He was glad when they'd left the dining room and were settled back into the wagon. The children slipped to the back, lying on top of their suitcases with a blanket they'd pulled out of one, Wolf nuzzled down beside them and Amanda sunk comfortably in the front beside him, her long legs a foot away from his thigh.

Gazing up at the twinkling stars, he took a deep breath of chilly night air and decided not to concern himself with business tonight. *Don't borrow worry,* his pa would always say, *it'll find you when it needs to.* Pa's gentle way was one of the many calming things Tom liked about his father.

Tom turned his ear toward Amanda, comforted by her easy, melodic tone as she explained the landmarks to the children. "And here's the turn in the road where you head for school. I'll show you tomorrow, Margaux. But we'll take it slow, and until you've made your decision about staying or going, we'll hold off on school. And that cabin there is where the O'Haras live...."

When they reached her shack, a light flickered in the window, the curtain fell closed, then Grandma stepped through the door. "Amanda? Did you bring the children?"

"Yes I did, Grandma."

Amanda waited for Tom to help her down. Her warm fingers heated his cool palm as she slid down his length. He liked the feeling of her hand tucked in his, but it didn't last for long. Wolf and the children came tumbling out of the buckboard, followed by warm introductions made to Miss Clementine.

Lugging the suitcases inside the shack, Tom set them down inside the door. He'd forgotten how cramped it was inside. His shoulders barely fit through the opening, and he had to dip his head beneath the beam.

"I pushed the beds together. We can all sleep across the beds, instead of lengthwise." Miss Clementine pointed to the six-foot bed that nearly spanned the eight-foot width of the shack. "It was the only thing I could think of in a pinch."

It would do for now, Tom thought, but not for long.

"We'll stuff pillows in between the children and ourselves," Grandma explained to her granddaughter. "You and I have to curl up our legs because the bed won't be long enough, but it's better than sleepin' on the floor."

"It'll do nicely," Amanda said.

Why hadn't Tom thought of something better? He'd had a few hours to think of it, but it hadn't crossed his mind. He edged his body closer to Amanda. "Tomorrow, I'll see if I can arrange something more comfortable."

He was well aware that for whatever reason, Amanda

couldn't bring herself to meet his gaze. Flustered, she likely wasn't used to men observing her bed, or discussing her sleeping arrangements. *Hmm...sleeping arrangements with Amanda Ryan.*

"I best be going," he said, interrupting his own train of thought.

"Wait, I'll walk you out," she said to his dismay.

As they left, the children were removing Sunset from the crate and introducing her to Grandma. Tom liked seeing the older woman with the orange kitten nestled at her heavy throat.

Outside, as Tom and Amanda wove along the forest, the wind had stilled. Crickets chirped and the soft call of mountain lions echoed in the distance. The fragrant scent of wild mountain orchids drifted through the air. When they reached his buckboard, Tom spun around to say goodnight, but didn't realize Amanda was following so close. His nostrils filled with a heady scent of her skin.

Her nearness kindled feelings of desire. The moonlight caught one side of her face and drifted over the curvy shapes, the delicate valleys, and the firm chin. She stared up at him, hugging her arms to her shawl. "Thank you for tonight. For helping me to pick up the children, and for dinner."

"My pleasure," he said. His gaze riveted to her vitality. The pride in her downy cheeks. Her full, rich lips. "Are you going to the ball?" The question surprised him, even as it left his mouth.

She was a bit startled, too, and stepped back. "No, Tom."

He tingled as she said his name. Her mouth softened, perfect for kissing, he thought, and his body ached to touch hers. "What if someone asks you?"

She swallowed tightly, her eyes glistening in the golden

light. Was he about to ask her? He didn't know himself. *Was he?*

Looking back to the shack, she said, "I've got more important things to spend my money on than a stuffy old ball gown."

He smiled at her assessment. "Yeah, I guess you do. And you see," he murmured tenderly, referring to the children, "you were worried, but they like you."

She laughed gently, barely audible, but her hushed moan rippled through him.

He couldn't resist her. With one smooth step, he closed the gap between them, dipping his large calloused hand, caressing her satiny cheek. He heard her intake of breath, felt the rise and fall of her breasts against his chest. With one hand at the back of her neck, pressing her silky hair, he lowered his head and pulled her tight.

Their lips met and his hunger exploded. He felt her shudder beneath him and his entire body quaked in response. Why did her touch upset his balance? Why did a mere glance in his direction send his pulse careening to the clouds?

What was it about Amanda Ryan that drugged him?

Their hearts beat faster together. She allowed her shawl to fall to the ground as she reached up and wrapped her arms around his neck. Her breasts flattened against him and he moaned with the pleasure of her heated curves in his.

His arms encircled her and she was weightless as he lifted her. Swirling her around, he pressed her supple back into the wagon and their urgency doubled. His long, muscled legs crushed against her lean ones.

Her lips opened and their tongues met in delicious exploration.

He was drawn into a passion he'd never felt before. He

wanted to make love to her, right here and now, to cover every inch of her body with his urgent lips.

She was a beautiful, enthralling, selfless woman.

When their bodies shifted and his thigh brushed her hip, he felt a change in her. She wrested free of his grasp, struggling for air.

"Amanda—" he gasped, entwining his rough fingers in her mass of hair "—what is it about you? You send me spinning."

"Tom, I don't think—"

Faint voices from the cabin distracted them. They listened, but it was only laughter.

"Don't worry," he murmured, taking her chin in his hand, feeling her relax, "they can't see us."

Her hair was tousled around her shoulders and her lips raw from his kiss, and when she smiled up at him, she was the most captivating vision he'd ever seen.

He wanted to prolong the moment, to say something to please her. "Margaux and Josh are lucky you found them. You're a natural mother, and one day your own will also be blessed."

Her face sobered so quickly it was as if someone had struck her. Her trembling lips fell open. She pulled away.

"Did I say something wrong?"

Stooping to pick up her shawl, she could barely speak. "I—I need to go in."

He heard the dejection in her voice. The distress in his own escalated. "What's wrong?" He reached out for her, but she'd already slipped through his fingers, running, escaping to the shack. "Amanda, what did I say?"

Even three days later, every time Amanda looked at Tom and his icy, rugged profile, her heart turned over.

Would she ever be able to accept herself the way she was?

What she yearned for most in the world, she would never have—a child of her own, a child to share with a husband. There, she said it, if only to herself.

She sighed in the late afternoon wind, feeling heavy with the burden of truth. Was she destined to be alone for the rest of her life? She knew there was more to *her* than her ability to bear children, but would a man see it that way?

Would Tom?

She glanced from beside the porch where she was helping Margaux climb onto the bicycle seat, to where Tom and Donald were laying another squared-off log onto the east wall of the emerging cabin. Such a stoic jaw and stubborn set to his lips.

"I think I can do it this time," said Margaux.

With an emerging smile, Amanda steadied the bicycle. It was her good fortune to have a profession where she worked with children, even if they weren't her own. Behind her, Josh's mumbled laughter echoed off the trees as he played tag with Wolf, filling Amanda with pleasure. Tom and Donald looked up from their four-foot wall. Their workday would soon be over.

"Hold on tight," Amanda said, trying to force thoughts of Tom from her mind. "Try to steer straight down the path." She released the bicycle for the tenth run, and this time Margaux was able to hold her balance. "Good girl, keep going!"

If anything soothed Amanda's spirits, it was that Margaux and Josh were taking to her. Her letter to the orphanage had been sent as planned and Mrs. Hawthorne hadn't raised further objections. Thanks to Tom, who had his men build a tiered bed—similar to the ones they had in trains and ships—the children had their own sleeping nook. Margaux's was on top and Josh's on the bottom. The children had regained color in their cheeks, Grandma was tickled to have tiny laundry to wash, and even their kitten, who was at first frightened of Wolf, had relaxed.

But what of Amanda's practice? Since Fannie's leaving, no other patient had taken her place. In addition to everything else that weighed on Amanda, was it time again to worry about finances?

"Howdy." Ellie's voice cut through the wind as she came to pick up her husband. They could stay for only five minutes; long enough to clap for Margaux on her bicycle.

When they left, Amanda waved goodbye, watching Ellie stroll away. Would Ellie be her first delivery? How would Amanda respond to holding her first baby since that tragic night? It comforted her to realize that her hands never trembled during her appointments with other women; it was only thoughts of her own loss that affected her.

Tom had seen her tremble. First in the mercantile when Mr. Langston had handed her the kerosene jug, then later when he'd mentioned the word mother and she'd gone running.

What did he think of her? Was he wondering? Or was he troubled by his own problems? She glanced at his profile as he tapped and hammered a log in the wall, checking his work for the day. Yesterday, he'd brought the law with him, and she'd explained everything that had happened between her and Mr. Finnigan to Constable Graham Robarts. But come to think of it, Tom had been distracted by something.

Were those darker circles beneath his eyes? What was troubling him? Those receipts from the blacksmith?

Tom slid his hammer into the carpenter's belt around his waist. Although perspiration drizzled from his temples and stained his denim workshirt, he looked like a solid statue of brawn and sinew. He unhooked his belt, lay it to rest on a board, then stooped low beside Josh, draping his casual arm across Josh's shoulder as the boy petted Wolf. "Look at your sister ride."

They watched Margaux yelp with glee on the shaky bicycle. When she got to the end of the path, she fell over, unharmed, yanking the fabric of her skirt that was caught in the broken leather. She gave a proud smile of success to her brother.

Tom looked in Amanda's direction, and for a brief moment the air charged between them, ripe with emotion. Amanda's stomach clenched. She could see the hurt in his deep green eyes. That long dimple in his cheek that normally ran clear to his jawline when he smiled only flitted across his face. His black brows were set deeper, in a gruff line across his forehead. Obviously he didn't understand her withdrawal.

Three nights ago, their drive to pick up the children had bonded them in an indefinable way. Amanda had felt the smoldering pull between them all evening, the double meaning of his glances, the rush of excitement when she'd accidentally brushed his knee beneath the table. When it came to saying good-night, she'd shamelessly melted into his arms.

Now, as she met his eyes, the memory of their warm embrace brought a tingling to the pit of her stomach, a galloping to her heart. Did he feel anything, staring at her behind that mask of indifference? *Her* lips still burned where he'd kissed her. Those strong, chiseled arms, muscled from lifting logs and chopping wood, had wrapped around her and felt wonderful.

But her *situation* wasn't an easy thing to explain. How would she even begin? *Tom, I'm sorry, but do you really*

*think you should be kissing me? I have something impor-
tant you should know first.* It was just a kiss, for heaven's
sake! No deep sentiments. Not that she wanted any. Lord,
after William had left her, she'd never thought it possible
to be interested in any other man.

But beyond a doubt, she had been interested in kissing
Tom.

It just created more problems. For at what point should
she tell him she couldn't have children? Now, after their
first kiss? Perhaps after their second? Before any public
outings? How about before she met his brothers, but right
after she'd planned their first meal together? It was all so
convoluted and ridiculous!

She and Tom weren't even close.

Did she want to be?

She gulped and glanced away from his resolute glare,
back to Margaux on the bicycle. Deep down, her worst
fear was…even if she mustered the courage to tell him,
how would he respond to her problem? Would he react the
same as William had? William had accused her, in a court
of law surrounded by their family and friends, of being
barren.

In a town where farmers, ranchers and businessmen
prided themselves on the size of their families, what would
Tom think of her? Not only was it a matter of masculine
pride to have many children, but one of economics. Men
needed sons and daughters to help with livestock, to plant
seed and harvest crops, to continue their line of work. Tom
would need them to carry on his sawmill, to cut logs, to
handle customers, to care for him in his old age. How could
she expect him to be any different in his needs and desires
for a family than any other healthy, red-blooded male?

Barren. What a lonesome, forlorn word. One she couldn't divulge to anyone. The midwife's secret, she thought. Her chest rose and fell with despair. She wasn't the right woman for Tom.

Chapter Seven

"Please say you'll stay longer," Margaux begged Tom. She stood in the half-cut entry to the new cabin, playing with the fishing reel the O'Haras had lent her yesterday. "You're done early today, so we know you have time."

"I've got things to do at home," Tom answered, removing his muddy work boots and replacing them with the black cowboy boots he'd begun stashing in the wagon, trying to reduce the amount of mud he brought home. But quite frankly, he could use a diversion from his own problems. If he went home alone, he'd just get all worked up again.

He glanced from Margaux's windswept features to her thin brother, who was dangling a piece of yarn in front of Sunset. Wolf looked on, his white head cocked in amusement. When the kitten pounced on the string, Josh buried his face in her russet fur and Wolf barked in approval.

It was getting close to the end of the children's first week here, but Tom knew they hadn't made their decision yet about staying. He hoped they'd say yes, for their own well-being.

Margaux was right about finishing early. It was only around three in the afternoon. Donald had already left because they'd gotten an early start this morning, cutting and stacking more logs today than any other. Good thing, too, because judging from the incoming clouds, it looked as though a rainstorm was heading in.

Tom's biceps ached from strenuous labor. Last night, he'd gotten another load of furniture varnished for the big hotel, and his men had delivered it this morning. A day of rest would do him good.

With a rustling of her skirts, Amanda came striding out of the shack, dressed in a freshly ironed white blouse and narrow black skirt. If he said yes to the youngsters, what would she have to say about it? "Done for the day?" she asked.

Tom nodded in reply. "Yeah." He felt a slow trickle of sweat ease its way down the back of his neck. Was it hot today, or did he only notice the heat more when he gazed at her?

A thick belt cinched her narrow waist, emphasizing her jutting breasts and fine hips. An escaping curl tucked itself over her creamy forehead, deepening the color of her blue eyes.

Why did he wince, looking at her? Why did the memory of her frosty response the other night make him feel…well, *awful?*

She didn't want him here, that's why. It was plain to Tom. Gazing at her solitary figure, he couldn't imagine why he'd thought she wanted him to kiss her. He'd overstepped his boundaries, but he damn well wouldn't do it again.

Not so she could put him in his place. After all, he was the worker, she the paying boss.

He felt Wolf nuzzle his leg. His only true friend.

"Margaux, be careful with that rod please," Amanda

warned. "I asked you not to practice with it around your brother. Someone might get hurt."

"Okay, I'll remove the hook," Margaux said. She looked very comfortable reeling in the line, untying the sharp hook, and Tom wondered where she'd learned it. "I was just practicin'. Please say yes," she said, tugging at Tom's dusty pant leg. Adjusting her wire spectacles, she turned to Amanda. "Please, Amanda, you ask him. Josh and I thought we could take you both fishin'."

"Fissin'," Josh echoed.

With a rosy tint to her cheeks, Amanda opened her mouth, but nothing came out. Tom lowered his head and stared at her. He'd like to hear her ask him.

She didn't.

He tried to tell himself he didn't care. Glancing at the boy's sun-kissed cheeks, Tom's lips dragged up at the corner. He tugged Josh by his gray suspenders, then lowered himself to the boy's level. *"Fishing,"* Tom repeated, enunciating slowly. "Can you say *fishing?"*

Tom watched Josh's mouth try to form the words. "Fissin'," the boy replied.

"He used to try to talk a lot more," Margaux said wistfully. "People used to make fun of him. Now he only speaks one word at a time."

Tom wasn't sure what surprised him more about Margaux's statement—Josh's terrible situation, or Margaux's matter-of-fact understanding.

Josh had the stilted vocabulary of a two-and-a-half-year-old, despite being four. What sort of life would Josh lead when he grew older?

Tom swallowed hard at Margaux's comment and glanced at Amanda, who met his eyes with open dismay.

"Sweetheart," Amanda said to Josh. "We'll practice together. I'll help you."

Maybe the children needed an escape from their problems more than Tom did. To Josh's giggling delight, Tom scooped the boy into his arms, then nestled him on top of his wide shoulders. "Fissin' is close enough." He turned to Margaux's exuberant expression. "How come you know so much about fishing?"

"My mother and father used to take us on their boat. Josh doesn't remember, but I do."

Again, Tom and Amanda exchanged a tender glance. Margaux didn't seem to have any difficulty talking about her past, even though Tom knew her folks had drowned. He tried to bury his sympathetic moan, but Amanda pressed her moist lips together and shook her head.

"Whaddya say?" Tom said to Amanda, deciding to forget about their personal differences. She didn't have to like *him* but he wanted her to like the children. He liked children, too, maybe because he grew up as the oldest and was always tending to one brother or another. Whatever the feelings between him and Amanda, he respected her for caring for these youngsters. *With no man to help her.* "How about we take them down to the river for an hour? Before it rains."

Amanda cupped Margaux's shoulder. "That's a nice idea. Grandma's taking care of supper."

The children whooped with excitement.

"But," Tom added, "I'll only go as long as Josh promises to bait my hook. I don't like worms," he said, pretending he was squeamish, making the children laugh.

After Amanda had told Grandma where they were headed and they'd gathered their other supplies—another fishing rod from the shack, a basket filled with weights, tackle and equipment for scaling fish—Tom slid the forty-pound boy off his shoulders. "The trees on the path are too tall," he explained. "I'll have to set you down so you don't bump your head."

Glancing at Amanda's rosy cheeks, he told himself he was doing this for the children, not for her.

"You look tired," Amanda said to him as they wove through the pines and poplars to the river. She dipped her body beneath a blossoming branch. He tried to ignore her lovely shape.

Was she concerned about him? He ran a hand along his cotton sleeve. "I guess I am." He realized with a snort that he'd never felt this tired. Exhausted from working, but he ached more from thinking. Twigs cracked beneath the shiny silver toes of his boots. Up ahead, the children raced between the trees, insisting on independence, carrying their own rods. Wolf and Sunset tagged along at their heels.

Amanda craned her neck, lifting her face up at his. "Are you working too hard?"

Was that why she was concerned? Did she think he might be too tired to finish her cabin on time? "Don't worry," he said, "I'll get your cabin built. Maybe even a couple of days early, and you'll get your dollar bonus."

She pressed her lips together in frustration. "That's not why I asked." He watched the rise and fall of her breasts. "How did…how did it go for you last week, when you met with the blacksmith about his receipts?"

Tom shoved a hand into his denim pocket. "Fine. I handled it." He didn't feel like confiding in her. Besides, it wasn't something he was proud of.

He owed Bill Seger and Sully Campbell money. Finnigan had cheated them for a combined total of two hundred and three dollars. Neither knew about the other's overcharge, and Tom, so far, had been able to keep it confidential. When the bank manager came to call, expressing concern for what he'd overheard at Ruby's, Tom had no choice—he placed his home up for collateral and repaid the two men.

Now his sawmill and his house were both in hawk.

Tom cursed under his breath. Gabe's law tuition was looming. It was Finnigan's blasted fault. Yesterday, the Mounties had received a sighting of him in the far north, in the town of Edmonton. Where the hell was he hiding? Was Clarissa still with him?

Tom stopped when Margaux crouched beside a spruce tree, her hem trailing the dirt.

"What's this set of animal tracks?" Margaux asked. The children had been quizzing him about animal and bird tracks for the past few days, and he was amused by their questions. So was Amanda.

Tom fingered the single line of paw prints, marked with claws, that led behind a boulder. The tracks were several hours old, judging by their dryness.

"What do *you* think it is?" Tom asked, pushing thoughts of Finnigan out of his head. "I'll give you a clue. It's an animal that walks on four feet."

Josh tapped his wool cap, then pointed to Wolf, who was sniffing the tracks. "Woff. Awggie."

"No, it's not Wolf. Dogs don't walk in a straight line like this. They imprint all four paws, side by side."

"Are they kitten tracks?" Amanda asked, her face enraptured by the puzzle.

"That's close," said Tom gently. "The tracks of a cat's hind feet fall exactly in the tracks of their front feet, so it looks like they're walking in a straight line. But cats retract their claws when they walk, so they don't leave behind these claw marks."

"That's why cats are silent when they walk across a plank floor," Amanda offered. "Because they retract their claws."

"Just like Sunset," said Margaux. "She's quiet."

"That's right." Tom nodded. "And dogs can't retract their claws, so they click across the floor."

Josh thought for a moment. "Foss," he mumbled.

They all glanced up at Tom, waiting for his response. "Fox?" How in tarnation did the boy know that? Tom rubbed his bristly jaw in amazement. "That's right," he said, sharing a proud smile with Amanda. "How did you know that?"

"Because he's smart," Margaux simply said. Josh beamed.

Amanda's eyes twinkled at Tom, making his pulse hum.

"You sure are," Tom said to the boy. "A fox walks in a single line, like a cat, but it leaves claw marks like a dog."

When they were finished, they walked in amiable silence to the riverbank and gazed over the rushing water.

Tom wanted the children to show him and Amanda all they knew of fishing. He sensed their independence was particularly important to Margaux, so he decided to step aside and let them lead.

The children removed their boots and socks and traipsed around in muddy feet. Amanda sat on a boulder and watched as Margaux proudly raced to show them what she knew. That's how he and his brothers used to race, Tom thought as the tension left his muscles, when they were younger, trying to prove themselves to each other and their folks. Ma had now been gone for twenty years from her heart illness, but Tom still warmly recalled racing to her with his first trout.

Margaux caught the dew worms on her own. She and Josh baited their J-shaped metal barbs, but when she swung the rod over her shoulder to toss the line into the river, Amanda reared back, out of the line of fire. "Be careful, sweetheart, I know you want to do a good job, but those hooks are sharp.''

"They're fine," said Tom from another boulder. "I'm watching them."

But instead, he was distracted by Amanda's warm smile as she interacted with the children. He should have heard the reel unwinding, he should have heard the line snap.

But all he felt was a sharp jab in his left biceps. Then an excruciating yank that shot down clear to his fingers. He'd been hit. "Ah-hh."

He pulled hard on the line to stop Margaux from reeling further. When he looked down, the fishhook was imbedded in his left sleeve. Blood seeped through his torn checked shirt. The worm had fallen onto his boot, luckily, so it wasn't impaled inside his flesh. A dirty cut, nonetheless.

"Ah, hell," he groaned, trying to rise to his feet, but stumbling back on his behind instead.

"Tom," Amanda shouted. She dropped to his side, blocking the view of both children.

Beneath Amanda's elbow, Tom saw the rod tumble out of Margaux's hands. "Oh, no, did Tom get hurt?" Her face paled and her body began to shake. "I'm sorry…"

Josh began to cry, but Amanda was still blocking them.

"It's all right. I'm okay," Tom tried to tell them. But when he looked down, he wasn't. More blood had poured out, his upper sleeve soaked. Dammit! He tried to cup his hand over the wound, knowing he should clamp pressure on it to stop the bleeding, but how could he press down with the hook still imbedded? His arm throbbed like thunder. His head ached.

"Don't move," Amanda whispered over him, ripping at the shirtsleeve.

Tom felt woozy. Bile bit at the back of his throat.

Amanda glanced frantically to the basket of fishing supplies, looking for *something,* then commanded the children. "Margaux, take your brother! Run along the riverbank then up to the O'Hara's!"

Margaux and Josh didn't move. "It's my fault," sobbed Margaux. "I was showin' off."

Amanda raised her voice and then they scrambled. "Honey, it's no one's fault. Please run!" The leaves beyond their heads vibrated with her shouts. "Tell Pierce to get my medical bag from the shack, and tell Mr. O'Hara to get Dr. Murdock!"

Amanda steadied her breathing, barely noticing her thumping pulse as she examined the jagged tear. The wire fishing line was still attached to the hook, and it all combined to bulge out of the muscled, bleeding hole. "You're bleeding an awful lot. It must have snagged a large vein."

Tom moaned. She noted that his face was white, but his heartbeat and breathing were steady. Propped on the grass with a boulder behind him, he braced his arm against his body.

With speedy hands, she removed her white cotton petticoat then grabbed the basket of supplies. Above them, clouds moved over the sun, casting them in shadow.

"Pull the damn hook out, will ya?" he groaned.

"I can't."

"I can." When he went to yank on the wire, she caught his hand.

Amanda met his eyes and tried not to show that she was trembling. "Don't. You can't remove a fishhook the same way it went in. The barb would rip your flesh and cause more injury. You might lose the use of your arm if nerves are damaged."

"Then how are we supposed to get it out?"

She choked down her queasiness. "I have to push the

hook through the skin on the other side of your biceps muscle, then cut the barb off, then slide it out from where it came.''

"Like hell you will."

It would be easier and faster to help him if he were under chloroform. She prayed he wouldn't fight her. "Fortunately, it's gone through muscle, not bone. But to stop the bleeding I need to remove the hook."

"Are you sure of what you're doing?"

"Positive." Her lips went dry. Blazes, it must hurt. She peered into the basket, spotting a set of cutters. They were the snips she used for removing fish heads.

She picked up the cool metal grips and groaned when she spotted the sliver of rust along one blade. "We've got to use these to cut the tip. We can cleanse the wound later when my bag or your brother arrives, but what we can't do is pour more blood into you once you've lost it." Besides, she couldn't wait here forever.

What if Quaid Murdock never arrived? What if no one could find him?

Tom needed treatment immediately. The longer the dirty hook was in, the greater the chance of blood contamination.

His muscled body went rigid. "Do it now."

"I'm sorry, it's going to hurt. You'll get pain medication later. Take a deep breath."

He took one.

She pressed against the end of the hook. Tom groaned with the pressure and, steeling herself, she told herself to be quick. The brown point of the metal hook appeared beneath the bronzed skin. When she gave it extra pressure, the barb pierced the surface. In a slippery pool of blood, she clipped the jagged top, slid the hook out, then pressed her petticoat to the wound.

Tom heaved with the assault.

"I'm sorry," she whispered, brimming with compassion. "Help's coming. Hold on."

She was still applying pressure when five minutes later Pierce came running down the riverbank with her black medical bag. "Amanda! I'm here!"

"Thanks, Pierce." She unbuckled the bag, removed a linen pad and asked him to pour diluted carbolic acid on it. She soaked Tom's wound. He jolted with the sting. And again when she repeated it, he didn't pull away. Lord, the man was stoic.

"Pierce, put pressure here while I measure the morphine."

The young man did as she asked. After she filled the syringe, she injected it into Tom's good, right arm. Thank God, she could finally help ease his pain.

"I'll clear up the fishin' tackle," Pierce said when everything had settled. He rose and scanned the area. "I don't think Margaux and Josh should see this mess if they come down. They were cryin' pretty hard."

"Where are they now?" Amanda asked.

"Watchin' you, up through the crest of that ridge."

"What?" Amanda and Tom groaned together and looked up to the forest's edge.

"Grandma insisted on comin' in case I needed help, but didn't want to bring them closer in case…he looked bad."

Tom waved weakly with this good arm, but the sister and her brother looked like they were still crying. The sky rumbled with muted thunder. Grandma waved, indicating she was taking the children back to the shack. Amanda would soothe them later. Right now she concentrated on her work.

Pierce walked downriver, headed to the two discarded rods lying on the ground.

When the medicine took hold, Amanda sutured Tom's wound, the entry and exit holes, nine stitches total. With a wisp of sadness, she realized he'd have permanent scars on his biceps. "I'm sorry this happened to you." She suddenly noticed how close they were sitting, dark heads almost touching.

"It was an accident."

She felt his body slacken beneath her own. The morphine was helping. Her body, in turn, relaxed with his.

When she finished with Tom's sutures, she took a good long look at him. Her hair, pinned loose over her back, dipped low over her shoulders. "Are you feeling better?"

He'd regained his color and managed a weak smile. "Yeah."

She quirked a brow at his expression. Something about the pleasant sparkle in his eyes, the agreeable tug at the corner of his well-defined mouth.... Sometimes, people reacted strangely to the morphine.

She'd seen it three or four times in Grandpa's practice, but there was nothing she could do for the patient once it started except let it ride. Tom became talkative.

"Why did you leave me standing at your door that night?" His voice was husky at her ear, his breath warm at her neck. Her heart began to race. His skin smelled fresh, like the wind and the river. "You know the night I mean."

Her chest tightened beneath his scrutiny. Now that the emergency was over, she was abruptly aware that beneath her long skirt, her knee was pressed between his firm legs and she was almost straddling his warm thigh. Good heavens, how had she gotten into this intimate position?

She lifted her knee and swung her legs over to the medicine bag lying beside her on the grass, hastening to tidy her bottles. "Now I know you're feeling better," she said, trying to sound casual. "But next time, I'll give you laudanum instead of morphine.'' Even though they were both derivatives of opium, she had used the morphine initially because it was more potent.

He reached out and touched the back of her hair, weaving his fingers between the black strands and her spine, sending waves of pleasure tumbling through her skin. ''Why did you flee? Don't you want to answer the question?''

''No,'' she whispered, completely still beneath his stroke.

''Then how about this one. If you were going to run away, why did you tempt me?'' He reached out and grazed her cheek, gently turning her face to his, arousing her to his burning touch. ''Why, Amanda, did you bother to kiss me back?''

''Please,'' she said, pulling away, feeling herself shiver, ''it's the medicine speaking.''

''No it's not, it's me.'' He sounded so wounded, so vulnerable.

''It's complicated.''

''I want to hear it anyway.''

She couldn't speak; gazed down at the brown bottle sliding between her fingertips. Her stomach tightened, half with fear, half with the possibility of telling him.

''What are you so afraid of? Are you afraid of me?''

A raindrop pelted her cheek. ''No.'' *Yes.*

He hesitated, measuring her beneath half-hooded lids. His voice was low and raspy. Were her senses deceiving her, or was he beginning to slur his words? ''Your former husband. What did he do to you?''

She tried to manage a feeble answer. ''Nothing.''

''Yes he did,'' Tom said evenly, tearing down her carefully built composure with his deep, dark gaze. ''And I'm going to find out what it was.''

He *mustn't*. It was too painfully private. "How do you...how do you intend to do that?"

"You're going to tell me." His silky fingers traced a path down her temple, then over her softly parted mouth, sweetly draining her of all resistance. "When you're ready, you're going to come to me and I'm going to hear it from these gorgeous lips."

The bottle of solution dropped from her hand and smashed on the stones between them.

Chapter Eight

"Tom!" A man's voice boomed from the trees, echoing above the gush of the river, startling Amanda. "Blazes, man, what have you gotten yourself into?"

Not yet recovered from Tom's intimate questioning, Amanda whirled to face the man running toward them. His tall, skinny body pounded the shore. A droopy, walrus mustache etched his young face. In his late twenties, wearing a bowler hat, white linen shirt, suede vest and brown silk cravat, he carried a leather medical bag. Help was here.

"Quaid," Tom called, then clamped a hand on Amanda's pivoting shoulder, anchoring her to the spot with his possessive hand. "We'll continue this later," he murmured, strumming another chord within her.

"How are you, Quaid?" Tom asked when his brother reached them. They looked similar, thought Amanda, except Quaid had brown hair instead of black, and his nose was larger.

Quaid laughed and nodded politely to Amanda. "How am I? Why you devil, you've frightened everyone—" Quaid stopped and stared at his brother. "Uh-oh. You've got that wild look in your eyes. You didn't give him morphine, did you, miss?"

Amanda rose to her feet and glanced down at Tom, with his tousled black hair, shadow of a beard, the irrepressible green eyes framing the handsome square face. His snug denims and silver-tipped boots added to his charm. ''I'm afraid I did. He's handling it pretty well—''

''That means the worst is yet to come—''

''Don't talk about me like I'm not here,'' Tom interjected with humor, trying to rise to his feet. This time his words were definitely slurred and he was swaying. Both Amanda and Quaid sprang to help him. Tom took their hands and yanked hard, nearly toppling them both. Then he laughed. ''Oops.'' He was as strong and tough as an ox.

Amanda bit down on her smile, but it was good to see he'd conquered his pain. He'd be fine. She could see it.

Quaid ignored Tom's comment and kept talking about him. ''He had a toothache a few years back and when I gave him morphine, he was dancing around the room on one leg. Why didn't you tell this woman—''

''I never thought of it.'' Tom's mischievous grin set off the deep groove that ran to his jaw. Why, he was teasing her.

''Well, it doesn't matter now,'' said Quaid. His good humor seemed to darken. ''Although I wish she'd given you laudanum. Let's see your arm.''

Tom held out his arm for Quaid to examine. Amanda was struck by the picture they made, two brothers deeply caring for one another. ''Amanda's already fixed it,'' Tom said, ''and she did a great job.''

''Hmm,'' said Quaid, ruffling his brow.

Amanda shifted uncomfortably in her boots while he prodded at the arm. The sleeve was ripped from the cuff to the shoulder point, exposing Tom's bare flesh. The hairy forearm flexed with deep veins and hard muscles, definitely cultivated from working hard. At least Tom didn't wince as Quaid pressed over the sutures, which meant the morphine was more than effective.

"*I* can take care of my brother now," Quaid said abruptly, releasing the arm. He glanced down at the moist dirt that was streaked along Amanda's black skirt.

She felt temporarily deflated. "Well...of course..."

"Thank you, Amanda," Tom added, frowning at his brother. "Come on, Quaid. Amanda Ryan, meet my brother Quaid Murdock."

She stepped forward, expecting to shake Quaid's hand at the introduction, but he didn't offer one. Instead he stooped down to pick up the basket. "Fannie told me about you."

Amanda felt herself color. Of course, Fannie Potter.

Quaid glanced down at the broken glass by her high laced boots and frowned. Then he peered into the basket and picked up the rusty wire snips. "Did you use *these* on my brother?"

She licked her dry lips. She'd known the dangers, but she'd weighed them carefully before making her decision. Beside her, Tom staggered on his feet.

"Let's help Tom up the riverbank," she said, wrapping her arm around his right side. Quaid did the same on the left. Pierce was already thirty feet ahead of them, carrying their medical bags. She'd return later to clean up the glass.

"I needed to remove the hook," she explained, puffing her way up the hill then through the forest, allowing Tom to lean on her. "And those snips are all I had to cut it with. But as soon as I got my medicine bag, I assure you, I soaked the wound with carbolic acid—"

"The snips are rusty," Quaid accused. "Haven't you read the current journals? Do you know anything about Louis Pasteur's theories? Something called *infection?*"

"Quaid," said Tom gruffly. He smiled at his brother in exaggerated friendliness. *"Lay off."*

Well, blazes. Amanda could take care of herself. She didn't need Tom's chivalry. "Yes, I've read them," she said with confidence, tugging Tom's arm tighter around her neck, causing him to smile, which she ignored. "Including last year's article of Joseph Lister's theories in the *British Medical Journal.*"

Quaid gasped from beneath his brother's wide shoulders. The doctor's mustache dipped well below his chin. "How dare you try to pass yourself off as a doctor—"

"Quaid," said Tom, "get off your high horse. Sorry," he slurred in Amanda's direction, with an apologetic grin. "My brother thinks he needs to protect me."

Raindrops pelted the leaves. Amanda surged forward. "I never claimed I was a doctor. I'm a midwife, with two solid years of book training, and another three combined with practice." *More clinical training than new doctors,* she wanted to add, but didn't have to, for the words clung to the air.

They reached the clearing of the shack and both let go of Tom so he could stand on his own.

Amanda asserted, "I'm well experienced, Quaid—"

"Quaid?" the man asked in horror.

It was an improper slip of the tongue. She should have addressed him as "Doctor."

Before she had a chance to respond, Tom tottered in front of her. "I hereby authorize you to call him Quaid." Rain trickled off his brow, along his straight nose, down his chin. Warm rain splashed them, but no one seemed to notice. Tom waved his finger at his brother. "Nothing else but Quaid. I insist." He nodded extra hard at his brother, like a schoolteacher chastising a wayward student.

She gazed from Quaid's stark disapproval to Tom's

thunderous smile. When Tom winked at her, the brothers struck her as funny. A gentle thread of laughter caught at the back of her throat.

"Tom," said Quaid, "if you talk to me like that, how the hell am I supposed to get any respect in this town?"

Tom turned his palms upward and splayed his arms at the sky, letting the rain splash his face. "How is *she?*"

"She treated you with rusty instruments and gave you morphine," Quaid said in a condescending tone. "Thank you, miss.... Is it *Miss* Ryan? Or *Missus?* I'm not quite sure how to address a woman...of your stature."

Amanda's mouth fell open in surprise. That was uncalled for. "It's *Missus!*" Miss was fine with her, too, but she wouldn't give him the satisfaction of choosing.

That was enough for Tom. He lunged at his brother. "I warned you. Now I'm forced to defend her. And this won't be the first time I've walloped your behind."

Quaid ducked out of harm's way. "Stop that! Or I'll have to come after you!" The two circled each other, fists drawn.

Mortified, Amanda watched. What had she done, calling for Quaid Murdock? She thought Tom's brother would help. But the doctor was fighting with his patient! The family was insane!

She heard the shack door open. Grandma sidled up next to her and planted an open umbrella above their heads. "Why, they're crazier than we are."

Tom hollered at his brother. "Are you going to smarten up and treat her better, or do I have to teach you a lesson?"

"I will *not* fight with you," said Quaid. "Drop your fists." But they both kept circling.

When Margaux and Josh cuddled up to Amanda's skirts, Tom must have noticed them, for he looked in their direction then suddenly sobered. "Howdy, Josh, Margaux. You see, I'm fine."

Margaux buried her face in Amanda's skirt and sobbed.

Amanda stroked her hair. "He's fine, Margaux. It wasn't your fault." Amanda's eye caught the porch, at the two worn leather suitcases. "What's this?"

Grandma spoke up. "I tried to stop them, but they insisted on packin' their things."

"Why?"

"We're leavin'," said Margaux. It was then that Amanda noticed the children were dressed in the clothes in which they'd arrived. "We knew you wouldn't want us to stay around, once…once Mr. Murdock got hit."

"It was an accident, sweetheart," Amanda said, clutching the children to her side.

Margaux's shoulders heaved with her tears. "We'll go back into town with Dr. Murdock and see ourselves to Mrs. Hawthorne's house. She'll help us find the train to Calgary. Sorry we caused you so much trouble, Mr. Tom."

Tom came wobbling over. "No, honey," he said to Margaux. "I'm fine. See?" He twirled around in the rain as Margaux and Josh peeked out from her side.

"Your shirt's all torn up," Margaux said.

"Ah," Tom huffed. "It was an old shirt."

It didn't look old to Amanda, but she was grateful to him for saying so.

"I've got two people lookin' after me, so you don't have to worry. There's Amanda, and then there's my brother here, the doctor."

"Are you sure he's a doctor?" Margaux asked in disbelief.

Quaid scowled.

Tom grinned. "He doesn't look like one or act like one, but he is."

Margaux giggled.

Amanda looked from Margaux's face to Josh's. "I'm still hoping you'll stay here with me. My original offer still stands."

"It does?" Their faces brightened.

Amanda smiled and nodded.

"Then we'd like to stay, instead of going to the Calgary orphanage at all, wouldn't we, Josh?"

"Ya," said Josh.

Amanda clapped her hands in surprise. They wanted to stay? Here with her?

"You know what?" said Tom when the hugging was over, drops pouring off his tanned face, soaking his clothing. "I think we better take cover. It looks like it might rain."

Josh was the first to start laughing, followed by the rest of them. Tom did have a pleasing way with children, thought Amanda.

"I better get you home," said Quaid, mounting his stead. "Getting wet isn't doing you any good. If I ride alongside the wagon, can you control your horse?"

Tom snorted in disgust. "Can I control my horse...."

"Maybe I should come with you," said Amanda.

Tom's eyes lit up. "Maybe you should."

"He'll be fine," Quaid insisted. "I'm here now."

Tom shrugged with disappointment and she laughed softly.

As much as she wanted to go to take care of him, she knew it was better that she stay here to comfort the children.

Where would Quaid take him? Back to his own cabin, or to stay at Quaid's overnight?

Tom lurched his way up the wagon.

"Goodbye, Tom," said Amanda. "And goodbye..."

What should she call Tom's brother? If she called him Quaid, the man would be furious. If she called him Dr. Murdock, Tom would be. "Goodbye *you all*."

Tom winked at her again, and she felt a warm gush of pleasure. She was growing to like him. He was likable, wasn't he? And, Lord, so good-looking.

They were just heading out when a stranger on a small horse, a pinto, rode up the path. "Is this property number D ninety-five?"

"Yes," said Amanda, wondering who he was. "It is my lot."

Was he a government official?

A bearded middle-aged man, he looked weary in the late-afternoon mist, as if he'd been traveling for days. He looked down at a piece of paper between his fingers—the same yellow color and size of Amanda's deed. A sickening wave came over her. Finnigan wouldn't have—couldn't have—sold it twice over.

In a mutual panic, Tom looked to her and she to him.

"Well, then," the man stormed, "why in thunder are you building a cabin on *my* property?"

"I don't know. I don't know," said Benny Jones, the tender-faced clerk in the land registry at ten after eight the next morning. "As soon as you people leave this office and give me a moment to send the telegram to Calgary, I'll let you know when the magistrate will arrive to hear your case."

Tom sighed and glanced at Amanda's stubborn profile as she stood next to him at the long pine counter. He didn't have to ask how she'd slept. One look at the puffy eyelids and the swollen creases in her cheeks told him she'd tossed and turned all night. Beside her stood Miss Clementine, equally agitated, then Pa and Graham Robarts. The newcomer with the deed, Lorne Wilson, had separated himself at the far end of the counter.

Tom had barely recovered from his day yesterday. The morphine had worn off and he'd tried not to take any laudanum, or willow bark crystals, until sunrise when the throbbing became unbearable.

Right now he watched Amanda battle for her land, and his frustration level equaled hers. It wouldn't be fair for her to lose it. She was a good woman with good intentions.

They did have one thing on their side—the stranger's deed wasn't properly dated and it hadn't been sold using a lawyer's services. Tom wondered if that meant anything. Graham had told them he thought it did. It had to.

The stranger from Edmonton, pounded on the counter. "I demand this be settled. I paid good money for this land!"

"But your deed's not dated. It just says May 1888," Miss Clementine argued. "Amanda's says April seventeenth, 1888."

"It don't matter what day!"

"I told you, sir," said the clerk, "it's not my decision, but the magistrate's. Tom's is the first property that's been resold in Banff. The law's not clear about the particulars of the date. And may I remind you, this is Canada's first national park? The land is rented in perpetuity, but the buildings themselves are bought and sold. We're all still new at this. The laws aren't clear."

Wilson grumbled about the good-for-nothing laws and stalked out of the office. In his Mountie uniform, Graham leaned over the desk and tried to reason with the clerk. "They have similar deeds, Benny. Both with Finnigan's signature."

"Goin' over it with me again won't solve anything. Let

me fill out the papers, will ya?'' Benny held up his quill pen.

Amanda backed away from the counter, inches from Tom, and fought to control her emotions. ''Let's give the man an opportunity to do his work. There's nothing more to be said.''

She left, but Miss Clementine and Pa began to argue with Graham and Benny again. Tom followed Amanda's resolute figure out the door into the morning sunshine, desperately plowing through ideas of how he might help, but coming up short.

The sunshine hit him square in the eye. ''What are you going to do?''

''I don't know.'' She searched his face. The shadow from her bonnet cast a line across her suntanned nose. ''I can't believe everything I've worked for...might be gone.''

''It won't,'' he said, trying to console her.

Amanda rubbed her temples. ''How many deeds do you think Finnigan sold? Even if I win this time, what if another man comes along, with another deed, a better one?''

''I don't know what it all means, Amanda, but I'll do whatever I can to help you.''

With what? With what could he help her? He was drained of resources. This morning, the tinsmith came calling with another one of those padded bills of Finnigan's. To boot, Gabe's letter from Toronto arrived, wondering where Tom's bank draft for Gabe's June rent at the boarding house had gotten to.

She leaned into the handrail of the boardwalk, glancing down the street at the early morning shoppers. ''Thanks, Tom, but it's out of your hands.''

Amanda was right.

Who owned the parcel of land? And who owned the half-built log cabin?

"I guess we'll have to stop building for now..." Amanda choked on the words. "And if I should...should lose the land, I'll have to move back to Calgary to my family there. I—I've got Grandma to think about, and now the children."

Tom silently cursed Finnigan. Where in Sam Hill was the blasted man? How could he have done this to all these innocent people? Why had Tom been so blind to the man's deceptions? Had he been that greedy for Finnigan's influx of cash?

He took a breath of needed air. He was too tired to stay furious. "Do you need a lift home?"

"I rode my bicycle. Grandma came with your father, but I wanted—needed—to be alone."

"Let me walk you, then. Where's your bicycle?"

"Around the corner of the mercantile, in the shade."

Grandma and Pa exited the land registry just then, walking behind Amanda and Tom, heading to Pa's horse and wagon hitched up the road.

"Don't you worry," said Miss Clementine, patting Amanda's shoulder blade. "We'll get this mix-up sorted out."

When they passed Fannie and her father, James Jefferson, Tom nodded hello, but the tinsmith and his daughter looked down at the boardwalk as they continued walking.

"And imagine," Mr. Jefferson muttered, "the old woman rides the contraption, too. Independence! At her age, gallavantin' around town like a circus performer on a unicycle."

Shocked to their boots, Tom and Amanda turned around in time to see Grandma's jaw drop open. Her long gray braids started flying. "Circus performer? Why, that little weasel—"

"Leave him be, Clementine," Pa said, placing his hand on the older woman's elbow. "He's an old fool."

"Well, I never," Grandma gasped, adjusting her black dress. "How dare he say such a thing. I'll show him circus performer—"

"I'll speak to him later," Pa vowed. If he didn't, Tom sure as hell would. The man had some nerve insulting the two women, and right under Tom's nose!

They left the old folks by the wagon, Amanda still shaking her head at Jefferson's remark, Tom distracted by the crowd up ahead that was forming around the mercantile's alley.

"What's going on?" asked Amanda, stepping through with Tom right behind her.

"Is this your bicycle?" asked an Englishman, dressed in wool knickers and jacket. By his checkered wool hat with its long red feather, he was obviously a tourist. An agreeable older woman stood by his side, presumably his wife.

Tom looked down to the ground where the man was pointing. Amanda's bicycle lay in the dirt. "What happened to the bicycle?" Tom demanded, jumping forward to yank it up. Fortunately, it looked unharmed. "Who did this? Did you see—"

"I saw a couple of men passing by," said the Englishman, "then it was in the dirt. It must have fallen in the breeze. No harm done. My brother in Dover has one like this. It'd be wonderful for my wife and I to ride one while we're here for the summer. Is it for sale?"

"I'm afraid not," said Amanda, standing above Tom as he checked the wheel.

The stitches tugged in his left arm, reminding him he'd need more medication soon. "Looks fine."

The man reached into his pocket. "But I'll give you—"

"No, thank you," Amanda repeated kindly. "I much prefer my freedom to any amount of money."

"I totally understand," said his wife with a smile.

Tom did, too. Who would give up their freedom for a lousy twenty or thirty bucks? It couldn't be worth more than one third the price of a good horse, and a good horse was going for about a hundred.

"Good day, then," the couple said as they left.

It appeared there was no damage done, so Tom dismissed it as an accident. Amanda did, too.

Sliding onto the seat, she rearranged the green twill fabric of her split skirt. Tom tried not to notice the sleek outline of her legs as she perched beside him—her trim waistline, the pronounced swell of her breasts behind the fabric of her blouse. He was reminded of how good she looked in the rain yesterday, when he'd fought over her with Quaid.

"Do you feel well, Tom? You don't look it. You may need another dose of your drug."

She mistook his sudden desire for her as a need for more medication. Truth was, he was feeling great, being here with her. His biceps hurt, but his mind was clear. As she shifted her weight from one foot to the other, wriggling her bottom on the seat, he could think of only one thing she could do for him. Naked on top of him. Naked beneath him. Naked standing up—

"Tom? What are you thinking about?"

"A cold tub of water."

"To soak in? Can I get you anything? Something you need?"

I need you.

"Nothing?" she asked, mistaking the blank expression on his face.

Everything, he thought.

"Tom?"

How had he gotten so mixed up with Amanda Ryan? Why did he want her so badly? "No thanks."

"I hope you feel better tomorrow. You know what's the worst thing about all of this?"

I want you but you don't want me?

She continued, "I hate to stand idle and wait for the magistrate to arrive to seal my fate."

Tom glanced away from her bewitching body, toward the diner. "There must be something we can do."

"Finnigan's got a brother in Canmore," she said tentatively, as if exploring his reaction.

Tom squinted down at her, hesitant to even glance her way. She had such a hold on him. "Graham told me that, too."

"The Mountie who questioned him wasn't able to pry much information out of him. Said the man was poorer than dust, and not likely involved with any schemes of his brother's."

He scratched his eyebrow. "Yeah, I know. Finnigan's only relative."

Amanda's blue eyes shot up to his. "I wonder if he'd talk to a woman." The wind kicked at her loose hair.

"A woman? What are you thinking?"

"Canmore's not far. Less than an hour by train. A person could take it tomorrow morning and be back before suppertime."

Tom stared at her. That independence of spirit glowed in her skin. That same spirit that gave her the strength to move to Banff, to start over without a husband, to help her grandmother and then the orphans.

Normally he'd insist she not go anywhere near trouble, but if there was anything the two of them could do to extract information from Finnigan's brother, shouldn't they take that chance? What did he have to lose? One day on the train? He wouldn't even have to worry about a chaperone since they weren't staying overnight.

"I'll go with you," he said.

Her gaze dropped to his stiff shoulder. "But you're not well."

"How could I let you face this man alone?"

"I could ask someone else. Your father, maybe. Or Donald O'Hara. Or Pierce."

Tom gripped the bicycle handles. He didn't trust her protection to anyone else, even though the Mounties had told him the brother seemed harmless—a family man with five young children and hardworking wife. But Tom was good with a gun, and fast on his feet. Whether he could keep his distance from Amanda was another matter. "I'm going."

"What makes you think I have anything to say to you?"

In a dilapidated barn, standing alongside Tom who was dressed in a red shirt, denim pants and double holsters, Amanda watched Frank Finnigan milk his cow. Although they'd been here with him for five minutes, and another fifteen with him and his wife inside their home, it hadn't taken Amanda more than a second to realize the man was angry.

Two of his youngest children, barefoot and wearing dirty overalls, chased three cats around the stall as their father held a teat in one hand and shot milk three feet away into the mouth of a fourth cat. He laughed at his daughter's giggle. The creases at his eyes were gentle. Was he a co-conspirator with his brother?

Amanda didn't think so. Then who was he angry with?

She dangled a piece of straw over one of the cats, who lunged at it, enthralling the children. She stepped back against a ladder, careful not to soil her only peach-colored suit. "Are you upset with us, sir, for coming to see you?"

The question took him by surprise. Tom, too. He removed his black Stetson and furrowed his brows. She was only trying to get a response. They didn't have much time left before the train returned, and Amanda usually found that good, honest people responded to point-blank honesty.

The man glanced up from his stool and grimaced. "It's your waste of time, not mine." He turned away again to concentrate on milking, pressing his dark forehead into the cow's flank. The squirt, squirt, squirt echoed from the tin bucket.

"The Mounties told us you're Zeb Finnigan's only kin," said Tom.

"When the Mounties come calling, people have gotta answer," he said sarcastically.

"Do you know where Zeb is?" Tom asked again.

Frank Finnigan laughed without humor. "Isn't that the question everyone would like to know?"

"Yes it is," Amanda replied, making sure the children were again out of earshot. "He cheated me for the price of my property, and stole from Tom's business."

Finnigan kept working, unruffled, but Amanda noted a muscle had tightened in his jaw. The words were getting to him.

"I don't have any more time to spend with you," he said. "I told you and the Mounties all I know."

They'd come all this way for nothing? Thirty questions had led to nowhere? She looked to Tom, his angular shoulders profiled in the slanting light.

"Just one more thing," said Amanda. "What was it that Zeb stole from you, sir?"

The tin bucket clanged. The milking stopped. The gruffness in his voice matched his harsh expression. "What makes you think my own brother would steal from me?"

Amanda didn't want to humiliate the man, but he was living in poverty. Five children and a very thin wife, all living in a shack no bigger than Amanda's. No other livestock except the cow, no horse to plow the fields, no crops planted. "Your wife told me your property was rented. It wasn't that I was snooping, it's just that when I asked whether you'd planted the wheat yet, she mentioned the land wasn't yours."

Fury and shame burned in the man's eyes. "He took it all from us. He…he…gambled away our deed."

Amanda's heart sank with compassion. "I'm so sorry. He shouldn't have done that."

"No, he shouldn't have. I'm his brother, for God's sake. His *brother*."

"Zeb is a gambler?" Tom asked. Amanda knew this was something the Mounties hadn't discovered.

"Yeah. It's a sickness with him. Like it was with our mother." The man watched his children climb the haystack. "I don't want him put behind bars, though. You aren't going to do that, are ya?"

Amanda didn't want to answer. Zeb Finnigan was ruining lives. He had to be stopped by the law.

Tom stepped forward. "It's out of our control. It's out of yours, too," he said gently, placing a large hand on the man's shoulder. It seemed to comfort Frank.

"This land should belong to my children. I worked two years in the coal mines, nearly lost my arm doing it," he said, holding up the hand with the missing three fingers.

"I thought this farmland would be my salvation. Zeb took it, instead."

Tom rubbed his jaw especially hard. She'd seen him do that several times in the past half hour. Was it sore? "If you tell the Mounties, and they find your brother, they might be able to get it back for you."

"They'll only put in him jail where he'll rot away to nothing. I can't turn in my own brother."

Amanda had an urge to forget about the whole darn thing.

Tom nodded, looking to her to leave. "Is there anything else you'd like to tell us, Frank, before we go?"

"Yeah. Zeb always seems to come back for more. When he gambled away my deed, he came back two weeks later and took my wife's solid gold locket. That's all we had left, or he probably would have returned again." The man looked to Amanda. "You best watch out for him."

"Thank you," she said, sympathizing with his difficulty in telling her. "We have to be going now, we've got a train to catch."

They said goodbye to the children, and less than an hour later, they boarded the evening express to Banff. It was packed with passengers. The Canadian Pacific Railway had invested big dollars making all the cars luxurious for the summer tourists.

"Well, it wasn't a waste of time after all," said Tom, leading Amanda down the plush corridor of the drawing room. "We found out Zeb's a big gambler."

They sank into the red velvet seats across from each other. Tom rubbed his chin and jaw again, then massaged the back of his neck.

"You okay?"

"A headache. I need a glass of water."

They asked for one and the barman brought it. Beneath

the table, there wasn't a spot she could find where Tom's long legs didn't touch hers. With every lull and sway of the train, his knee brushed hers, and she felt a jolt of lightning. He seemed to notice it, too, and tried to pull away.

When she noticed his arm stiffen and sweat collect at his brow, she slid her arms closer. "Is it time for your laudanum? You look like you could use some."

"Yeah," he said, sliding his calloused palm into his jacket and removing a small brown bottle. "I can't put it off any longer."

He'd been sitting here all this time in pain? He removed the salts and measured a spoonful.

"I feel sorry for Frank and his wife," said Amanda, setting her bonnet and gloves on the wooden table.

"So do I. That's why we've got to tell the Mounties what we've learned. They'll start looking for him at gambling and flop houses."

"I know it's not possible, but I wish we could forget about the whole thing, seeing how much pain it's causing Frank Finnigan."

"It would be difficult for any brother to talk against his own, that's why the rest of us law-abiding citizens have to do it for him. If Zeb has any money stashed when the Mounties find him, Frank will get a portion of it back. We've got to continue this for him and his family."

It was unselfish of Tom to look at it like that. But then, unselfishness seemed to run in his character.

"When you put it like that, it makes me feel better," she said. He always had that effect on her, she thought with a start. Whether he was fighting with his brother in the rain, or making her and the children laugh, or being by her side when she faced Frank Finnigan, Tom was a man unlike any other.

Would they grow closer yet?

What did the future hold for her in Banff? Would she have to pack her bags and leave the friends she'd made? If she thought too much about it, her fears and trepidations would rear up again, so she chose not to.

She checked to see if the laudanum was helping Tom. He was quieter. Still restless, though. Every jostle of the train seemed to disturb him. Thank goodness the ride wasn't long. Another twenty minutes and he'd be safe with Quaid again.

Peering out of the huge glass panes, she watched the mountains rush past them in their springtime glory. Fields of purple flowers sprang to meet them; buds in orange and pink and red infused the planes. If you looked closely, you could see animals scamper from the path of the train— beavers, elk, two bald-headed eagles soaring high above.

Although neither of them was elaborately dressed for such a posh car, she enjoyed sitting here with Tom. She in the same peach suit she'd worn when they'd dined at Ruby's, and Tom in a dashing red shirt and suede jacket, his hair slicked back like a boy on his way to choir. Their silence was easy and comfortable.

Tom cleared his throat and looked at her. "I haven't had a chance to apologize for my brother's behavior. The things he said to you in the rain."

"There's no need to apologize—"

"Yes, there is. On one hand, my brother is as smart as a whip. On the other, sometimes he's as dumb as a nail."

She smiled. Maybe once Quaid got to know her, his opinion would soften. "He was just saying what the rest of the town is feeling. You can't blame the man—"

"Sure I can. And I do."

"All right, then, apology accepted."

"Quaid's all right, you know. You'd probably get on well with his wife."

"He's married?"

"Yeah. Beth is visiting her folks in Winnipeg at the moment. Her mother's not well."

"That's always difficult."

He took a moment to compose his thoughts. "I'd like to ask you something. About the ball."

A wave of panic washed over her. Where was this headed?

The clump of dark hair that grazed his forehead framed the strength in his face. "Would you consider going…with me?"

Startled, she blinked.

"I'd like to take you." His warm, direct gaze penetrated her calm facade.

How should she answer him?

Part of her wanted to go. Would it be fair to say yes without explaining her divorce and why it'd happened? Why William had walked away from her?

Even though Tom's was a simple offer to accompany him to one dance, she didn't want to lead him into a false direction. She knew the offer meant more. She *felt* it.

He leaned forward. "What's the matter?"

If she told him, would he run from her, too?

"Seven pounds, eight ounces," she said softly.

His face grew thoughtful. "What's that?"

She knotted her fingers together and carefully watched him. "That's how much my baby weighed when she was born…when she passed away…."

Chapter Nine

"*What?*" Tom whispered, staring into Amanda's grief-stricken face. He temporarily forgot about the pounding in his sore muscles and his stiff neck while he gazed at the smooth outline of her cheekbones. He couldn't believe he'd heard right.

When she didn't answer, instead looking nervously out the window then back at him, he asked again. "You lost a baby?"

She nodded, clamping her hands together in her lap. She couldn't disguise her pain, and he felt heartsick for her.

"When?"

"A year and a half ago."

He moaned. "I'm so sorry." He had no idea.

"That's why my divorce happened. It's why my husband left."

"You mean your husband left you because you lost your child?"

She nodded.

Tom's lips tightened in response. Her former husband was a callous bastard. Why hadn't he stood by his wife? "How could he?"

"I know it's no excuse, but William always wanted children."

It stunned Tom into silence. Shifting uncomfortably on the chair, he rolled his jaw, trying to unloosen the ache. Amanda's news had come out of nowhere to knock him off his feet. "That day at your log cabin, when I told you his twins had just been born, you must have—*I* must have devastated you."

Her face mellowed. "You didn't know."

Tom floundered, disturbed by the guilt of how he'd talked to her that day, and how she'd taken it. "There will be other children for you, though. Other babies—"

"I can't have more. There were complications.... I lost my uterus."

He swallowed hard. No more children?

"Now can you see why it's complicated between us?"

Complicated. Not simple. He stared at her. What did he know of women's problems? Nothing. "Are you feeling all right now? Are you in physical pain at this moment?"

"I'm fine. There's no pain involved. You almost wouldn't notice that I'm different, except that I can't have that time of the month." She sighed and looked away. "I used to always hate it, but now I wish…"

"It's nothing to be ashamed of, Amanda. You're a beautiful woman. *In every sense of the word.* Any man would be proud to be at your side."

And yet he struggled to grasp the meaning. No more children. Ever.

He wanted children. Didn't he? It had always been part of the equation when he'd thought of marriage. Babies. One-year-olds and two-year-olds who'd grow to be nine and ten, then young teens. Children he'd share his home and life with.

He silently cursed himself for thinking of what

Amanda's loss meant to *him*. His loss, his pain. The selfish thoughts sickened him, yet he couldn't get them out of his mind. He wasn't brave enough to handle this with Amanda. He didn't know how to handle it.

And what would it be like to make love to her? Would he feel pity for her? Would he be afraid to touch her? To consummate? Would his own body disappoint him and wither in response to hers? His body reaction was something he couldn't control, and if he couldn't satisfy her, he'd cringe with shame.

"I can tell by the look on your face that you're shocked. Really disappointed."

"That's not it," he said, but they both knew it was. He suddenly felt stifled, and he was sweating profusely. "It's hot in here," he mumbled, struggling to make his jaw work properly, "we need to open a window." Was he getting a toothache? Is that where the pain was coming from? He got up to unlatch the window, thankful for the fresh blast of air.

When he spun around, she'd turned away to gaze at the scenery. Even though she was beautiful sitting here in her neatly pressed clothes and dignity in her posture, he wished he could afford to buy her whatever she needed. New suits, new dresses, new shoes.

He snorted. What a frivolous thing for him to think of at a time like this.

Her former husband was a coldhearted son of a bitch.

Was Tom any better? Was he tough enough to handle this? He considered her a close friend. Over the past weeks they'd grown more intimate. He had ached to take it further. And now?

How could he even think he'd be good enough for her? She needed a decisive, capable man by her side, someone who was sure of himself, not someone like him.

"Amanda," he said, sliding onto the red velvet beside her, ignoring the stiffness in his arm. "I can't say that I'm not surprised by what you've told me. All right, shocked. But…"

When she peered at him with big, caring eyes, he felt as if she were looking directly into his soul. For answers. For support. What more could he say? That everything would work out for the best? How lame. It was something he couldn't promise.

How did she feel about her inability to conceive? If it was a terrible blow to Tom, he could only imagine what it must be doing to her. She adored children, he could see it in the way she cared for Margaux and Josh.

"Amanda, I'm amazed by you. How can you put yourself in the position of being a midwife? How can you put yourself right in the center of delivering babies, when it must be a constant reminder to you of your own child?"

"It's not difficult when I'm involved with my patients. When I'm up to my elbows and concentrating on my work, I think of them."

"You're fearless."

She moaned. "I've got plenty of fears."

How could she cope with the knowledge she'd never have children of her own?

How could he?

"I never got to hold…*Sharon Rose*…. But I'll cope fine. I know I will. I always do."

He ached for her. He should say more, he should comfort her in some way.

No words came. Only silence. His blasted head throbbed. If the headache didn't leave soon, cripe's, he'd have to go to Quaid.

Her gaze was a mixture of hope, then sorrow when he

didn't respond. "I'll have to decline your invitation to the ball."

The ball? The furthest thing from his mind.

With a stiffness to his body, he slid to her side of the seat and placed an arm around her shoulders in his own silent desperation. She fell into his arms and they pressed together, her body soft and warm. A cramp pulled in his arm. He clamped and unclamped his fist, trying to work the muscle.

He was glad he had her body to brace against, glad she couldn't see his face. What kind of man was he? A coward? He should speak up and *comfort her. Say something.* But what? That life was sometimes so goddamn unfair?

That ten minutes ago what he felt for her was so powerful he thought his heart would burst, and now he didn't know what he felt? Or what he should say?

"Tom, your hand is growing stiff."

"It's fine. It's just a cramp."

She looked up at him. "You're blue. And your hand...good heavens, your hand's shaking."

"It is?" He looked down and tried to stop its spasm. What in blazes? He jerked at the faint sounds around him. A dinner bell in the car behind them, the screech of train wheels, the nondescript laughter of the woman three seats down. His head spun with dizziness. What was happening? Something was wrong.

He tried to drag himself out of his seat, but his knees wobbled and his legs rocked. "What the hell?" The words mumbled together. He couldn't talk right. His pulse jumped with fear. What was wrong with him? Why wouldn't his mouth move?

With a good shove, he pulled himself up again, only to collapse on the floor.

"Tom, get up!"

In the ensuing panic of voices, Amanda tried to help him rise.

Passengers screamed. Charlie, the ticket agent, supported his body; the barmen rushed to help Amanda.

The train screeched to a stop. The crowd shoved around him, lifting him like a swarm of bees and moving him down the stairs into the station. He tried to talk, but his stiff jaw couldn't move.

Amanda's voice rang frantic above the others, urgently repeating the same words over and over, but he couldn't understand them. "Lockjaw. *Tetanus.*"

"Quaid," said Amanda, pounding on Tom's log cabin door for the fifth morning in a row. "Please let me in. I need to see him."

By the grace of heaven, Quaid had been located within an hour of the train's arrival. He'd been able to sedate Tom, but there wasn't much else they could do except wait it out.

She blinked in exhaustion. Would Quaid answer this time? She felt the tears well in her eyes again and the hot ache in her chest. Tetanus. An infection in Tom's wound where the toxins had spread throughout his bloodstream.

He'd made it this far though, five days, with no funeral procession, no whispered condolences from the neighbors, no arrangements of burial plots at the hillside cemetery. Tom was still alive.

She hammered on the door again, her hand stinging from the pounding, not caring if the men who were peering out the lumber mill stared at her the whole morning. "Quaid, please, I know you're here. I recognize your horse. You've been alternating with your father and the minister, and I know you're here."

She muttered in the ensuing silence. She hated funeral

processions, everyone dressed in black and as solemn as a thundercloud. She'd seen too many in the past year and a half. First, little Sharon Rose's, then Grandpa's, and now…? Were her prayers helping Tom? What else, in the name of heaven, could she do to help him?

The children were distraught at the turn of events, Grandma as silent as Amanda had ever seen her. And poor John Murdock, his face ashen when he'd passed Amanda's on his way home last evening.

The log door suddenly opened. "What is it I can do for you?" Quaid asked. Dressed impeccably in his silk vest and cravat, he poked his head through the doorway. His mustache bristled.

Startled at finally seeing him, Amanda pressed a hand to her apron and picked up her straw basket. "I've come with some chicken soup for Tom."

Quaid looked over at her bicycle, scowled, then glanced down at her basket. Was she being ridiculously hopeful, thinking Tom was out of his coma?

"Is he awake yet, Quaid?"

"He's grumbling this morning."

"Oh…" she uttered in shocked delight, unable to keep her voice from trembling. "Oh, that's good."

She met Quaid's eyes and sent him a tremulous smile. His eyes began to water. He turned away, embarrassed, but she saw he was crying.

Stepping inside the door, she pressed a firm hand to his shoulder. "It'll be all right. He'll get better, you'll see."

Quaid took a deep breath. "I can see why Tom likes you. You're an optimist."

"If you only knew…"

"I blamed you, you know, for the first three days. Every time his body racked in spasm and he could hardly breathe, I blamed you for using those rusty snips."

"I blamed myself," she whispered.

Quaid looked at her in silence, then removed a hanky from his pocket and mopped his face. "It wasn't your fault, though, more likely that his wound got infected from the fishhook."

"I know," she answered. "I wish there was an anti-toxin we could give him, like the new one we have for rabies. But they've only just discovered the cause of teta-nus, no cure yet. Quaid, is he really grumbling?"

"Yeah, tossing and turning. An hour ago he said my name and talked to me. He was able to sit up to wash his face and brush his teeth."

The good news sent her spirits soaring. "May I see him, please?"

Quaid took a moment to decide, then nodded.

Thank you. Amanda took a deep breath and stepped over Tom's muddy work boots by the door. She wished with all her heart that she'd see him again soon standing tall in those boots, smiling down at her with that charming, dim-pled grin.

She'd never been in Tom's cabin before. It was a simple, square room, as cluttered and messy as she imagined any bachelor's would be. In one corner sat a cast-iron stove riddled with pots, a rough pine counter stacked with dish-cloths and a washbasin, and in the other corner, a narrow cot and armoire. One tall bookshelf rested against the wall, crammed with books, one silver clock, and two rolled-up shirts.

As she passed by the table she noticed a stack of old newspapers turned to the same page. They were word puz-zles, neatly filled out in ink, sitting beside Tom's Stetson. He liked word games?

Imagining him all alone by the fire on a Friday night,

struggling with a word, brought a warmth to her heart she couldn't describe.

He had to pull through.

When she reached the bed, she was taken aback by his appearance. He'd lost at least five to ten pounds, she could see it in his unshaven face. His lower half was covered by a coarse wool blanket, but his upper half was naked. A flaxseed poultice covered his left biceps, drawing out the infection. The lightly matted chest rippled with muscles. He was evenly tanned.

Laying at the foot of his bed, Wolf raised his head and moaned at Amanda.

"Wolf, I nearly didn't see you."

"He's been laying there for five days straight," said Quaid. "He won't hardly budge. The dog's been drinking, but he won't eat anything."

"Good dog," she whispered. "You'll be able to eat soon. Tom is better now."

Wolf wagged his tail.

"Tom," she said, kneeling beside the bed. Gently she reached out for his warm hand and squeezed. "Tom? It's me, Amanda. I've come to see how you are."

When he grumbled, she pulled back in surprise, then stroked the moist hair at his temples, trailing her fingers along the washcloth that Quaid must have put there. Such warm, wonderful skin. "Tom," she whispered, "come back to me."

His eyes fluttered open. Those gorgeous green eyes, lined with slanted black lashes, looked at her.

She grinned wide. "Hi."

He swallowed hard. His dry lips cracked. "Hi."

They stared at each other for a full minute.

"Hi," Quaid added from behind, making both Amanda and Tom laugh softly.

"What are you doing in my bedroom?" Tom asked weakly. "Am I dreaming?" He paused to muster his strength. "If I am, I'm taking advantage." Before she knew what was happening, he yanked her up on top of him.

She yelped, but very happy with his strength. He *was* going to be all right.

"Tom," said Quaid in disapproval.

"Quaid, get out of my dream," said Tom.

"You're not dreaming," said Amanda, sliding off his hard body and adjusting her skirts. "You've been in a coma for days. Do you remember our train ride?"

He went pale again, likely from the overexertion. "No, I don't."

"We went to see Frank Finnigan, then...then you started perspiring and rubbing your jaw. You collapsed in the train with lockjaw."

"Hell, now I remember."

Did he recall everything? Did he recall their discussion about Sharon Rose?

He looked at her with inquisitive eyes, but she sensed his withdrawal. He remembered something.

Did he remember asking her to the ball?

The thought of being asked, of being wanted... It was a dream that seemed to be beyond her grasp, but even if she could never have Tom Murdock, she was utterly grateful he was alive and someone else would.

"You look like hell," Tom said to her.

"I do?" she said, adjusting the kerchief over her head. "Just what every woman likes to hear."

He cleared his rough throat. "You haven't been sleeping. Were you worried about me?"

She couldn't deny it and so nodded in agreement. The tension and exhaustion she'd felt for the past five days came rushing to the surface. It felt good to finally let it ease.

Tom's arms suddenly stiffened with a spasm. Amanda winced and placed a soothing hand on his waist until he recovered.

"What on earth was that?" he asked.

"The spasms will subside in the next two to four weeks," Quaid answered. "Hopefully they won't be frequent. They were very bad during the first two days. I had to sedate you with chloroform so you could sleep. Your age got you through this, you know. If you'd been very young or very old, you wouldn't have made it."

"Well, thanks to the two of you, I did." He pulled back from Amanda in alarm. "Can I spread this to you?"

"Lockjaw isn't contagious."

His body eased.

Amanda glanced down at the floor to avoid his gaze and Quaid busied himself with the chicken soup she'd brought. He took it from the jar she'd brought it in and dumped it into a pot, then threw another log into the stove. Amanda knew Tom would be angered if she told him Quaid hadn't allowed her in until today, and she didn't see the point of telling him.

Tom swung his long legs over the bed and for the next hour they helped him slowly wash up, brush his hair, then helped him to a bit of soup. They left his shirt off so not to disturb the poultice. Amanda tried not to admire his physique, tried not to flush every time her eye caught his.

Wolf took a biscuit from Tom's fingers and she was thrilled to see the dog eating.

Quaid grew restless in his chair. "Cripes, man, why didn't you tell us you were in so deep?"

"What do you mean?" Tom said, bringing the spoon to his lips. Amanda sat there and watched him, enjoying every movement. The way his arm flexed as he lifted the spoon to his lips, the unshaven, dark aura of his face, his bulky presence, the kindness in his voice when he talked to Wolf.

"The bloody banker was here yesterday," Quaid said.

Tom set his spoon down with a clang. "The banker? What did he want?" He looked to Amanda for answers, but she wasn't sure what Quaid was getting at.

"He took the house—"

"What?"

"The house. This house. He took it for payment."

Tom swore beneath his breath. "Why did you let him do that?"

"There was nothing me or Pa—"

"Pa knows about this?"

"Well, yeah."

"How could you tell him—"

"He was here when Thimbleton arrived."

"While I was in a coma?" Tom asked incredulously. "Thimbleton took my house while I was in a coma?"

Amanda couldn't believe the news. She had no idea Tom had financial problems. Why, she thought his life ran as smooth as silver. And didn't she once tell him so? The heat from that argument rushed to her cheeks now.

Quaid shrugged.

Tom picked up his spoon again, thinking carefully. Slowly, his dimples appeared, then his cheekbones went up, the corner of his lips rose, and he stifled a deep laugh. When Quaid joined in the laughter, Amanda thought they were both mad. Tom had just lost his house!

"He must be awfully scared of you when you're awake," said Quaid, sending them into another round.

Amanda reeled away from Tom. "You laugh too much."

Tom settled down and peered at her across the table. He reached out and traced a pale finger down her cheekline, sending shivers down her arms. "You frown too much."

"But you've lost your house," she added.

He sobered. Tom was in deep financial problems and she hadn't known it? He was struggling, and yet he'd kept it hidden?

"So he took it?" Tom asked his brother. "I no longer own it?"

Quaid nodded.

"I used to like the other banker a lot more than Thimbleton. He was fair."

"Too bad he moved away," Quaid agreed.

"Well, at least I've got my bed. And what kind of a guard dog are you?" Tom asked Wolf. "You're not supposed to let the bad men in."

Wolf tilted his head and whined. Tom patted the husky's head and both man and dog sighed.

"When am I supposed to be out of the house?" Tom asked.

Quaid frowned. "Day after tomorrow, if you're out of your coma or not."

Tom smiled again. "What in blazes was Thimbleton going to do if I was still unconscious?"

"Wheel your body to the sanitorium, I suppose."

The brothers thought this was funny again.

"How can you joke?" asked Amanda. But watching the two brothers, she began to wonder if William had been able to laugh more at life like Tom did, then maybe they could have survived the hard times of marriage.

"Because I woke up and I'm not dead," Tom answered. "And I still have my sawmill. Don't I?" he said to his brother.

Quaid threw his hands into the air, a gesture of frustration.

"They didn't take that, too, did they?" Tom's voice rose a notch.

"You still own it. But why don't you give it up, Tom? What's the use of going on? I don't have a dime to spare right now, but I'll be on my feet in another year. Then I can help you out, and Pa for whatever he needs, and Gabe, too. Come live with me and Beth in the meantime."

"I'll take my bed and sleep in the back room of the sawmill. Behind the office."

"Why don't you sell the sawmill?" Quaid continued. "Why keep torturing yourself, holding on to a lost cause?"

Tom flinched at the insult. "Because if I've got the sawmill, then goddammit, I can still get it all back. You're done with your schooling but Gabe needs to finish law school."

"What the hell are we going to do?" Quaid asked, leaning against the counter and crossing his arms. "Thimbleton told me about the credit note for my instruments. That's why he took the house. You missed two payments. I'll give them back—"

"Don't be silly. You need them. How can you practice without the proper tools?"

"That's why Thimbleton took the house, goddammit. My instruments for your house. If my own home weren't mortgaged, I'd—"

"Don't panic, Quaid. Just don't panic. Let's take it slow and easy. I'm going to get it all back with the sawmill."

It was then that Amanda realized just how strong and resilient Tom was. He was a complex man, the center of his family. He kept everyone together. He schooled his brothers, he looked out for his father, he employed a dozen of the town's men. She fought her overwhelming need to depend on him, too.

"How can you get goodwill back?" Quaid asked. "People in town trusted you and Finnigan. Now they don't. How do you plan on regaining that after so many of them were overcharged? And it doesn't look good, your house being repossessed. People will worry that if they hire you as a builder, they'll lose money if the rest of your business goes under."

"I'll continue the way I always have. Working hard, talking to people, letting it be known that we're looking for Finnigan and that it was him, not me, who stole their money."

"It'll take too long to build up that trust again."

"Then I've got to do something fast."

"Like what?"

"Like continue to seek their business at every turn. I've got to go to the ball and say my speech, as planned, and get as many people on my side as I can. I'll look guilty if I cower here."

"I'm not sure you're still invited to speak, or if they'll have you."

"They'll have me. I know Stanlowski at the big hotel. He's the assistant to the CPR president and owes me more favors than I can count."

Tom turned to Amanda, as if suddenly realizing she was still there and listening. "Is there any word on the magistrate? On your property?"

"He'll be here the Monday after Saturday's ball."

Tom nodded and pushed away his empty soup bowl and faced Amanda. "You know, I'd still very much like to take you to the ball."

Her stomach rolled at the question, at the intensity of his dark gaze. How could she say yes?

How could she say no?

Quaid sprang from his seat. "Tom—Amanda, no offense—Tom, think of what you're doing. Amanda's not exactly the first choice. She's got some difficulties of her own in this town, and not everyone is happy to greet her. Sorry," he said again to Amanda.

Tom ignored his brother, in the humorous way she'd come to admire. A muscle in his temple throbbed. "As I was saying, Amanda, I'd still very much like to escort you to the ball."

"That's very kind of you, but maybe you should listen to your brother—"

Tom placed a large hand over her small one, which was resting on the table. His heat seeped into her fingers. "I remember everything about our conversation on the train. Everything," he said gently. "And you're right. It's complicated between us. But we'll take it a step at a time. This is simply one night out. No commitment."

He still wanted to take her. That alone sent her senses spinning. But Quaid was right. If she went with him, she might ruin his chances with the rest of the town.

"Even if I wanted to, I don't have anything appropriate to wear. And I can't—*won't*—spend that kind of money on a ball gown when Margaux may soon need new glasses. Her wire frames are bending."

He grinned and his whole demeanor changed. "You are one woman in a million. Let me take care of everything—"

"But how—"

"Trust me," he asked.

Trust was the one thing he desperately wanted from her, but she was unable to give. "I can't," she said, rising to leave.

He tugged her back by her hand. "You can."

"I need some time to think about it," she said, wrenching free, ignoring his moan of frustration. And with that, she strode out of the cabin, reeling for fresh air, more confused now about Tom than she'd ever been.

Chapter Ten

Tom had never bought clothing for a woman before, but he'd do his best for Amanda. After he took care of his pressing business affairs today, he'd visit the dressmaker. It had been three days since he regained consciousness, and he couldn't lie around another day.

He threw his legs over the bed and sat up. A coughing spasm shook him. When it subsided, he tugged on his pants. How could he coax Amanda to the ball?

He hated what had happened to her. He hated the injustice of her losing her only infant. He hated that her husband had walked out on her, and he hated that she could never have any more children. *His* children.

But just because Amanda couldn't bear children didn't mean he could stop liking her. As a midwife, she put herself in the center of the most painful situations he could imagine, delivering babies in order to help other women.

If the situation were reversed, would he be able to do the same thing? If he were sterile, could he help other men to celebrate the birth of their children?

Not likely. He wasn't as generous, or as tough.

With a groan, he got moving. After breakfast, he gave his men instructions to move his furniture into the sawmill, then with Wolf at his side, he strode down the street toward the big hotel to speak to Stanlowski. Tom's arms and legs felt stiff as he moved, but the soreness would ease as the day wore on. He allowed the morning sunshine to warm his skin, concentrating on the cool, easy feel of the invigorating spring air as it slid into his lungs, instead of his deep financial worries.

As for Amanda, did they have to think about the future? Couldn't they just go to the ball and see how they felt about each other? Didn't they owe themselves the pleasure of discovery?

He stumbled in the street. Wolf yelped. Leaning against a hitching post by Ruby's Dining and Boarding House for support, Tom glanced through the dining window and spied Ruby. He saw an opportunity to create business. The place was jam-packed with tourists for lunch, and he knew from experience that business owners had less difficulty spending their money when it was pouring in.

An hour later, after he'd discussed Ruby's extension—which they'd been discussing for half a year—and she finally agreed to start next week, he visited with Stanlowski. If there was something amiss, the well-groomed gentleman didn't act like it, welcoming Tom with an arm around his shoulders and questions about his health.

Tom deliberately left his visit to the bank till the end of the day, to give his temper time to cool. Thimbleton, true to character, was miraculously unavailable to speak to him. Muttering a few choice words beneath his breath, Tom found him holed up in his office.

"I'll move out of the house," Tom snapped, "and give you the deed as payment for Quaid's instruments, but I want you to agree you won't sell it until the end of the summer. You can rent it out to tourists, but not sell."

The creases on Thimbleton's forehead grew deeper.

"That'll give me some time to buy it back," Tom insisted. "You know you won't have any problem renting it out. Ruby told me she's turning away boarders every day."

"All right. August thirty-first, but not a day later."

After another stop at Ruby's for an early dinner, Tom felt rested enough to approach the dressmaker, Mrs. Hanna Warren, whose shop adjoined her husband's laundry.

Last year when her husband had broken his leg and his laundry business had suffered, Tom had let the payments slide on the massive wooden laundry tubs he'd installed, insisting he'd take payment when times were better for them. Well, he hoped times were better now because he needed a favor.

Wolf waited outside while Tom picked up his laundered shirts—and his father's while he was at it. When he walked across the hall and squeezed his tall frame into the dress shop, middle-aged Mrs. Warren poked her head through the back curtains. "Hello, Tom, what brings you here?"

He peered at the hanging dresses in the window and realized he had no idea how to go about this.

"My companion for the ball needs a gown."

One of Mrs. Warren's young assistants stood up from the corner, where she was stitching a hem. The pin cushion tied around her wrist slid lower. "But it's less than a week away—"

"You're too busy?" asked Tom, his hopes sinking.

"We're busier than a henhouse and Madeline is working double time. But for you," Mrs. Warren said with a smile, adjusting the buttons at her large bosom, "for you, anything. And," she lowered her voice, "no charge, I insist."

He grinned and tipped his hat. Goal accomplished.

Luckily, Mrs. Warren had seen Amanda only yesterday on her bicycle, so guessing her size was not a problem.

"How tall is she?"

"She comes to here." He indicated his chin.

"How big are her heels? The shoes she's wearing with the dress?"

Tom hadn't thought of it. He'd only seen Amanda in boots. "I guess she'll need new shoes, but I haven't been to the shoemaker's yet."

"I'll arrange for matching shoes if you tell me her size."

He scratched his head. "I don't know." The first time they met, when he'd chased her around the sawmill and she fell off her bicycle, her insole had slipped out of her boot. "I have her insole. Could you use it as a pattern?" The dressmaker smiled coyly and he felt his neck flush. "This whole thing's a surprise. You'll keep it that way, won't you?"

"My lips are sealed. My husband's, too. We're very discreet in our business. If you only knew who was picking up whose laundry in this town. The stories we could tell." She took out her sketchpad. "Have you got a certain style in mind?"

Tom smiled with pleasure, imagining Amanda. The whole evening could be a lot of fun. "Something fancy. Something she'd never in a hundred years pick out herself—"

Mrs. Warren giggled. "I know just the thing. I'll sketch it for you, and you can tell me what you think. And the color?"

"I'll describe it to you when I come back with the insole." He whirled around to leave.

Mrs. Warren tugged him back by his vest. "What about you? Do you have an evening suit?"

"I've already got one good suit, no need for another."

"You can't take the lady to the ball dressed in that faded thing you wore to Parson's funeral last month. Heavens!

You need something suitable to match. Get in there behind that curtain, drop your drawers and let us take your measurements!''

"Why won't you go with him?" asked Grandma.

Amanda pulled her lips together and kept sweeping the inside of the half-built log cabin. Sunshine bore down on them. Work had come to a frightening standstill since Lorne Wilson had arrived. The magistrate would be here in less than a week to decide her fate, and the furthest thing from her mind was Tom Murdock.

Well, maybe not the farthest, but she sure as heck wished he was. "I'm not going anywhere with him. I've got things to do here. The children need me. And who wants to go to a snobby ball where everyone will be comparing the size of their gold rings?"

Grandma swiped the broom from Amanda's hands. "Me and John can look after the children for one night. And you *do* want to go the ball, especially with *him,* and no one will be comparin' the size of your anything! You're a midwife who helps lots of women with their problems, but you're afraid to talk about your own."

"My problems can't be solved."

"Maybe not the way you hope, but Tom Murdock is not the same man as William was. He knows your problems, but still wants to take you to the ball. Maybe you should trust him."

There was that word again. Trust. "I'm...I'm not ready."

Grandma sighed. Amanda took her broom back. She knew it was wrong of her to think so, and she knew she was blessed with so many good things in her life, but at this moment, she wished she weren't Amanda Ryan. She wished she were anyone else in the whole world except herself. Someone who was capable of having a full relationship with a man. *With Tom.*

The sound of horse's hooves caused her to glance up the path. Tom came riding in on his mare, his profile chiseled in the morning sunlight, his upper body flexing beneath his brilliant red shirt. The cherry color brought out the dark tone to his skin, and depth to his brows and eyes. Her body came alive. What now?

She leaned her broom against the corner and walked out to greet him. He dismounted. She noticed he was walking steadier and had regained a pound or two. "You look a lot better than the last time I saw you."

Tom's eyes swept over her. "And you look just as good."

Grandma elbowed her in the back. So subtle, her grandma. Amanda bit down on her lip.

"Fine morning, isn't it, Miss Clementine?" Tom said, removing his hat. His black hair glistened with warm tones of brown and rust. It had been almost two weeks since he'd taken ill, and he looked close to full recovery.

"Gettin' finer by the minute," said Grandma, leaving the area, ignoring Amanda's look of alarm. "I'll go see what the children are up to."

Why had he come? The Saturday ball was—

"I'm here to see Margaux and Josh. I haven't seen them since I took ill and wanted to see how they were."

The tension in Amanda's stance softened. "They've been asking every day, and you know how Margaux is, she's concerned it was all her fault from the very beginning, with the fishhook."

"That's what I suspected."

Three feet separated them, but it might as well have been an inch. Every movement in her body seemed to respond to his. The soft beating of his pulse, the flicker in his eyes, the warm tilt to one side of his mouth that was neither a smile nor a question.

"Have you moved yourself into the sawmill?" Amanda asked.

"Yup."

Her throat tightened with sympathy. It was unfair for him to lose his house when he only wished to help his brother. "After all the things you do for people, you deserve better."

His green eyes shimmered with the compliment. "Sometimes people don't always get what they deserve. Do they?" He furrowed his brows into that tender line of black that she'd come to know. She knew he was referring to her problem, and she quivered with anticipation that he'd speak of it. Not here, not now. She turned away in awkward silence to look for the children. They were coming up from the river with Grandma.

"When the magistrate comes to town on Monday," Tom continued, "I'd like to be there with you."

"Why? You don't need to. Constable Robarts will be there. He'll explain everything."

"Would you mind, though, if I came? In case you need me? I can bring my wagon around and pick you up."

It would be easier, she had to admit. Ellie had promised to look after the children, and it would be easier for her and Grandma to get a ride with Tom than to walk the mile to town. "You're turning into a very dependable friend. All right, thank you."

He smiled at her consent.

Josh and Margaux came running toward him, hugging him at the knees. He laughed and put out an arm to stabilize himself.

"Be careful, children," Amanda said with breezy laughter in her voice. "He's still recovering."

"He looks fine to me," said Margaux. The girl's obvious joy at seeing Tom in the flesh, standing solid in one piece—*very solid,* Amanda might add—touched Amanda's heart. She'd been worried about the girl for the past few days, so quiet and unresponsive except to ask about Tom.

Tom seemed to realize the significance of their embrace, for he glanced up at Amanda, grinned and nodded. Gooseflesh rose on her arms at the gentleness in his embrace.

He was so carefree and jovial with the children. How could she rob him of children of his own?

"I missed you kids," said Tom, tossing Josh in the air. Now Amanda knew for certain he was feeling better, for he did it with ease.

"We missed you, too," said Margaux.

Josh mumbled. "Mmm-hmm."

Margaux cupped a hand over her spectacles to shield her eyes from the sun. "Want to come down to the river for a bit?"

"Sure," he said, not stopping to ask for Amanda's approval. Could she blame him for not looking in her direction? She'd only scowl and say no.

After they'd marched down to the Bow and settled themselves on the same rocks where he'd had the accident, the children began skimming stones off the river. Tom helped them collect the flat ones that were best for skimming, then eased back into the grass beside Amanda. She was sitting with her knees pulled up against her, and carefully made sure there was at least a foot between them.

Tom peered out at the horizon. "You know I'll keep asking until you say yes, don't you?"

And there it was, out in the open again. Her shyness crept up on her. "I know."

"And will you?" He reached out and touched her calf, stroking the cloth of her skirt. Her breath caught at the contact of his warm hand on her leg. At the impropriety of his touch. Tom Murdock never did anything the way other men did.

"You mustn't do that…"

"I can't stop myself."

She couldn't, either. It felt so good to be near him. It didn't matter. She abruptly withdrew her leg.

He tugged her close again by the same leg.

A smile rose to her lips, and she pulled away again.

When he reached out the third time, she thought she'd outsmart him and dip her leg out of his grasp before he could reach it, but he surprised her and caught her by her arm instead.

"I win," he said.

Laughter escaped her. "What do you win?"

"You. I win you."

"Tom, how can we continue when you know—"

"All I know is how I feel. Can you deny you feel something for me?"

"I can deny it," she said, pulling herself taller, looking straight ahead at the blue sky and ripples over the water.

"Look me in the eye and deny it."

Cautiously, she swiveled her face toward his. His lips were partly open, his features riveted on hers. What she saw in his face was goodness. An aching. "I can…I can…"

"You can't resist me."

She laughed again. It might be true, but he didn't need to know that. "You've got a big head."

"We can take it nice and slow. I won't pressure you into anything. You're a *vital* woman, so full of life, who has more to offer than any—"

"Tom, look at this!" Margaux called. As they turned to watch the children play leapfrog, Tom's hand slid off

Amanda's arm. A coldness remained where he'd touched her. Why did she feel so much better when his hands were on her?

"I'm worried about Josh's future," said Tom.

"I know how you feel," Amanda whispered, staring at the four-year-old who seemed happy playing in the sunshine. She was very concerned about him, too, but surprised that Tom thought so deeply about him. "It's one thing to get through childhood with his speech problems and the troublesome way people look down on him, but quite another to face the challenges when he becomes an adult."

Her voice drifted to a hush and she opened up to Tom, saying the things she hadn't been able to share with anyone else. "Yesterday when I took the two of them to visit the school, I heard two of the older children whispering names as he passed."

Tom reached out and cupped her shoulder, easing her burden, letting her go on without interrupting, just listening.

"Josh didn't understand, but Margaux did. I saw her turn white and stiffen. Josh is too young to go to school yet for a couple of years, but how long will it be until he understands what they're calling him?"

Tom sighed and kept rubbing, kept listening.

"The O'Hara children are really good to him and treat him like the normal boy he is, but as he grows older... I don't know who'll hire him, or how he'll make his living. Or how he'll cope with aging. Or even if he'll ever find a woman to love him."

Tom was obviously shaken by her words. "I've thought of it all, too. He's a smart boy. When you spend some time with him, you can easily see it." Tom whistled, calling the children to his side.

Margaux squatted near Amanda, and Josh sat on Tom's lap. Tom gave the boy a hug, allowing his lips to rest for a second on the boy's forehead before asking, "Can you say 'My name is Josh'?"

Amanda watched the interplay, touched by Tom's compassion for Josh and his desire to help.

The boy mumbled something incomprehensible.

Amanda tried next. Josh still couldn't get it. "Face me," she said gently, staring at the boy's mouth. "Try again, sweetheart." When his mouth tried to form the words, Amanda gasped.

She stared into his mouth around his tongue.

Her pulse skipped a beat, comprehending what she was seeing.... He had a medical problem that was causing his speech impediment. One that was treatable!

"What is it?" asked Tom.

A cry of joy broke from her lips. She jumped to her feet. If she was right, Josh's world was about to change. She *was* right, she knew she was, and she trembled right through to her bones. But she didn't want to startle the children and couldn't say. "Why don't you children go on up to the shack? Right away. Get cleaned up. We're going into town for a little adventure. We're going to visit Tom's brother, Dr. Quaid."

"Quaid?" asked Tom, rising to stand tall above her. "Why Quaid?"

"Is Tom comin' with us?" Margaux asked.

"Yes," said Amanda, feeling buoyant.

When the children scrambled up the hill, Amanda turned to Tom. "Josh can't speak properly because the lingual frenulum—*the membrane beneath his tongue*—is holding it down, obstructing his speech. I should have seen it earlier. Good Lord, the boy's not mentally imbalanced, he's only tongue-tied!"

Chapter Eleven

"Josh's speech will be normal?" Tom asked Quaid two hours later, still amazed at the whole turn of events, especially thrilled at Amanda's perception in exposing the problem.

"It'll take you two years to catch up with your speech," Quaid said to Josh while he examined the youngster on the leather padded table. "You didn't go through the regular babble and gurgle sounds you would have as a baby, so you'll have to learn those now."

"We'll help you through it," said Amanda, holding on to Josh's hand on one side, her arm around Margaux's slender shoulders on the other.

Quaid helped the timid four-year-old rise to a sitting position. "You'll be fine, Josh."

Tom's gaze turned to Amanda again. His appreciative eye traveled from the laugh lines at her eyes to her upturned mouth. Pride filled him. She had just accomplished something incredible. She'd turned Josh's future around. Tom ached to reach over and touch her, to kiss her in congratulation.

Margaux's face appeared beside her brother's. Her lips

paled. Was she frightened? "What do you have to do to him?"

Amanda got down to her level. "See this piece of skin holding down my tongue?" Amanda stuck her tongue in the air and twirled it up so the girl and boy could study it. "Dr. Quaid is going to make a small adjustment underneath Josh's. He's going to make a little stitch, much smaller than Tom got in his arm." She explained to Josh. "The doctor's going to give you medicine to make you fall asleep, so it won't hurt. When you wake up, it'll all be finished."

"Boo-boo?" asked Josh.

"No boo-boo, we promise," vowed Tom.

Margaux peered at the long waxed tips of Quaid's mustache. "You have a funny mustache."

The group laughed, and in his exuberance, Tom reached out and allowed his arm to trail down Amanda's. His touch seemed to upset her calm. Although she reclaimed her arm and color rose to her cheeks, her eyes sparkled with an inner excitement.

Tom reached to the shelf for an oval mirror and passed it down to the children.

"What's this?" asked Margaux.

"It's a fancy mirror," said Tom. "Have you ever seen one?"

"No," breathed Margaux, clutching the ornate silver handle.

Tom grinned at their amused expressions. "Go ahead, make some faces."

Margaux hugged her little brother, then the two of them raced to the leather wing chair in the corner to examine their tongues in the mirror while the adults talked.

Amanda cleared her throat and glanced around the room, at its well-polished oak furniture, the lines of labeled bottles above Quaid's head, the brand-new leather examination table. "My cabin's not built yet, Quaid, so I don't have the sterility or facilities you do here. And you know how difficult it would be for me, working on a patient who feels like part of my own family…I can't do the procedure. Could you do this for us?"

"Of course I'll do it."

"I could assist you."

"It's not necessary."

"I'll have to make payment another—"

"Amanda," Tom interrupted. He shifted in his boots, towering over the other two, glancing at his brother. "There's no need."

"I agree with my brother." Quaid turned to face the wall, fumbling, making as if he were checking his stethoscope, but Tom knew how difficult it was for Quaid to admit Amanda's brilliance in discovering Josh's problem. "This is for the boy," Quaid said.

"I should have noticed his problem earlier." Amanda played with her fingers. "I didn't look for it—"

"Neither did I," said Quaid, very quietly. "And I've seen him a few times myself."

Say you're sorry, thought Tom of his brother. *Admit how skilled Amanda is.*

Quaid said nothing more.

Tom leaned against the table, squeezing his large injured shoulder past the wall shelf. The sutures were out, but it was still tender. "When can you do it?"

"Well, that depends." Quaid looked at the clock. "I've got to make a house call in two hours to remove a splint. I'm free now, but I'd have to use chloroform and put the boy under. His stomach has to be empty," he explained to Tom, "so that he can't choke during the procedure. When was the last time he ate?"

"This morning." Amanda sprang forward, as if she were prepared for the question. "Around seven. I didn't have them eat lunch before we came to you, in case—"

"You thought of everything," said Tom.

Quaid's jaw flexed. What was it with him? thought Tom. Did he feel threatened by Amanda's expertise? He was being ridiculous, and Tom would tell him so as soon as he got him alone. Why, Quaid had nothing but the best money could buy in this office, while Amanda made do with old medical supplies, in a shack! With no complaints, he might add.

He wished he could give Amanda the same advantages Quaid had. She was unbelievable.

"It'll be easier on the children if we do it now," Amanda continued. "It'll only upset them if they have to worry about it for tomorrow, or the next day."

"Fine," said Quaid in approval.

"Can I stay to assist?"

"Suit yourself."

Amanda and Quaid stayed with Josh while Tom took Margaux to the waiting room. Tom hoped—prayed—that it went well for the boy. Hell, Tom admitted, he was more than a little anxious knowing Josh would be put to sleep. But at least he was in there with the two people Tom trusted most to perform the operation.

Twenty minutes later Amanda poked her head out the door. Tom jumped when he saw her. She was flushed and radiant. "It's all finished. He's fine. He's still asleep, though. Quaid says he has a bedroom for his patients down the hall. Would you mind carrying Josh to the room?"

With Margaux bouncing at his side, Tom strode toward the office. "Not at all."

Amanda smiled at Margaux. "Come see your brother."

They sat by Josh's bed for two hours while he slept.

There was packing beneath his tongue, so his mouth looked full, and Amanda said he'd be groggy and feeling nauseous when he awoke.

Tom got up and walked to Quaid's kitchen, and with the help of Quaid's elderly housekeeper, Mrs. Garvey, he brought back a loaf of rye and smoked meat. Even though Amanda declined, Margaux ate heartily.

"You've got to eat, Amanda," said Tom, waiting for her to bite into her sandwich before he attempted his own. "When Josh wakes up, he'll need you." He sat beside her on the bench, with Margaux nestled on the rug between them.

Amanda began eating, never taking her eyes off the little boy.

Tom watched her. Her head was capped by a mass of lustrous black hair. Although her dress was simple, the woman beneath was anything but. "What you discovered about Josh was amazing."

Amanda leaned her back against the wall, straightening her thighs beside him. When she broke into a wide smile, he felt a sensual pull between them. "Unbelievable news, isn't it?"

"Incredible."

Quaid knocked on the door then, checking on Josh, going over his care treatment with Amanda, then retrieving Tom to the hallway, out of earshot. "Will you take them home?"

Tom crossed his arms. "I'll take care of them, you go to your house call. Thanks for what you did in there. I'll let the housekeeper know to lock up when we leave."

Quaid nodded and glanced at Tom's shirt, at his injured side. "How are you feeling?"

"Fine. All set for dancing tomorrow."

Quaid frowned as he slid into his jacket. "You're still going to take her?"

"She's still saying no, but I've got a few hours left to convince her."

"I really think you should reconsider—"

"I don't need your advice. Besides, you're not even going to be there. Your train to pick up your wife leaves tonight."

"God, you're stubborn. Just because you're the oldest, you treat me and Gabe like we don't know anything."

"Me?"

"Fannie tells me Amanda hasn't picked up any more new patients because no one in town knows what to make of her—"

"That's not true. She's still looking after Ellie, and Donald told me that the Smythes called her for one of their children in the middle of the night—"

"Well, yes, Amanda lives closer to them than I do."

"Amanda diagnosed mumps and quarantined the children."

"I know."

"Why can't you work *with* her, instead of against her? She could be a help to the folks in town. She's a big help already. There's enough work for the both of you—"

"That's not what it is." Quaid's voice rose.

"I think it is. And I'm not sure I know you sometimes."

"Your business affects all of us in this family, but it's *you* I'm worried about. Once I get on my feet, I can help you, but not for another six months. As a person, I think Amanda seems all right, but people are looking at you strangely, and Fannie and her father keep asking me what you're doing with her. Why can't you back away from her until your business is back on track?"

Tom scoffed. "Because it's not my style to back away."

Quaid clicked his tongue with exasperation. "I've got to run." Shaking his head, he reached out and playfully punched Tom on his good shoulder. "I should really stay and kill you, but I don't have the time. I'll have to do it when I see you next."

Tom's irritation at his younger brother melted. "Have a safe trip to Winnipeg. I'll pick you up at the station when you get back. Monday evening, right?"

Quaid nodded.

"Say howdy to Beth. Tell her the baby cradle is finished, one month ahead of schedule."

"She'll be happy to hear it," said Quaid as he raced out the door with hat and bag in hand.

As he watched his brother leave, Tom knew Quaid only had his best interests at heart. But sometimes his advice was misdirected, particularly with Amanda. Didn't Quaid have enough to worry about with Beth eight months along and the two of them expecting their first?

Quaid had initially balked at Beth traveling so late in her confinement, but her mother had been gravely ill and Beth had thought it might be the last time she'd see her. So Quaid had accompanied his wife to Winnipeg two months ago, and in the end, her mother had recovered from her bout of pneumonia.

Tom had been excited at their announcement that they were expecting. He was going to be an uncle and a godfather for the first time, and he'd cherished the news, anticipating the day when he'd become a father, too. At the time of the announcement, he'd thought it would be with Clarissa.

But Clarissa was gone, and Amanda was here.

And Amanda would never have his children.

Pulling himself together, he walked back into the room and watched her. She gently coaxed a groggy Josh to a sitting position, giving him ice chips to suck, then broth to drink. She made sure Margaux was allowed to help care for her brother even though Tom knew it would be faster and easier for Amanda to lay the pillow or to tie the boy's shoes.

While they recuperated, he slipped away from them for more than an hour, saying he needed to check on his men, but really making his secret calls. He visited the dressmaker, then dropped off the packages to Miss Clementine, assuring her Josh was fine, pledging her to secrecy for the afternoon but seeking her help in his other plan concerning Pierce.

In the late afternoon, when they all left Quaid's, he pulled the wagon to Amanda's door, taking Josh inside and laying him on his cot.

Amanda came outside to say goodbye to Tom. They were both quiet, both anticipating the other's move, he reckoned. Should he ask her again? Had he asked too many times already?

Could he handle it if she said no?

When he simply nodded goodbye and slid into the darkness with his horse and wagon, he wondered what she'd do when she opened the packages. Would she show up at the ball?

Did she care at all about him?

Beside the crackling woodstove, after the children were settled in their beds for the night and their heavy breathing echoed off the beams, Grandma uncovered her bedspread to reveal two brown packages.

"What's that?" asked Amanda in dismay, looking at Grandma's tender expression. Both of them wore their flannel nightshirts. "Where did they come from?"

The huge one rested on a hanger. Grandma lifted it and slid it over the top of the door. The package nearly touched the floor. "Tom brought them this afternoon."

"But he was with me." Then she realized. "Except for that hour."

"That's the hour he was here. I believe these are your clothes for the ball."

"Mine?" whispered Amanda. He'd thought of the ball, after all he'd done for them this afternoon? She hadn't thought of it once since Josh's problem was discovered.

She knew she wanted to go with Tom. Deep in her heart, she knew she wanted to, to dance in his arms, to feel those muscular arms pressed against her back, to breathe the scent of his skin.

How had he arranged for a *gown?*

"I can look after Josh while you go. John promised he'd help, and Ellie said she'd stop by to call on us. Tom arranged for Margaux to be invited to the ball, too, to accompany Pierce. Ellie's already been over with a hand-me-down dress for her, if she'd like to attend. Pierce will wear his father's suit."

"Tom arranged for Margaux to come, too?"

Grandma nodded. "Apparently, there's a group of older children going together. You know how much the girl would love to go."

"I'm sure she would." A thirteen-year-old girl would adore the ball. Dear, kindhearted Tom had thought of Margaux as well as her.

What did the gown look like? How had he known her measurements? How could he afford it, when he was so strapped himself? Stepping to the package, she removed the visible note, attached to the paper by a stickpin. Her hand trembled as she opened the parchment.

Sometimes, people do get what they deserve. Come with me to the ball, Amanda. It starts at eight. I'll send a carriage.

With a long, limber stride, Tom stepped out from the crowded ballroom into the foyer of the Banff Springs Hotel, peering over the dozens of heads making their way down the marble corridor. The grandfather clock in the corner read seven forty-five. Still no sign of Amanda.

Wearing a double-breasted black gentleman's suit with tails, Tom headed toward the grand entrance, saying hello to passersby, soaking in the wealth and splendor of his surroundings.

Hand-cut crystal chandeliers from Austria adorned the arched ceilings. Gleaming mahogany chairs lined the corridor, Spanish-carved railings curled their shapes up the massive spiral staircase, and wall candelabrum cast dancing shadows as he passed. His black high-topped shoes marched over squares of Italian terrazzo, their echo combining with the orchestral sounds wafting from the ballroom, mixing with the chatter of English noblemen, French aristocracy and his fellow countrymen.

The violinist standing at the entry directly ahead of Tom began to play, welcoming the guests as they disembarked from their carriages and made their way through the doors. "The Blue Danube," Tom recognized with a smile, by Johann Strauss.

Pierce had already arrived with his friends, and Tom had seen to it they were settled at a table close to the front of the ballroom, hoping young Margaux would arrive with Amanda to keep Pierce company and enjoy herself for one lovely evening.

Heads turned in Tom's direction as he strode, women mostly, but he took notice only because he was scanning faces, searching for Amanda. He had no guarantee of when or if she would arrive.

He went out to wait by the carriages. Some folks had chosen to come in buggies, being practical in the rough terrain, also knowing the hotel's carriages would be very busy this evening. When he thought he caught a glimmer of blue inside a buggy, his heart began to pound. Was she in it?

He strained his neck to see. No. It was Ruby and her husband.

The transfixing sound of horses on cobblestone played in his ears. More carriages, more people Tom knew, but no Amanda.

When the fifth carriage pulled up and wheeled around him, its back to him, he thought he spotted an ankle he recognized, descending from its depths.

A glimmer of blue satin and lace. She was here!

Her delicate, high-buttoned leather shoes with slender high heels looked better on her sensuous legs than they had in his hands. The gentle curve of her ankle made him swallow hard. While the footmen helped her and Margaux disembark, Tom's awestruck gaze followed up Amanda's legs to the rest of her.

Blue satin clung to her curves. A deep, plunging-V caressed the swell of her breasts. Another daring-V exposed her beautiful bare back, one he longed to strum with his fingertips. Her short sleeves were capped, but little skin was exposed on her arms because her long gloves, made of the same blue satin as her gown, gracefully met with the sleeves at the line where her arm muscle curved. It was the same blue satin, he realized, that Mrs. Warren had used to tailor his cravat.

The pleats at Amanda's waistline accentuated her femininity, and the curled, silky black hair that flowed down one side of her front made him ache to feel the silky strands wrapped around his body.

While Margaux, dressed in a long green velvet gown,

raced around to help Amanda straighten her satin train behind her, Tom didn't move.

Amanda dipped her face to Margaux's, her delicate cheekbones curving upward as the two laughed about something together. Swirling in her gown, turning toward the entrance, Amanda glanced up the stairs, and finally, after his eternity of waiting, found his quiet face in the crowd.

Chapter Twelve

When Amanda spotted Tom standing at the top of the stairs in the golden moonlight, one tanned palm resting on the rail, the other tucked inside the pocket of his black jacket, her heart reacted with a beating flutter. She'd never seen him looking more imposing.

A starched, white collar stood out against his neck, and a cool blue cravat—made of her own gown's satin, she realized proudly—contrasted with the warm tones of his face.

His thick, black hair was slicked around his ears, but a few uncompromising strands slid to his brow. Those friendly lips she was used to seeing smile bore no smile now as his bold eyes swept over her. His clean-shaven jaw tightened. She was dismayed at the magnitude of her own response, and extremely aware that she must look different to him, too.

And he was her companion? For the entire evening?

She pulled her soft angora shawl tighter around her shoulders and watched as he walked down the stairs to greet them, every muscle moving with an easy fluid motion, culminating in a graceful stride.

He cast his eyes on Margaux first. "I didn't realize you were such a pretty young lady."

Margaux smiled and adjusted her spectacles, and Amanda felt herself glow at Tom's thoughtfulness. That a grown man would take the time to think of a girl's feelings, to make Margaux feel accepted in this town with other teens her age, was undeniably appealing.

"How's your brother doing tonight?"

"He's fine. He's already sleeping."

Tom chuckled. When he took Margaux's white, gloved hand and bowed, she beamed so brightly, it made Amanda catch her breath with happiness.

She met with Tom's twinkling eyes.

"And you," he said, ever so softly, bringing her gloved hand to his lips, "are breathtaking."

The pulsing contact of his warm hand on hers, even through the cloth, made her yearn for more. His lips coaxed an involuntary quivering which raced from her fingertips to her toes. "Thank you. And thank you for inviting us both."

"I'm glad you came." He spun around to stand between them, cupping their hands in the crux of his elbows. The confident way he carried himself gave him an aura of fearless pride. "Shall we?" he asked, motioning to the stairs.

They passed through half a dozen doormen, some holding lit torches in one hand while opening heavy doors with the other. Tom stood head and shoulders above them. Amanda noticed the interested gazes of other women following his movements, and she felt elated to be at his side.

When the threesome stepped through the doors, listening to the violinist, Amanda gaped at her surroundings. She'd never seen anything so plush and regal. "Are you sure we're invited?"

His dark brow wrinkled with humor. "Of course you are."

Margaux's eyes widened as she raised her head to the chandelier. "Uh-hh...."

"Right this way to the ballroom."

With a possessive hand at Amanda's waist, he wove his way expertly through the crowd, seating them at a table near the front, next to friendly folks Amanda didn't know. She spotted Pierce in the corner with his friends, a group Margaux said she'd join later, after the speeches. For now, Amanda recognized that the girl felt more at ease by her side, like a shy daughter might by her mother's.

There were perhaps eight-hundred people here this evening. Not only tourists and townsfolk, but vice presidents and engineers of the Canadian Pacific Railway, all the way from Edmonton, Toronto, Quebec City and Halifax.

When William Van Horne, the CPR president, rose to give a toast, the crowd followed. Amanda stood beside Tom, trying not to react to his striking presence, trying to concentrate on the awe that filled everyone around her.

They were bathed in splendor. While some drank the finest champagne from France, others authentic port from Portugal, Tom and Amanda sipped cognac from Venetian goblets imported directly from the island of Murano.

Three more speakers rose to the podium, then finally Tom. He bowed slightly to Amanda as he left her side, then made his way to the front. As she listened to his marvelous speech—describing the grit and determination of the townsmen during construction of the grand hotel, his pride at being involved in Canada's first national park, how smitten he was by the mountains and the unrelenting human spirit of Banff—she realized Tom was a born leader. He did his best under the most difficult of circumstances, caring for the folks around him as deeply as he did his own brothers and father.

When his eyes penetrated the crowd and found hers, she swallowed tightly. It was a good thing she intended on taking this evening one step at a time. No promises, no commitments, just as he'd said to her on the train.

No commitments. She sat mesmerized, watching the chandelier lighting capture the curve of his dark cheek. Why did that leave her with an emptiness?

Why had she come tonight? Was part of the reason she was here because of Margaux? So that the young girl could experience this once-in-a-lifetime evening?

When the speeches were over and Tom was again attentively by her side, the tables were cleared for dancing while the orchestra began to play. She and Tom rose with Margaux and encouraged her to join her classmates. Two of them were lovely girls Margaux had mentioned before, and of course, Pierce O'Hara.

The sixteen-year-old boy rose to greet them. With a gangly awkwardness, his father's suit a bit too large in the shoulders and legs but nonetheless looking charming on him, he handed Margaux a little white box and grinned.

Margaux took it and smoothed her hair. "What's this?"

"A present. Tom helped me pick it out. He said we should get you somethin', since you weren't gettin' a new gown."

Amanda looked to Tom. She was again caught off guard by this unpredictable man. He shrugged his broad shoulders and with a quirk of his full lips, tilted back his head to watch Margaux's and Amanda's reactions.

With a small gasp of delight, Margaux opened the lid and pulled out what looked to be one shiny piece of inexpensive jewelry. "Earbobs? For me?"

Pierce gazed shyly at the girl's face. "I thought they'd

match your eyeglasses. Gold and gold. You look much older with spectacles, you know. I thought you were at least fifteen when I first saw you.''

Margaux flushed, obviously pleased. "You did?"

Amanda lost herself in the comfort of being with the teens. Margaux obviously felt relaxed, and Amanda realized how important the girl's happiness was to her. She hoped she had much more time to spend with Margaux and Josh before anyone took them away.

Tom nudged Amanda's shoulder and lightly took her hand. She tingled with the excitement of being this near to him. His exploratory gaze traveled over her face then descended to the bare expanse of her throat, to the string of smooth pearls nestled there that had once belonged to her other grandmother. His tantalizing look could almost seduce her to do anything.

His grip tightened. "Would you care to dance?"

Her lips quivered. In order to dance with her, he would have to touch her body. *Touch her everywhere.*

She succumbed. "I'd love to." Glancing to the orchestra, a dozen men and women who were playing piano, harp, violins and flutes, she placed an arm around Margaux. "And the children?"

"They'll be fine, won't you?" Tom asked.

"Yeah," replied Pierce.

With her new earbobs dangling from her ears, Margaux brushed at her green velvet dress and nodded.

"And you remember now, Pierce," Tom continued, tugging his long fingers in between Amanda's, making her heart race. "The return carriages and chaperones begin at ten-thirty for you young people. That's roughly an hour and a half. The adults are staying later, but you're to start home without us. Eleven o'clock at the very latest."

"I'll remember, sir."

A new waltz began. Tom clenched her hand and wove ahead of her, pulling her through the throng of heated bodies. Facing him on the dance floor, she could barely keep her heart from beating wildly beneath her breast. Did he notice how nervous she was? Would he be able to feel how sweaty her palms were? Looking down at her, he lifted his left hand for the dance, she slid in her right and they began.

She gulped at the desire she saw in his eyes. Would this be a night of heartache, or would this be a night of surrender?

"I'd like to thank you for this gown," she said, trying to think of other things, trying to concentrate on the six-inch space between them rather than the parts that were pressed together. But every dip of his muscled body stirred a reaction in hers. "However did you manage it?"

His long lashes swept over her. "Mrs. Warren made it."

"The town dressmaker?"

Her steps slowed. He suddenly tugged her closer and spun her around to the music. "I called in a favor."

"Well, I'll have to thank her, too." His broad hand tightened around her waist and her body arched toward him. "And the shoes, Tom," she whispered, "I've never owned a pair that were made simply for dancing."

"It's about time, then." With the next fast twirl, she had to hang on tighter to his back. His eyes flashed and his mouth responded with a slight smile of flushed approval.

They moved gracefully around the others, his palm flat against her lower back, over her gown. Some of the men from Europe were wearing gloves, but he wasn't. Many formalities in the West had been done away with for practical reasons and for less fuss, and she liked it better that way.

They danced without speaking, in time to the rush of

music. Other people on the dance floor, both men and women, turned to watch them. Her pulse quickened at the speculation of what she was doing, of what might happen between them. She had a need to press her body closer, but with tense control, kept her arms at the proper distance.

When Tom moved his palm higher on her back, then lower again, adjusting his hand ever so slightly, she realized he was having difficulty knowing where to place it. She hadn't thought of it, but the fact that her back was exposed made it improper for him to place his hand directly on her skin.

During another swirl, he guided her around the floor, but his hand must have been sweaty, too, for it slipped off the fabric of her gown. When his hot fingers dug into the curve of her naked spine, his touch seared her flesh.

She shivered.

He shuddered.

Their eyes locked.

He didn't remove his hand! Heat rushed to her face. He let his fingers sit where they'd slipped. She should say something, she should object.

His eyes challenged hers, but she said nothing!

As the music continued and the melodic chords vibrated through her body, she let his hand slowly stroke her skin, letting it caress her, letting it mingle with the sweat and salt of her own body.

She wanted him in every sense of the word. To make love to him, to explore his body and linger over every part of it like a turbulent lover would. When his breathing grew raspy, he tore his gaze down to her open lips, looking as though he longed to bury his mouth there.

She wanted to surrender. She felt the desire race from the tips of her breasts down her trembling stomach.

It would never happen here, in this public forum. Would it happen anywhere?

The dance ended. He whispered into her hair, but she broke free of his arms. How could they continue this?

Excusing herself, she grabbed her reticule from the table and rushed to find the powdering rooms. Just a moment was all she needed to bring her senses back from the clouds.

The wooden privies were indoors, she remembered as she tore down the hallway. She raced into the crowded rooms with a sigh of relief. How far would she let this go with Tom?

Porcelain bowls filled with water sat on top of carved walnut counters, and she headed that way to splash water on her face. Hand mirrors lined the countertops for women to attend to their powdered noses, and those lines were full.

She saw Ruby enter the room from the other door, waving hello to her through the throng of women. But Amanda couldn't face anyone and hoped Ruby would keep her distance.

What she needed was to catch her breath. Why had she come here tonight? Was it only for Margaux's sake, as she'd rationalized earlier?

No, her heart answered. She'd come for Tom. For herself. She'd come for what she'd wanted all along.

She wanted to be with Tom and to see how it felt to be held in his arms. She wanted to imagine for one moment that there was a man out there for her, beyond her devastating divorce, and that maybe, just maybe, she wouldn't have to spend her life alone.

Her hand trembled on her reticule. The room was hot. Stepping into the shortest line for a mirror to straighten her hair, she waited for the seated woman ahead of her to finish at the counter and wondered how on earth she'd go back out there to face him when she was obviously so affected.

"Good evening," the woman said above the chattering voices in the room, glancing at Amanda in the circular mirror that rested in front of her. "I'll only be a moment."

Amanda nodded and pressed her hands to her hot cheeks, trying to calm down. Tom wanted more from her than just a dance.

But if not a commitment, then what?

A small tin canister clattered on the counter, distracting her. She glanced up at the woman again, who was rubbing a pale cosmetic from the tin then applying it to her lips. Amanda tried not to stare, but her medical background made her curious about the woman's health.

The young woman was very pretty; curly chestnut hair fell down her shoulders, some of it tied up in stylish twists on her crown, but she was brushing powder over one cheekbone that looked slightly swollen and lightly bruised. How had she sustained the injury she was trying to hide?

She was dressed in an amazing burgundy gown, shimmering of sequins and silk. Her jewelry was distinct. Diamonds glittered at her throat, and the silver bracelet on her wrist clanged against the counter as she applied her elegant powders.

"Are you with someone?" the woman asked, peering at Amanda through the mirror again, her large brown lashes amplified.

Amanda cleared her throat, trying to regain her composure. "A good friend."

"A good friend? If you find a good friend in a man, you should keep him." Something about her tone seemed very sad. The older, made-up woman standing beside her, waiting for her to finish, nodded in agreement.

Amanda was suddenly overcome with the mixture of

strong perfumes in the crowded space. She hadn't thought to wear any. Even if she had, she'd left her three bottles behind with her mother and sister in Calgary. She remembered thinking, why would I need perfume in Banff?

"Are you here with someone, too?" Amanda asked them, uncomfortable in the stilted silence and trying to fill it.

"We're here only for the dancing. We skipped the speeches altogether. Quite frankly," the pretty woman said, "I didn't come with someone, but I plan on leaving with him."

Her friend chuckled.

The directness of the response silenced Amanda.

While the woman stood up to leave, Ruby squeezed to Amanda's side, huffing in exaggeration at the crowd she had to tame to get here.

Catching sight of the brunette, Ruby stopped abruptly, staring in surprise from Amanda to her. Then Ruby recovered quickly, running her thick hand over her yellow and blue taffeta gown, stepping to the brunette to kiss her cheek. "How nice to see you again, Clarissa."

Amanda was taking an awfully long time, thought Tom, gazing down the hallway again, past the bobbing heads, but no sign of the black-haired beauty. He reentered the ballroom and listened to the orchestra weave their magic, nodding to Graham and the other constables standing at attention in the corner.

When he'd held Amanda in his arms on the dance floor, he'd felt the harsh uneven rhythm of her breathing, and he knew what she felt for him was not as casual as she'd led him to believe. He'd looked into her eyes and he'd seen the passionate message swirling in the deep blue depths. His heart was still thundering.

Amanda Ryan wanted what he wanted.

Luckily, things were going better this evening than Tom had expected, on all fronts. After his speech, two men had come to him, requesting his bid for a new restaurant they hoped to build before the end of the tourist season, and Graham told him that his sergeant wanted to get a bid on a larger stable for the Mounties' horses.

Payroll might be met again this week, Tom thought with a surge of relief.

At the sound of his name being called, he glanced to the door. Amanda was finally walking through it in her magical swirl of blue satin. She looked upset; her face was drawn and solemn. He straightened, taking his hand out of his jacket pocket. What was wrong?

Then he noticed another figure following close behind, encased her in her trademark family jewels and a glamorous new burgundy gown, talking to Ruby and waving to him.

For cripe's sake, Clarissa Ashford.

His gut clenched. In a predatory response, he scanned the room. Was Finnigan here, too?

No, of course not, he thought, trying to make quick sense of the situation. Finnigan was a wanted man. Clarissa wasn't wanted by the law, not technically. She wasn't charged with a crime. But why in hell was she here and what was she doing with Amanda?

And how exactly did he feel about it?

He rose to full alert. His gaze was transfixed as they came closer. Amanda was slightly taller and more slender, walking with determination in her stride, whereas Clarissa was softer, with more curves and twists to her hair and body. But not half as appealing.

Tom leaped to Amanda's side, offering a silent look of

condolence. Her body withdrew and her gaze was cool. *Great.* What had Clarissa told Amanda?

"Clarissa," he said, trying to restrain his anger as he peered down at her smiling face. The last time he'd heard from her was that blasted note she'd left him in the sawmill. "What are you doing here? Where's Finnigan?"

Clarissa frowned.

"I think I see my husband," said Ruby, looking uncomfortable. As she walked away, she squeezed Amanda's shoulder, and Amanda bent her soft face to Ruby's hand, acknowledging the tender gesture.

Tom felt nauseated. The last thing he wanted tonight was to hurt Amanda. She knew part of the story, but not all of it. Hell, he didn't know himself how the story with Clarissa would end. And this wasn't the time or place to confront her.

Clarissa's rosy lips puckered. "That's a fine way to greet me." She studied Amanda with curiosity, as if wondering why Amanda was still standing there. "It was a pleasure to meet you, Amanda," she said in dismissal.

Amanda didn't budge. Annoyance hovered in her expression. She braced herself, showing no signs of leaving, bringing her reticule to her midriff in quiet defiance.

So Clarissa didn't know Amanda was his companion?

Clarissa tried again. "I'll...I'll catch up with you later if you like, and we can have another nice conversation then."

Tom walked to Amanda's side. He draped an arm around her shoulders. She stiffened beneath his touch. He silently swore. "Amanda's here with me tonight."

Clarissa's lips parted open as she stared at Amanda. Amanda blinked.

Clarissa's thick brown lashes flew up at him. *"With you?"* Her eyes narrowed for a moment of contemplation, then she blushed. A deep crimson crept up her neck. Tom had never seen her blush before. She tilted her head at Amanda, the glossy brown coils shifting on top of her head. "*He's* your good friend, I suppose."

Amanda's voice was strained, but deliberate. "I didn't realize we were talking about the same man."

They'd been talking about him? About what? His neck grew hot beneath his tight cravat.

"Oh, really?" whispered Clarissa.

"That's enough, Clarissa. I'll ask you again. What are you doing here, and where's Finnigan?"

"Can't we have this discussion in *private?*"

Tom dropped his arm from around Amanda. "You can speak frankly in front of both of us. Amanda herself has been affected by all this business with Finnigan."

"Has she been affected by the business between *us?*" The sexual insinuation was obvious.

Amanda gasped, then stepped away. "I should let you talk."

"Please stay," said Tom, reaching out and grabbing her by the arm. Clarissa's eyes followed the movements of his possessive hand on Amanda.

"I don't think there's any *business* left between us," he said pointedly to Clarissa. All he felt for her right now was frustration. "If you remember, you left me a note?"

Clarissa paled at the reprimand. When she clamped her lips together and tilted her head, candlelight from the nearby table hit her face.

Did she have a bruise?

Startled at the prospect, Tom stepped close and cupped his fingers beneath her chin. She seemed to bask in his touch, mistaking it for a forward gesture. He kept his distance to let her know it wasn't.

He tilted her jaw to the light. "What happened? How did you get this bruise?"

With a sudden look of shame, she pulled away.

Tom felt his blood run cold. "Blazes. Finnigan didn't—"

"It's nothing. I ran into the carriage door when I arrived."

Tom didn't believe her. The bruise looked older; already blue. Finnigan was a son of a bitch. "Why did Finnigan do this to you?"

Clarissa looked to Amanda and Amanda looked away, allowing the woman her dignity. When Clarissa turned back to him, she sagged. "I don't know. And I'm sorry that I...that I...left you when I did. I should have stayed with you, not him."

It was too late, he thought. When she fell against him, he opened his arms to comfort her, more from pity for an old friend than anything. When he looked up again, Amanda was gone.

Hell. He had to find her. But who could blame her for leaving? What a sticky mess.

He allowed Clarissa the respect of not shoving her away. Being rude wasn't right, especially when someone was hurting. Tom should listen to her explanations, if only to get his answers about Finnigan. For Amanda's sake, too.

Clarissa was wearing the flowery perfume that used to be his favorite. Now all he could think of as he smoothed the back of her hair was how sorry he felt for her.

No one deserved to be beaten, and when he got a hold of Finnigan—and he damn well would—he'd let him know how it felt.

What a terrible mistake she'd made, getting messed up with the likes of that man. Only a few weeks ago, *Tom* might have been the one to fall into her soothing arms, but a lifetime had passed since then.

What Clarissa had done to him was brutal. She'd left him for his business partner and he thought she'd broken his heart. Now he realized she'd only broken his pride.

Tonight when she returned, had she really expected that things would fall back into place?

He scanned the faces of the crowd past Clarissa's looming hair. Where did Amanda go? He'd stay and get his answers from Clarissa, and deliver her to Graham, but Tom wasn't about to let Amanda slip through his grasp. Not after what he'd felt in her response to him tonight.

His heart didn't belong with Clarissa, it belonged with Amanda.

Chapter Thirteen

"Where are you going, Amanda?"

Startled to discover Tom was still at the ball an hour later, let alone standing behind her and Margaux and Pierce in the hallway, Amanda could only nod.

Beyond the breadth of Tom's dark shoulders, a crystal chandelier flickered high above them, its candlelight casting shadows over his face. The scent of burning wax curled around them.

She held her temper in check. She knew it was a good thing Clarissa had arrived, that it could only help their cause in finding Finnigan. But Amanda had spent the past long hour with Margaux and her young friends, teaching them the steps of the waltz, trying to pretend she was enjoying herself, that Tom Murdock didn't matter to her. She'd danced with the men who'd asked, all the while wondering where in thunder her own escort was.

She'd had no polite means of escaping the curious looks of the adults who knew she'd arrived with Tom, and for those who questioned her, all she could do was simply shrug. It was left to her imagination where Clarissa and Tom had escaped to together.

Then, of course, there was the guilt she felt for being

mad at Clarissa—the poor woman who'd been beaten by a man they all now despised.

"I asked where you were going?"

Her gown swished as Amanda pulled away from Tom. She clasped her lacy handbag closer to her bosom. "I'm showing Margaux and Pierce to the carriages. We're going home."

His confidence seemed to dampen. "All of you?"

She kept her voice and her features composed, although inside she was secretly delighted and relieved that he'd finally appeared. She scolded herself for caring. "Yes, all of us."

Towing the children down the corridor, she motioned to the doorman. He pushed open the door and she exited into the star-filled night. Her group spilled out behind her.

A mountain breeze whispered through her tangled hair, easing the harshness in her stance.

"Please don't go," said Tom, standing tall beside her.

"Why not?" she asked in a suffocated whisper, descending the stairs.

He studied her face for a beat. "Because we're not finished."

"I think the evening's over." It had come crashing down around her when Clarissa Ashford had appeared.

With irritation at herself, Amanda wondered why on earth she should care who in tarnation Tom spent his time with. No commitments, she reminded herself.

Standing beside Pierce, Margaux grabbed her by the elbow. Margaux's face held an expression of concern. "We'll be fine getting home on our own. You don't have to go on our account."

Amanda's gaze softened as she looked at Margaux, wishing the girl wouldn't worry about her. She glanced at the lineup of adolescents on the cobblestones. Ten people ahead of them; it would only be a five-minute wait for a carriage.

"Don't worry about me, Margaux." Amanda pulled her soft angora around her arms, and with a deep breath, faced Tom. "We've had a lovely evening tonight, thanks to you. But I've got an early appointment in the morning, and I'm really not used to staying up all hours."

"It's not that late," Tom insisted, shoving his hand into his pocket, looking up at the limestone facade and the clock nestled in the wall. "It's only quarter to eleven."

Her mouth grew dry. Why did he want her to stay? To get more details from her to corroborate with Clarissa's stories? "Is this about Finnigan?"

"There's more to it. I want you to stay *for us*." The color deepened in his face. His jacket parted open and the muscles beneath his white silk shirt quickened her pulse.

What had he and Clarissa talked about for a solid hour? Did he still care about Clarissa as much as he had a month ago?

It was obvious what she'd wanted. *I didn't come with someone, but I plan on leaving with him.*

He ran a hand along his cheek. "Let the children go on ahead. Listen to what I have to say, and what I've learned about Finnigan's whereabouts. You do want to know, don't you?"

He knew the right words to make her fumble. But couldn't she wait until tomorrow to hear the news?

"Stay, Miss Ryan," Pierce prodded. "I can take care of Margaux. I'll make sure she gets home all right."

"None of the other adults are going home yet," Margaux begged. "Our friends are all going home on their own. Why can't we?"

Amanda opened her mouth to protest, then glanced around her. It was true no other adults were leaving, and she supposed the children would feel proud, making their way alone. "All right. I'll stay a while longer. Just a little," she directed to Tom, who happily nodded and stepped back for the carriage to pull up beside them. "Margaux, tell Grandma not to wait up. It's been a long night for her already."

"I will, ma'am."

As Tom and Amanda watched the carriage leave, the two youngsters sharing the carriage with three of their friends, Tom leaned in close and whispered to her temples, "Finnigan was hiding out in Canmore."

She whirled around to face him. "Where his brother Frank lives?"

He stared at her in the moonlight. The direct way he was gazing at her made her wonder what it'd be like to relive the velvet heat of his kiss. "Apparently just down the road," he said. "Frank must have known where he was all along."

She breathed through parted lips. "He didn't tell us the truth."

"He probably couldn't."

"Poor Frank. No wonder he looked so tormented."

Tom was so incredibly attractive in his black suit, she lost track of the people jostling around her. Tom raised his arm to her shawl, leading her away from the hotel. "Are you ready for the next bit of news?"

She waited for his answer as her shoes padded against the stones. Holding her train of fabric firmly in her hand, she enjoyed the cool slick feel of satin against her arms and breasts and thighs.

"Clarissa had no idea he'd stolen money from my account, or overcharged for lumber."

"Do you believe her?"

"Yes, I do." With tanned, sensitive fingers, he ran a

hand over his jaw, which was already developing a dark shadow, Amanda noticed, even though he'd likely shaved hours before.

"How could she not know? It was right beneath her nose."

"It was right beneath mine, too, and I didn't know." When he stopped walking to face her, his eyes glistened with regret. The collar at his neck parted, revealing the hollow curves of his throat. "She just discovered it now, when I told her. They'd been gambling all over the prairies, but she thought it was with his money. She told me she hadn't checked in with her family because she needed time for them to adjust to her choice of Finnigan...over me."

Emotion spilled into his voice, and she realized he must still have deep feelings for Clarissa.

Hurt and longing filled her, making it difficult to speak. "I'm so sorry, Tom. But now that she's back maybe you two—"

"What?" His lips twisted. "She never gave me a second thought, leaving with a man she thought had more money lining his pockets than I had."

Starlight glimmered over his firm lips. With a calm, assured grip, he led her off the stone path and turned to the deserted country road that led to town. The closest carriage was a hundred yards ahead of them.

"Where's Clarissa now?" Amanda asked, trying to understand what this all meant.

"Graham's talking to her."

"But she's been beaten. You need to help her. You should...you should be at her side."

When they cornered a clump of fragrant, fifty-foot-high pine trees, he stopped. They were shielded from the hotel and everyone's line of vision. "God, Amanda, you're so much more than she is. Where I should be *is* right where I am. Here with you.''

When he gazed at her, his tender look pierced her heart. He stepped closer, bridging the gap between them, making her crank her neck to look up at him. That sweet erotic pulsing began to beat within her. When he carefully lifted his heavy arms to rest them on her shoulders, she felt the heat of his body course down hers.

She'd never felt for another man what she felt for Tom. William's touch had never awakened her the way Tom's did.

With a low guttural moan, he lowered his demanding mouth on hers. The touch of his persuasive lips sent a wave of arousal through her body.

She let him take her. She wanted it, yearned for it. It'd been so long since she'd felt the warmth of another human being pressed against her, she yearned for more than a kiss.

They explored each other with abandon, the feel of their mouths, their lips, their tongues. When his bare hands slid down her naked back, she gasped with pleasure. This was what it was like to come alive and feel something.

A crack of gunpowder exploded in the sky.

She jumped at the sudden sound, but he laughed softly and pulled her back into his protective arms. His feverish lips brushed hers. ''The fireworks have started.''

''At the hotel, or between us?''

''Both.''

Breathless with excitement, they laughed into each other's mouths, then he devoured lower, planting kisses down her throat, over her curvy shoulder, one delicate earlobe, lower to capture the sliver of creamy flesh at her cleavage. She felt her nipples tighten beneath the satin of her gown, her breasts swollen by the graze of his hot lips.

Could she stop this?

No, never.

Squeezing her waist with renewed vigor, he crushed her body to his. When he broke free of her lips, his mouth was bruised with passion. "Come with me."

"Where are we going?" she asked, drunk with eagerness, knowing that at this tumultuous moment she'd go anywhere with him, all he had to do was ask.

"A place where we can watch the fireworks in private."

Tom led Amanda up the overgrown pathway, halfway up the mountain to a patch of thick grass he knew there, nestled between the trees and foliage, overlooking the town. He loved how good she felt in his arms.

Surrounded by the sensations of moist dew and fragrant leaves, Tom fought to restrain himself from simply grabbing her, wrestling her to the ground, and working his way up her delicious body with his mouth. But in his soul he knew the invitation had to come from her. Her silent agreement to follow him here was a big step in her faith in him and he didn't want to overpower her.

"You were right," Amanda said, peering at the town's flickering lights below, a sheen of perspiration highlighting her pretty face. "There's nothing like the view from a mountainside."

Glancing through the full branches, past her shapely profile on the hillside, he took a moment to savor the extraordinary evening. In addition to the lights from the boardwalk, fires burned in the backyards of folks who couldn't make it to the ball themselves but who still wanted to see the fireworks. Kerosene lanterns lit up the path of the hotel, and candles inside the hotel windows illuminated the shadows of moving people.

Most spectacular of all, hundreds of people gathered on the grounds, heads turned up, watching another bowl of light explode in the sky, then cascade into rivulets to the earth. It was all done in the open grass, as a precaution against fire.

Amanda stared with awe. The curves of her throat glistened in the starlight, against her string of pearls, and as the gunpowder crackled above them, circles of golden light danced across her forehead and cheeks, illuminating her beauty. His heart pounded in reaction.

"The children will see it, too," she said, her body heavy and warm alongside his. "On their ride home."

A hot ache grew in his throat. "I imagine so," he murmured, entranced not only by her radiance, but by the way she always thought of the children. What a bloody waste she couldn't have any of her own. But what a joy she'd found Josh and Margaux.

"Did you bring me here to see this view?" She turned around, and he found himself inches from her face.

"I brought you here to share my favorite place in the world."

She stared at him in his new black suit, with her quiet oval face, moist, full red mouth, a flush to her skin that he couldn't believe he was responsible for putting there. He thanked whoever it was in the stars above that had led her to him.

"It's lovely, and very private. No one would know it's here unless they came looking for it. I understand why it's your favorite."

"I come here when I need to think."

"It that often?"

"A lot lately." A sense of urgency drove him, but he tried to control his desire. Removing his long jacket, he spread it on the dry ground, then stood up straight in front of her. "If we sit, we can watch the fireworks."

She didn't make a move to sit. When she slowly slid

her gaze over his ruffled shirt, then collar, then up to his face, he could hear her soft inhale, feel the uncertainty in her.

He reached out with one strong hand and tugged her down to the grass. His pulse hammered when their skin met. She perched on the hillside, her angora shawl as smooth as a downy feather, spilled around her full hips.

What he wanted to say to her was, *Pull me down beside you, lay with me and take me and touch me. Touch my hair and touch my mouth and touch my neck, and touch me lower. Let me explore your body and show you what it's like to make love. Let me make your blood pound and let me make you cry my name.*

Instead he said none of those things. Curling his fingers into the velvet green grass beside his leg, he stroked the soft blades, wishing he were stroking her bare, soft skin, her bare, soft nipples.

Another cannon of fireworks exploded above them, striking the air with tension. The charge seemed to arc through her. "You come here to think."

"Yes."

"What about?"

His voice strained. "You, mostly."

He saw her shudder in the blast of light. "What about me?"

"I've been wondering what's been going on with you, what you think about…late at night."

Humor illuminated her mellow blue eyes. "Lots of things. Josh's medical problem, Margaux's new school, my grandma, my log cabin and what's going to happen in court on Monday."

His gaze came to rest on her mouth. "I mean, what you think about men."

Suddenly shy, she turned away to look up through the

trees, but he followed her movements and captured her stubborn chin between his fingers. The dark black fringe of her lashes cast feathery shadows on her cheeks.

"I mean, what you think about *me*."

With teasing laughter, she escaped his grasp. When she shifted in her gown, her plunging satin neckline twisted, and he caught a glimpse of the most tempting cleavage. Blood coursed through his veins.

"I think...I think you're absolutely wonderful."

His soft lips pulled into a grin and his discretion left him. "I want to hear more. I want to know if what I feel for you is the same that you feel for me."

Biting back a smile, she smoothed her gown over her knees, still wearing those long blue gloves that clung to her shapely arms. "Well, then you'll have to tell me how you feel so I can compare."

He filled his lungs with cool, fresh air. "When I'm with you, I feel like nothing can happen that I can't handle. I feel like I can fight the world and win."

Her eyes grew gentle and yielding. "Do you really feel all that?"

"Yes," he murmured, his voice slicing through the night air. "Sometimes, I think about all you've been through in coming here to Banff, and it helps me to carry on when things aren't going well in my own life."

She moved toward him. Rising onto her knees, she positioned herself behind him, slipping her slender arms beneath his. Her breasts crushed against his shirted back. He savored the way she melted her warm curves against his, the way her warm breath nipped against his earlobe. "Do you know what I like most about you?"

"What?"

"You make me forget."

"Amanda..." He cupped her arms and tried to swing

her around to face him, but she resisted. Maybe it was easier for her to open up and talk to him this way.

"When my husband left me, I wasn't sure I'd ever meet a man again who I'd care to spend time with, and then...*you* arrived on my doorstep." She kissed along his neck and it made his flesh quiver with expectation.

"You make me sound like a sack of potatoes."

"Potatoes are my favorite. Fried with gravy."

A breeze rippled through the bushes beside them.

"I know you're a good man, Tom, and I want to open up to you, but..."

He stroked her arms and they rocked together, she pressed tightly behind him.

"Then open up to me, Amanda."

"I'm not sure I can. Sometimes I feel like part of me shriveled up and crumbled in the wind when William left. I don't know...if I have anything left to give you."

"You have so much left to give, if you could only see yourself the way others who know you do. I'd be lying if I said I never wanted children. I'd also be lying if I said I could walk away from you."

She buried her warm face into his neck and sighed. "I'm not sure that I'll ever be able to enjoy that sense of intimacy, that...physical bonding...between a man and woman, ever again."

They grew silent with her soft confession.

He realized it had taken a lot for her to share that private fear with him. This time, he took her by deliberate, gentle force, and whirled her around to lay on the grass, sprawled at this feet. She struggled, then collapsed with a sigh of pleasure, her arms spread wide at the sky.

"I'll help you enjoy it."

"Can we take it slowly?" she asked. "No promises?"

I'm not inexperienced at this, but you may feel differently afterward. And I—I might feel differently, too.''

His emotions whirled at the invitation. ''No promises. I promise.''

She laughed, the warm rumble melting into his.

He couldn't resist her any longer.

Sliding along her body, he caught her in a soft embrace, rolling her on the ground beneath him. ''I love it when you laugh. You look beautiful.''

When she reached up and wrapped her arms partly around his shoulders, returning his affection, he felt his body weaken.

''It's the gown that makes me look good. *Your* gown.''

His hands moved gently down the length of her back. He enjoyed the cool, satin feel. He had a devilish new thought. ''It is my gown, isn't it?''

''Mmm-hmm. And your shoes, too.''

''They are, aren't they? All mine.''

His mouth descended. She parted open for him, and he quivered when their tongues met. His hands caressed their way to her bosom. He cupped the curve of her breast, over the satin fabric, and found the nipple round and firm.

He hardened in response.

Raining kisses on her neck and throat, he planted one on her nose. ''Since they're mine, perhaps I'd like them back.''

''The clothes? I could get them back to you tomorrow—''

''I'd like them back right now.''

She broke free of his kiss to laugh. ''Now?''

''Right now. Give them back to me, one item at a time.''

She laughed in a long, surrendering moan. ''You want me to remove my clothes for you, one item at a time?''

He sensed her thrill of arousal. In quite a state himself,

he ran a hand through his tangled hair. "That's right. You can do it. I have confidence in you."

His hand locked against the fabric of her shoulder while she buried her face into his muscled chest. The warmth of her soft flesh was intoxicating.

"Thanks," she said, gently slapping his ribs.

When she fell back into the grass, gazing up into his eyes again, he knew it was a moment of reckoning. Would she do it? Did she trust him enough?

"What comes off first?"

He swallowed hard. Oh, blazes! "Your shoes."

She slid through his arms, moving upright in splendid glory, reaching seductively beneath her gown. When he heard the snap of her unbuckling the five leather buttons, he stilled with the exquisite torture of knowing that she'd soon be naked.

Bending forward, he cupped her slender foot in one large palm, kneading and rubbing the delicate muscles through her white lace stockings. Pressing his lips to her ankles, he felt her tremble beneath his fingertips.

"What's next?" Her thick, dark hair hung around her shoulders in graceful curves, dipping around the swells of her uptilted breasts, and he couldn't believe she was peeling for him.

"Your stockings."

Blue satin tumbled around her legs as she reached higher and higher, lifting her skirts way beyond his wildest dreams, even lifting one edge of her bloomers to finally plant her hands around a gorgeous peach-colored thigh, rolling the white lace of her stocking expertly down her skin. Her creamy round thighs cried out for his hands. He gripped her waist with both palms, tugging dangerously, roughly, toward him. Long, luscious legs curved in front of him. Beginning with her ankle, he pressed his mouth against her flesh and kissed around the ankle bone, up the calf, then he bent her knee to kiss behind it, somewhere in the hollow. She moaned with animal pleasure, and it drove him madder. His hands trembled up her soft thighs, to the edge of lace at the bottom of her ruffled bloomers.

"Now what?"

In the watery starlight, her sleek, soft face radiated the wonder she was feeling. Soft crackles of fireworks sounded behind him, but he didn't turn to look. "Your gown."

"You don't ask for much, do you?" She teased him with her hands, sliding them down his shirt, unbuttoning as she went, pulling out the shirttail from his pants.

"I ask for what I want."

"Why settle for less?"

His smile widened in approval. Despite the cool summer chill, perspiration erupted at his brow. "My sentiments exactly."

"Then before I remove my gown, I believe I should ask you to remove your shirt."

He laughed as he regarded her. Wrapping his fingers around his cravat, he tugged until it came undone. Her eyes never left him. When he undid his collar, she sat up on her knees and trailed her cool fingers down his bare chest.

"Mmm," he groaned. She helped him undo the last buttons, less inhibited than he'd imagined she might be. When his one bronzed shoulder pulled out of its sleeve, then the other, she slipped her hand to the soft, smooth skin beneath his arm.

He rocked back with uncontrollable delight. She lowered her head and kissed his matted chest, running her warm mouth over his rib cage, across his hardened nipples, then up to his throat.

"You might just drive a desperate man further to desperation."

When she slid her gown up over her luscious hips, yanking it high above her head, her breasts nearly spilled out of her boned, white corset. The worn but well structured linen bodice was laced up the front with leather, and her breasts perched over the top. Would he really have her? This entrancing woman?

He removed the undergarment for her, flicking each crisscrossed string of leather as it slackened at his touch. Heavy breasts spilled into his hands, satiny smooth, ripe for him. Her string of pearls shimmered against her skin, a stunning vision. His lips found a flat, rosy-pink nipple and he teased it to attention. His hands slid across her silken belly, then over to her other side, gently outlining the circle of one breast while sucking the other.

"Tom," she said, whispering into the stillness. "Why do you make me feel so good?"

Her words affected him deeply. "Because we were made for each other."

She trailed her heavenly fingertips over his back, and his reaction was swift. "All right," he said, ripping apart from her, "your bloomers come off next."

She obeyed willingly, sliding them off until she lay there, naked under the stars, her golden skin flashing in the new round of fireworks, the light rippling over her curvy breasts, tight belly, and the soft black curls of her womanly mound.

He couldn't fathom why he was entitled to her, but he wanted her more than any woman he'd ever been with. He hardened with need.

Removing his pants, he thrilled at the sexual way she watched him. Her gaze lingered down along his chest, then down along the rest of him to his shaft, and he quivered in response.

He caressed her cheek. "I want this to be good for

you... Tell me to stop if it's going to hurt...because of what happened to you...."

"Don't worry. I'm normal there, it's deeper inside where it differs, but you won't be able to feel it."

"The heavens had mercy," he whispered. "I'm so pleased for you sweetheart." That *she* would be able to enjoy this.

He couldn't believe that only two weeks ago he was worried he wouldn't be able to sustain an erection with her, that his fear of hurting her might make him wither...but those fears were gone. The problem now, he thought with unabashed eagerness, was that his need was so intense for her, he was afraid he'd spill before he was able to please her.

His hands roved her body, making her arch to meet his fingers. He wanted to drag it out for her until she couldn't resist, until she begged for mercy.

"Touch me *there*," she whispered.

"Aye, aye," he said, sliding his lips over her laughing ones.

He touched her *there*, and with mutual surrender, they gloried in each other's embrace. He plunged into the hot depths of her body, rejoicing it was Amanda beneath him.

She saturated him, enveloping him with intense moist heat, fulfilling him in every way imaginable.

Both drugged with ecstasy and exhaustion, she finally peaked, and he allowed himself to release, knowing there would be no turning back between them.

Chapter Fourteen

Although she didn't know for sure, Amanda guessed that an hour had passed since they'd begun. She wove her legs and arms between Tom's as they watched the final cascade of whistling fireworks above them. Turning over, her stomach met with his hips as she lay naked on top of him. Her loose, long hair tangled around her shoulders and dipped over his chest. The smooth necklace of pearls bounced off her pointed breasts.

"I'm not finished with you yet," she drawled, pulling herself up to a sitting position, one leg on each side of him to rest her bottom on his abdomen.

The sinews of his dark jaw flexed as he searched her face. She felt his abdominal muscles coil beneath her as he grasped under her arms and lifted her, his tremendous strength wedging her into place on top of his erection.

Sweet satisfaction rolled through her as she tightened around him, one thought hammering in her brain. Her spirit wasn't shriveled up inside, she felt alive and intense and burning with a mad fever for Tom.

The chill of the night air brushed her shoulders, while the hot pressure of his fiery palm cupped her breasts, making her climax quickly. She unwound her limbs, pinning him at the shoulders, feeling her breasts sway as she rocked against him.

He kissed along the tendrils that jiggled at her ear, along her temples, along her straight, smooth brows. Then he grew urgent, rocking faster, digging his fingers into her waist, pumping his hands around her hips, sinking them into the creamy flesh of her bottom.

She brushed her lips along his cool forehead. "I never knew you could do this to me." She rolled off him to the ground, collapsing into a delightful heap onto the soft fabric of her shawl.

His groan, his obvious pleasure at her words, made her smile. Having rolled with her, he swung off her now, revealing her bare thighs.

"I think it's you who's doing it to me."

He stroked a path beneath the arch of her neck, over the ribbons of her lips, up to the bridge of her nose.

A cool wind curled around them, settling on her arms. She shivered.

"Are you cold?" he asked.

"Yeah."

"Let's get dressed then."

"Do we have to?"

"We don't have to, but we'll look silly walking home naked. What would the neighbors say?"

"They'd say *lucky woman*."

His easy laugh rippled through the trees.

He tapped her hips then playfully tossed her her stockings and bloomers. As she tugged into her clothing, watching him step into his pants, one long bronzed leg after the other, she knew she didn't want this to end. She didn't want to face the real world again, away from this haven of...lovemaking.

Had this night been one in a thousand? Could either of them give themselves to a commitment?

While he studied her, she sensed he was waiting for her to speak of it first. "You surprise me," she whispered.

"How?"

"What is it about you that makes me react so strongly?"

Standing there, he loomed over her in the grass, his muscles flexing as he wove his belt through the loops of his pants, his black hair jumbled from rolling around with her. "Why, it's everything about me," he said with jest.

Stifling her smile, knowing it was true, she tugged at the laces of her corset. He paused in what he was doing and came to stand in front of her, gently coaxing her fingers out of the way so he could finish the lacing. She'd never had a man want to dress her before, and she allowed him, reveling in the newfound feeling of being cared for.

She grew wistful. "When I think about what happened in my life in Calgary, especially how my husband left me, I wonder sometimes why it happened. What reason did fate have?"

His fingers stopped moving. The lacing was finished. He wove his hand behind her neck to let it rest there, knotted in her hair, and looked softly into her eyes. "Because Amanda, fate sent you to *me*."

Her stomach fluttered with the words. He sealed them with a provocative kiss, then said no more.

She hestitated, wanting to reach out and to tell him what he obviously wanted to hear—that she was torn in her affections for him but that she desperately wished to continue with their relationship. But she couldn't give promises she might not be able to keep. She'd tried marriage once before, and it had failed.

Blanketed in his warmth, she helped pack up. They walked to his home, and the sawmill and the small barn where he was still entitled to kept his horses for the summer. After he hitched his mare to a buggy, they plodded along the streets of Banff to Hillside Road. The paths were filled with couples walking home from the ball, hand-in-hand, some in carriages, some in leather buggies similar to theirs. It was a dreamy, star-filled night; one she'd remember forever.

What would it be like, returning to her normal routine? How could anything be normal again after tonight?

In a strange way, she was glad she had tomorrow to herself, away from Tom and his influence, to think about what had happened and where it might lead. Would he feel differently, now that they'd made love and his desire had been quenched? How would he feel seeing her Monday, bringing her to the courthouse?

And what about all the other problems that intruded in their lives? Hers with her deed and the log cabin, his with the banker and his brothers…and on and on.

Her muscles ached with fatigue. Doubts and misgivings grappled with the bliss she felt for having made love with Tom.

Monday morning came with sunshine. The splendid heat soaked through Tom's shirt into his shoulder blades as he urged his horse and wagon onto Amanda's road. How would she greet him this morning? He grew nervous.

After two nights and one day of thinking about her, he still sang her name. Their night of lovemaking was all he could think of—the turn of her cheek, her tempting body beneath the firework lights, the smile and sigh when she'd uttered his name in the quiet of the forest.

His mind raced to what living with her might be like. How did she comb her hair for bedtime? What side of the bed would she prefer to sleep on? What, he wondered with a smile, did she eat for breakfast?

Could he imagine a fulfilling life with her, alone, just the two of them?

Would *he* be enough for her? That was the most pressing question on his mind. If they continued seeing each other and it blossomed into something more, something deeper, how long would it last before she tired of him? Most women would have babies and youngsters to fill their lives with hopes and dreams and love, but she might only have him.

He wasn't arrogant enough to believe that he could be enough for any woman.

Would she be satisfied enough, happy enough, to be involved with other people's children, even if they had none of their own? Quaid's maybe, and Gabe's once he finished his schooling and married, and then even the children Amanda took in—especially Josh and Margaux.

Tom hoped whoever adopted the two would live close by, no matter what happened between him and Amanda. The thought of the children moving away filled him with sudden gloom. He wanted to watch little Josh grow up to speak correctly, whose life was turned around because of Amanda, and he liked spending time with both children, teaching them things he knew how to do.

What was Amanda thinking about the future? Saturday night when he'd taken her home, he knew she was holding back whatever emotions were tumbling through her.

Then thinking about his banking troubles, he cursed softly. How could he possibly entertain the notion of any future with Amanda when his business was on the verge—

The O'Haras' cows mooed in the distance. The O'Haras were good people, and they'd befriended Amanda and Miss Clementine, but how was the rest of the town feeling lately? At the ball, there'd been no indication of trouble, but then not everyone had been there. Not Fannie and not her father, and not Mrs. Hawthorne.

The wagon rumbled onto the path and Tom pulled up beside the shack, searching for Amanda. She was nowhere in sight, but Miss Clementine was out front, putting her gloves into her bicycle basket. She was nervously chewing on gum.

He removed his felt hat. "Where you headed?"

She adjusted her knitted shawl across her shoulders. "It's such a lovely mornin', I thought I'd ride to the court-house."

"But didn't Amanda tell you I'd be here to drive you both?" He pulled the handbrake, then lurched out of the wagon.

"She did, but to tell you the truth, my old nerves kept me awake most of the night, and I need to calm them. If I don't do something to settle them down, I'm afraid I might stand up in court and start yelling at the magistrate. Or Lorne Wilson himself. The bicycle will tire me nicely."

The door creaked open and Amanda stepped onto the porch. Although neatly dressed with her hair pulled tightly into a bun, she looked pale. Of course, he thought, she was concerned about the outcome today. "Good morning, Tom," she said softly.

"Morning." He filled with a warm glow of seeing her again.

If he thought he might detect any indication of the evening they'd spent together, he saw nothing in her eyes. They flickered on him, then to her grandma. Nothing? he thought with disappointment.

He leaned against the railing of the porch, beneath Amanda's elbow. "Miss Clementine says she's not coming with us."

"I tried to convince her but it's hard to convince her of anything." Amanda smiled good-naturedly at him, then he saw by her warm feminine expression and the slight hue of color that flushed her skin that she *was* thinking of him.

His mouth dipped and they shared a private smile. Of course, how could he assume either one of them could ever forget Saturday night?

Miss Clementine mounted the bicycle. She rang a bell. "What's that?" He pointed to the rectangle of metal on her gripping bars.

"It's my new cow bell," she said. "Your pa had it hanging around his place and he said I could have it."

"What do you need a cow bell for?"

"Oh, Tom," said Amanda, stepping off the porch and removing her apron. Her nose pinched with concern. "She rings it at every opportunity to let everyone in town know she's coming."

"I'll show 'em a circus," Miss Clementine grunted, flinging her braid over her shoulder in defiance.

Tom stared at the old determined expression, stifling his laughter. "I bet old Jefferson's eyes bug out every time he sees you."

"They do," Miss Clementine whispered, as if they were in a conspiracy. "You should have seen him yesterday when I rode it to church. As I was barreling down the hill, I rang it in time to the church bells, and I thought the man was going to keel over."

She gave a friendly laugh, smacking her black gum.

"Grandma, I wish you'd be careful," Amanda said gently. "Not everyone in town might think it's funny."

"Ruby does."

"Ruby's special. She's nice and she likes us."

Tom looked at Amanda, standing high on the porch

above him. "A lot of people like you," he insisted, wishing more did.

"A lot of people don't," she answered.

His lips softened into a serious line. Dammit, he wished it weren't true. "Where are the children?" he asked.

"Margaux's in school and Josh is at Ellie's."

"How's Josh?"

"Good. He's eating soup and dumplings now."

Tom grinned at the news, wishing he could reach out and touch Amanda. But Miss Clementine didn't know how involved they were, and he'd promised Amanda to keep their involvement quiet, until they'd discussed it some more.

On his side of things, he couldn't wait for everyone in town to know how he felt about Amanda. He'd never treat her the way William had, but she needed more time to see it.

"Ellie said we can take our time coming home." Amanda smoothed the hair at the back of her bun. She looked so different from the other night—so prim and proper that he longed to take a hand and muss up her hair. "I'd like to pick up kerosene from the mercantile, and I need a new tin pail at the tinsmith's, if you have the time to wait for me."

"That's why I brought the wagon." He walked to it and began unloading his tools. "Just in case you needed it for errands, and because I'll need to start on construction this afternoon, right after the magistrate declares the land is yours for good. We have to catch up on lost time."

Amanda smiled at him.

"That's awful nice of you, Tom," said Miss Clementine, her eyes tearing up. "It's gotta work out that way."

Tom nodded. "It will." Picking up kerosene was good. It proved that Amanda was thinking ahead, that she thought the property *would* be hers at the end of the day, despite her doubts now.

Miss Clementine left, Amanda went inside to get ready, and Tom took the ten minutes to set up his tools.

When Amanda returned, he helped her up beside him in the wagon. "It feels good to touch you. I missed you yesterday." He clasped her hand and kissed it, enjoying the way his rough fingers laced into her smooth ones.

"I missed you, too." With a slow smile, she lowered her head, straightening her dark skirt, adjusting the row of white buttons down her blouse. She seemed a lot more detached than he felt.

He reached out and slapped her thigh. Just to show her who was who.

She laughed at that. They headed to town, both quiet, Tom feeling as though he shouldn't push her to talk. They both had a lot on their minds with the property dispute, no matter what they pretended on the surface.

When they pulled up to the town hall, there were already several buggies lining the road, around the grassy town square, with single horses grazing beneath the trees.

Amanda shifted beside him. "Why are there so many people here?"

"They're curious, I guess. We rarely have cases heard in Banff." And the outcome might affect many people, he thought, but he didn't voice it.

Inside, the place was packed. In spite of his words, Tom had no idea there'd be this many folks here. This was supposed to be a simple judicial hearing, mostly paperwork to discuss, he'd thought. Hell, at one point, he'd considered not even showing up himself. It didn't really matter, he supposed, because it seemed like an open-and-shut case to him. Wilson's deed wasn't dated, but Amanda's was, and hers was witnessed by lawyers.

They had to weave past Fannie Potter, her husband and her folks. Cripes, why were they here? Ruby was here, too—Tom supposed it was between her morning breakfast rush and the busy lunch hour—but didn't they all have better things to do?

Toward the front, on one side of the aisle, Miss Clementine sat squeezed between Tom's pa and Graham—in Mountie uniform, fiddling with the papers on his lap. On the other side sat Wilson, alone. Neither party could afford to have a lawyer represent them, but Graham had insisted he'd like to help with the talking, and Amanda had gladly accepted. It was just a minor civil case, Tom understood, with a community-appointed magistrate to preside.

In the far corner, at the end of one row, Tom caught sight of a familiar brown bonnet. Clarissa? She nodded solemnly in Tom's direction, and he twitched with discomfort.

When Amanda looked her way, he felt Amanda's back stiffen beneath his hand. Why on earth was Clarissa here? Graham had told Tom she was free and clear of any wrongdoing.

As Tom and Amanda took their places next to Graham, the constable whispered to them, "I asked Clarissa to come. She's directly involved, and her testimony against Finnigan needs to be included."

Tom glanced sharply around. His demeanor was shifting into one of alarm. And Graham seemed a bit overeager.

Amanda's mouth tightened in Clarissa's direction, but she didn't respond.

A side door opened. At the front of the room, next to the massive, raised walnut desk, Benny Jones jumped to his feet. "All rise for the Honorable Magistrate Nicholson."

The magistrate sailed in, black robes flowing behind

him. He was a short, clean-shaven man with a bulbous nose and well-groomed, long white hair. He walked past the flag in the corner—Canada's Red Ensign—then glanced briefly at the photographs pegged to the wall—Prime Minister John A. Macdonald, and the golden jubilee portrait of heavy-set Queen Victoria.

"Please be seated," he said as he took his own seat behind the desk. "I understand there's a property dispute here."

Graham handed the magistrate Amanda's deed.

When Lorne Wilson stood up to give him his, Nicholson glanced at his disheveled appearance. Wilson's clothes looked as though the dirt had been washed out of them, but no one had ironed them, so the wrinkles in his pants were remarkable.

The magistrate studied the papers. "I take it Zeb Finnigan is not here."

Tom heard the benches behind him creak from side to side, and voices began to titter.

"Quiet," the magistrate declared, and all went still.

"No, Your Honor," said Graham, "Zeb Finnigan is not here, but his business partner—*former partner*—is seated next to Miss Ryan. Tom Murdock."

Nicholson peered at Tom. "Why former?"

Graham began, "Because the two—"

"I'm asking Mr. Murdock," Nicholson interrupted.

Tom rose and walked to the front, thinking perhaps he should have worn a suit as Wilson had, as wrinkled as it was. Instead, Tom ran a hand down his denimed leg, and grew uneasy in his newly ironed, laundered shirt. He was being asked a direct question. He wished the crowd would vanish for the very private answer he was about to give. It was hot in the room, he noticed, feeling his palms sweat.

"Because, Your Honor…just before he left town, Zeb Finnigan stole my money."

"Speak up, sir."

"Zeb Finnigan stole my money."

Dozens of people gasped. It was out. The secret he'd hoped to keep to himself was out, and there was nothing he could do to take it back. Would it shake the confidence people had in him? In the sawmill?

The magistrate turned to Graham. "Has Finnigan been charged?"

"Yes, Your Honor. With robbery, fraud and larceny. He's wanted by a lot of folks. He stripped the sawmill's business account of all its money. Fourteen thousand, seven hundred and thirty-three dollars."

For cryin' out loud, why did Graham say that? The crowd murmured and Tom could hear their boots shuffling clear to the other side of the windows.

"Do you know his whereabouts?" Nicholson continued.

"He's hasn't been found yet. We've tracked him to Calgary and Edmonton. We think he's back in the area, somewhere between here and Canmore. Yesterday, he was spotted on the express train comin' in from Canmore. We can't be sure it's him, but the conductor's description sounds likely."

Amanda's gaze swung to Tom, but he was just as surprised by the news. What would Finnigan want here? It had to be someone else on that train.

"We have an eyewitness here, Miss Ashford, that can attest Finnigan was in Canmore."

"Miss Ashford?" said the magistrate.

"Yes, Your Honor?" She stepped forward in her stylish brown suit, nervous and ill at ease. The room went still again.

"What do you know of Zeb Finnigan?"

"I was with him when he left town."

Voices rose behind Tom. He rolled his eyes and tried to concentrate. He couldn't look at Amanda, didn't want to place her under the scrutiny of the crowd if he so much as glanced warmly in her direction. Their secrets were being aired, and he wanted to protect her.

"I'm urging all of you to keep your voices down," Nicholson said to the crowd. When they settled, he asked Clarissa, "Why were you with Finnigan?"

"He asked me to…to…go away with him. To marry him." As the crowd roared, Clarissa craned her neck to study Tom, bit her lower lip and looked away.

Tom heard Amanda's soft gasp. It was the first time she was hearing it, too.

"Quiet in the courtroom!" Nicholson banged his gavel. "It's not a formal trial, but I can still kick the whole lot of you out to the street." With a look of exasperation, he turned to Clarissa. "Did you marry him?"

"No, sir."

Nicholson looked to Graham. "Has Miss Ashford been charged with any crimes?"

"No, Your Honor. She didn't know what Finnigan was up to. There's no evidence she was involved."

Tom glanced at Clarissa's stark profile. She looked as though she wanted the floor to part so she could drop through it. How had it come to this between them?

The magistrate still hadn't asked Amanda any questions, Tom realized, and he was beginning to wonder why. It could only help her case.

Tom rose. "Your Honor?"

"Yes?"

"Forgive me for speaking out, but perhaps if you knew what Mrs. Ryan intended to do with the property—"

"It's irrelevant."

"I should say so!" bellowed Lorne Wilson, jumping to his feet.

"But Your Honor, an orph—"

"Irrelevant," Nicholson repeated in the storm of voices. "Sit down everyone!"

When Tom fell back onto his bench, the magistrate continued. "The crown can't show favoritism toward one individual. We're here to discuss the facts of the deed only."

Tom didn't like what he was hearing.

The judge addressed Amanda. "Is this is your deed, Mrs. Ryan?" He held it up.

Amanda stood. Tom saw her hands tremble and he wished he could reach out and soothe her. "Yes, Your Honor."

"Can you add anything more to the facts of the situation?"

"Only that I bought my property from Mr. Finnigan, and it was signed and sealed by a barrister and solicitor's office, and that I've already begun to build a log cabin."

The magistrate eyed her from behind the desk. "How far are you in construction?"

"About halfway. You can ask Mr. Murdock here, he's the builder."

"That's right," said Tom, standing up beside her, shoulder to shoulder.

"How much have you paid him so far?"

Amanda thought about it for a moment. "One hundred and seventy-six dollars and fifty cents."

"That's fine. You can both be seated."

That was it? That was all the magistrate wanted to know?

"Mr. Wilson?" The magistrate motioned to the wily man who Tom was disliking more by the minute. "Although your deed doesn't have a lawyer's seal, it's not necessary in these parts."

Lorne Wilson gloated in their direction.

"And as for the missing date, that is a deep concern, but one you'll soon see is irrelevant, too. We'll hear from the clerk now," said Nicholson, surprising the entire congregation.

Benny looked thunderstruck, turning cherry-red at being singled out. He stood and faced the judge.

"Have you read Subsection A of the Article of Property Lease and Sales?"

"Your Honor?"

"Have you read it? It's a simple question."

"Yes, sir, I've read it. So has my boss, so has everyone in the registrar's office."

Tom turned to Amanda. What article were they talking about? Her eyes darted around the room in confusion.

"Do you understand it?" Nicholson asked.

Two deep lines appeared on the clerk's pocked forehead. "I think so."

"Do you have it with you?"

"Yes, I do. I brought the entire book."

"Turn to that section and read it to the court."

Benny cleared his throat, leafed through the dog-eared handbook and read out loud in his squeaky voice. "'The properties shall be divided—'"

"Not that huge paragraph. Just the last sentence."

"'All lease and property sales must be approved by the government land registry before they are deemed valid.'"

"That's the sentence right there. Read it again."

"'All lease and property sales must be approved by the government land registry before they are deemed valid.' But...but we *have* been approving all sales at the clerk's office—"

"With all new sales, correct?"

"Yes, as people come in to lease the properties, we've been very careful to put our seal of approval on every one."

"That's good, Benny. You're doing fine job, too, as was demonstrated to me when I looked at the books this morning. But if I understand correctly, Mr. Murdock was the first person who transferred his lease and resold his building, outside the hands of government. And Mrs. Ryan and Mr. Wilson are the first two who've bought resold property."

"That's correct."

Tom shrank in his seat. He couldn't believe what this implied. He felt Amanda rear up to attention.

The magistrate waved the deeds in the air. "I don't see a government seal on these two deeds."

The crowd hushed.

"You mean *every* time a transfer of property occurs," Benny said weakly, "the government needs to approve it?"

"That's what the law states. We've never come across anything like this before, because Banff is the first national park, but that's the way it was set up and that's how I've got to make my judgment."

The magistrate looked in Tom and Amanda's direction. He held up the two deeds and fanned them in the air. "These deeds aren't valid. And if Finnigan sold any more deeds that we don't know about yet, those won't be, either."

Tom leaned over his legs and dropped his head into his hands. Amanda moaned in the ensuing commotion.

The magistrate strained to be heard above the buzz, banging on his gavel. "Therefore Tom Murdock still owns the property."

"What?" said Tom, rising to Amanda's defense, unable to control his shock. "What about the money Amanda's spent?"

"And mine?" shouted Lorne Wilson.

"Unfortunately," said the magistrate, "they were robbed by Zeb Finnigan. When that man's caught, his assets will be divided to make restitution. Until the time he is, you, Mr. Murdock, still own the property."

The crowd was out of control. This affected everyone. Every sale, every lease transaction needed to be approved? What kind of government involvement was this? It was beyond reason!

The magistrate banged his gavel. "As far as Mrs. Ryan is concerned, she's building a cabin on property that doesn't belong to her. Tom Murdock, the court further instructs you to pay her for the value of the cabin, so far under construction. By the end of this week. Value of one hundred and seventy-six dollars and fifty cents."

What? Tom spun to Amanda, who stood up beside him, pale and grappling for words. The property wasn't hers!

And he didn't have one hundred and seventy-six dollars! That was a month's payroll. He'd have to lay off half his men to come up with that kind of payment. If he did that, that would be it for the town's confidence in his sawmill, and confidence was *everything* in business.

Neither one of them could comprehend what had just happened. As everyone rose to their feet, the magistrate and Benny disappeared through the side door. Wilson cursed up and down at the other end of the room then ran out the back door.

While the mass of men and women pushed their way into the aisles, Miss Clementine dabbed at her eyes with a hanky, Graham tried to explain to Amanda, Amanda was consoling her grandma, Pa looked on in bewilderment and

Clarissa and Tom painfully eyed each other across the room.

"Amanda," said Tom more desperate than he appeared, staring at her shaken face, "we'll work out something."

"That's right," said his pa, patting Miss Clementine's hand with renewed vigor.

"But you have to follow the magistrate's decision," Graham reminded them. "You'll have to go through the legal channels and get approval before you can do anything."

Tom cursed. He rubbed his sore neck.

Amanda's eyes had lost their sheen. "I appreciate what you tried to do in here today—"

With a burst of determination, Tom slid closer and gripped her by the shoulders. "There's good news here, too, Amanda. Lorne Wilson doesn't own this property. One of *us* does. And we both know that it should go to you. I'll sell the whole thing back to you for one penny, and you can keep the log cabin in lieu of the money I'm supposed to pay you. We'll keep building, starting this afternoon—"

"You know I can't sink another dime of lumber into that cabin until…until I know it's rightfully and legally mine. With the proper deed."

"Then, dammit, I'll get you a proper deed—"

"Tom," Graham interrupted, "you've got to go through the proper channels."

"How long will that take?"

"I don't know. It'll take at least a few days for the magistrate's decree to settle in at the registrar's. They'll probably check with their government lawyers to confirm the ruling. They may even change the clause if it no longer suits them. You know the government, they always move slowly, on the side of caution. If they work at breakneck speed you might get a new lease in three weeks. Maybe three months. Who knows?''

"Three months…" Amanda's shattered voice dwindled into silence.

Tom's enthusiasm faded.

Amanda flopped onto the bench and rubbed her temples. "Maybe I should take your payment and leave Banff. I've got my grandmother to think about, and the children."

"No." Tom ignored the startled looks of the others as he nearly shouted the word.

"Why not?" she asked quietly.

"I don't want you to." To hell with whatever anyone else thought, he was saying his piece. He didn't want Amanda to leave, not when she'd just arrived into his life. And, blazes, he remembered again—he damn well couldn't afford to pay her.

Her face stilled, and he could barely handle the despair he saw there. His muscles hardened with anger, thinking of what he'd like to do to Finnigan.

"Let's go home, all of us." Amanda rose, leading her grandmother toward the door. "Let us give you a lift this time, Grandma, you're in no condition to pedal home. Tom can throw your bicycle into the back of the wagon, can't you, Tom?"

"Sure," he rumbled, pacing behind the others, making his way out into the sunshine. He marveled at Amanda's ability to get back to the practicalities, when he felt like putting his fist through something. He and Pa shared a look of disgust at today's ruling. "Where did you leave the bicycle?"

"Under that big fir." Miss Clementine pointed across the road.

Tom ignored the curious glances of the scattered crowd

as they crossed the square. He wasn't about to give up. Something. There had to be *something* they could do.

"It's right over here." Miss Clementine led them to the shade. She stopped in front of him and Tom nearly toppled over her smaller figure. Staring through the trees, she gave a startled cry of anguish.

Amanda peered in the same direction, then turned white. "Good heavens."

"What's wrong?" Tom pushed his way past the women, afraid of what he'd see.

Someone had destroyed the bicycle.

It was lying on its side, in the grass. The rims had been kicked in. The spokes were busted. The handle bars were twisted, and the seat had been yanked off, flung to the other side of the tree.

"Uh-hh," Tom groaned, feeling as if someone had punched him. *"Who could do this?"* His voice was a low, dangerous whisper.

Miss Clementine wept. Amanda fell against the tree for support.

Pa knelt in the grass beside the bicycle, his old bones looking stooped and broken. "They took the bell."

Tom's frustrations rushed to the surface and he reacted without thinking. His arteries pounded with fury. Racing into the street, he shouted, "Who did this?"

His voice pierced the sunny morning, bouncing off the walls of buildings. Women turned and stared. Men raised protective arms around their wives.

Tom went wild, pummeling the air. "Who in bloody hell could do such a thing? You coward! Whoever you are! You bloody coward! Come out and face me!"

Her cherished bicycle, the one that harbored her freedom and independence, was smashed to smithereens.

Chapter Fifteen

A terse silence enveloped Amanda and her Grandma as they watched the horrible scene unfold. People fled out of Tom's path as he leaped down the street hollering at the top of his roaring voice, his pa behind him carrying the wounded bicycle for all to see.

Against a backdrop of white-capped mountains, dozens of folks disappeared into their wagons, hiked up to the boardwalk, or squeezed between the log buildings, all escaping the madman.

Hadn't anyone seen anything? How could someone get away with smashing her bicycle without being seen?

Lacing her arm through Amanda's, Grandma pulled out a hanky from beneath her long sleeve. "They don't like us in this town, Amanda. Let's go home to Calgary. I'm too old for this. I want to live out the rest of my days in peace, among neighbors I can call my friends."

A storm of emotions battled in Amanda as she watched Tom stalk through the square, demanding answers on her behalf. Her mind swirled with disbelief that someone could do such a loathsome thing, at the same time watching her valiant Tom defend her. "*They're* our friends, Grandma, those two warriors out in the street. Look at them."

Grandma's sobs quieted. Amanda rocked her gently, feeling such...*love for Tom,* she realized with a start, at his defense.

After fifteen prolonged minutes Tom's demand for the perpetrator was futile. No one owned up to the dirty deed.

Who could have done it? Who, of the dozens of people who'd commented on her bicycle since she'd arrived in Banff, disliked her so much they'd destroy it? Names flew through her mind. James Jefferson. Mrs. Hawthorne. Lorne Wilson. Even perhaps Clarissa?

A woman wouldn't do such a thing, would she? With a weary hand, Amanda comforted her grandmother.

Tom came back to rest the bicycle at Amanda's feet. He straightened himself and gazed down at her, his swollen lips parted with heavy panting.

His shoulders blocked the sun, his dark eyes welled with sentiment, his powerful jaw trembled with sorrow, and she felt her own heart crack with the ache of his.

"Thank you," she said. "To you, and to John, as well."

Tom looked so very ashamed for what had happened, but she reached out and placed her firm palm over his, letting him know how much she appreciated what he'd tried to do. "Now, we've still got some supplies to buy. Perhaps your pa could take Grandma home in the wagon, then come back for us later in the day."

Tom ran a hand along his shirt. "You still want to stay in town to run your errands? After what happened?"

Her voice deepened with resolve. "Whoever thought that this would send me running in the other direction was wrong. This isn't going to beat me," she continued. "Grandma and I aren't going to cry defeat."

With a hoot and a holler, John Murdock laughed beside them. He removed his dusty straw hat and slapped his thigh with it. "You two women are tougher than two mules."

Grandma wiped her face with her hanky and managed a jittery smile. "I'm not sure that's a compliment."

"Sure it is," said John, old eyes twinkling.

Tom's eyes hadn't left Amanda's face, and she was well aware of it.

Love, she thought again. Was she *in love* with him? The thought made her shaky. "I still need kerosene from the mercantile, and a new tin pail from Jefferson's."

His dark eyes focused deeper. "Jefferson's?"

"That's right," said Amanda, acknowledging the question in his perceptive gaze. If James Jefferson was responsible for this, she intended to seek him out. "I believe I need to talk to him. Would you care to join me? We'll need to bring the bicycle."

"How can you be so calm?" Tom asked Amanda as they strolled down the boardwalk, she holding her head high as she carried the new jug of oil, he dragging the twisted bicycle. If they were getting strange looks from passersby, he no longer cared. His heart was pumping faster as they approached the tinsmith's, ready for battle, but she looked as if she were just making another call.

"I'm not calm on the inside."

"Well, you sure hold your temper well."

They reached Jefferson's, and Amanda stopped beneath the sign. "Promise me you won't fight with anyone."

He felt his muscles tighten. "I can't promise that."

She shook her head. "Then promise me you'll try."

"Okay," he said, trying to appease her. He held open the door for her in a civilized manner, even though it took extraordinary effort to walk through it himself, restrained.

Inside the store, another couple was talking to Jefferson. The man's back was to the door as he showed them a stack of nestled baking tins. It seemed Amanda and Tom would have to wait if they wanted to avoid a scene in front of the others. Tom tried to remind himself that maybe Jefferson wasn't responsible. Maybe someone else had done it, and Tom should give the man a chance to defend himself.

The store was cluttered with wares, and normally, Tom liked visiting the place. Hip washtubs were displayed in the glass windows, buckets and pails hung from pegs on one wall, while kitchen utensils lined another. A tall pine counter ran the length and width of the store, forming a large square in the middle, where Mr. Jefferson and his wife—not here at the moment—usually stood to serve their customers.

Tom slid the bicycle to the floor planks and glanced around, trying to control the nervous kicking in his gut. Amanda stood straight as a rod as she waited for the owner to turn. Unable to control himself in showing his sympathy, Tom reached out and put a limber arm around her, pulling her close for a gentle squeeze.

Her mouth lifted in a warm smile, and it gave him the strength he sought but didn't even know he needed. The thought that someone could take one of her possessions and kick the tar out of it got his fists going again. *He'd* take care of the culprit.

"Fine," Tom heard the woman say, "we'll take these."

Tom and Amanda straightened. All he wanted was a good look at Jefferson's eyes when he caught sight of them. Eyes didn't lie, and whatever Jefferson knew about this, Tom was certain he'd see it.

Jefferson turned around to his cash drawer to make the transaction, glanced up to see who'd entered his store, and his eyes fell on Amanda and Tom.

The old, brown eyes widened in shock and his whole body snapped back in alarm. The wrinkled lips dropped open at the sight of the bicycle. His cheeks and forehead flamed with red. Dammit, the bastard knew something.

Tom leaped forward. Amanda grabbed him by the arm. "Wait till he's through. Don't frighten anyone, please."

Jefferson continued with the sale, but his hands were shaking. When the other couple left the store, Jefferson began to inch away, toward the back door.

"Hold on a minute, Jefferson," said Tom, lurching forward. "What the hell do you know about this?" He held up the bicycle.

"Nothing."

"You know something. I can see it in your eyes."

Jefferson gulped. "How did it happen?"

"That's what you're going to tell us."

"How should I know?"

"Because I think you had something to do with it."

"I did not!"

"Graham Robarts might discover otherwise."

The threat made the man's color deepen.

Amanda stepped forward and placed her hands on his counter. "What is it that you have against me, Mr. Jefferson? What have I ever done to you?"

Jefferson stopped shuffling away. He rose taller and crossed his arms, clenching his jaw as he looked from Amanda to Tom. Was it a glimmer of guilt Tom saw in his eyes?

"Didn't I help your daughter in the early stages of her confinement?"

Jefferson refused to answer. He shook his head as if he didn't want to hear more.

"It was Fannie's choice to move along to Dr. Murdock, but isn't he Tom's brother, and don't you care about that?"

Jefferson seemed to weaken at that statement. He was struggling with something.

"We didn't come here for a fight, James," said Tom. "We came here to get some answers. And I stupidly believed that I might show Amanda that some folks in this great town of ours do care about her. When I demanded answers earlier in the square, and not one person stepped forward to help us, that fact shamed me more than what this culprit has achieved."

Jefferson said no more. Whatever it was that he knew or didn't know, he wasn't about to spill. Feeling defeated, Tom cupped Amanda's arm, and they turned to leave.

"Wait," Jefferson blurted. "It wasn't me. I saw who did it."

They searched the town. They notified Graham about the vandalism. They talked to anyone who might have been in contact with the man accused.

No one had seen Lorne Wilson since he'd stormed out of the courtroom earlier that morning.

"Where do you think he went?" Amanda asked, feeling that thread of anger wind its way through her chest again. She slipped another forkful of hot chicken pot pie into her mouth, seated in her favorite spot at Ruby's—the window where she could watch people passing by. The taste was heavenly on Amanda's tongue, especially since they'd forgotten to eat lunch in their haste to catch Lorne Wilson.

"I think he rode out of town on the same little pinto he rode in on, wrinkled pants and all."

That image brought back her sense of humor, and she managed a laugh. What else could she do at this moment but laugh at the whole extreme situation? Wilson couldn't have her property, so he'd smashed her bicycle.

Tom studied her. "You laugh too much."

She crinkled her nose. "You frown too much."

He grinned and took another sip of coffee. She realized

it was Tom who had that affect on her—to keep her going even when things looked hopeless.

Amanda watched him, the movement of his throat, down his neck to the matted hair that curled out from the top of his shirt. It was the first time in six hours that they'd had a moment to rest, and she was intrigued by him.

Was she in love with him?

How could she *not* be?

Her stomach tightened with an onslaught of butterflies.

He peered at her with an almost imperceptible grin tugging at his dimple. Lord, that look didn't help her. Warm gooseflesh rose on her arms and she felt like cushioning herself in his embrace.

"I do believe you're finally relaxed," he said, his gaze working its way down her blouse and lingering to the tight buttons.

She blushed fiercely, remembering what his hands had done to her two nights ago. Was it only two nights ago that they'd made love? She felt as though she'd known him, been friends with him, forever. "There's nothing more we can do about Lorne Wilson. We've looked everywhere."

Tom's profile stiffened. "Personally, I'd like to get my hands on him and even the score."

It was an entirely new feeling, having someone fight on her behalf, and even though she would never admit it to anyone, she delighted in the security of having Tom defend her.

Amanda reached for her napkin to wipe her lips. "I think the score's been evened by Mr. Jefferson coming forward."

"That was something, wasn't it?"

"You were right." Pausing, she tried to keep herself from spilling what was in her heart. It was too soon to speak of it. She wasn't sure yet of what she felt for Tom, or what she planned on doing about it. "There *are* some people in this town who *do* care about me." She was referring to more than Mr. Jefferson. She was referring to Tom.

He nodded slowly, his intense gaze causing her to look away.

Did she love him? Her heart beat rapidly beneath her corset. She drank from her water glass, hoping its coolness would also cool her heated palms. She wasn't the young and foolish girl she'd been when she'd fallen for William. She wouldn't make the same mistake of falling into the arms of the first man who'd said he cared for her.

"Too bad about your bicycle," Tom said, cutting the slice of steak on his plate. "Your grandma will miss it, too."

"Poor Grandma, she's had a hard day."

"She's a strong woman. So are you."

They continued eating.

"What are you going to do, Amanda?"

"I'm...not sure," she answered truthfully.

"You know you can stay in the shack for as long as you need, and my offer to give you the proper deed still stands. You own that property, not me. I considered it a loss the day Finnigan stole it. And when they catch him, *he'll* pay me back."

"Money doesn't mean a whole lot to you, does it?"

He shook his head and didn't even need to stop to think about it. "Only as a means of support for the people I care about."

He was so different than many of the men she'd encountered in her life. She nodded in agreement and sipped her water again.

''It's a good thing your bicycle wasn't worth a whole lot.''

The water pooled in her throat, and she nearly choked.

What would be the point of telling him how much the bicycle was really worth? It would only make him feel worse, and knowing Tom, he'd probably try to help pay for a replacement. He didn't need another burden.

Recovering quickly, she played with the boiled carrots on her plate. Bicycles were rare, which kept the price high, and most were hand-built, one-of-a-kind contraptions made from special steel and solid rubber.

She could buy three excellent horses for the price of that bicycle. Luckily, her grandpa had left it to her so she hadn't spent a penny. Once she'd received it, she realized how much cheaper it was to maintain than an animal, and in moving to Banff, how much money she'd be able to save by not having to build a barn, or buying feed or saddles.

Now that the contraption was gone, what would she do? Perhaps it *was* time to look for a horse, or a mule. She had a bigger brood to look after, with Josh and Margaux living with her. Should she take Tom up on his offer to let her stay on the property? Did she trust him at his word that he'd hand over the deed?

Looking into his honest face as he finished his supper, knowing how he'd fought for her today, she answered with a thundering, silent *yes*.

A train whistle sounded down the street. Tom looked up. ''There is one more place we could look for Lorne Wilson.''

''I just thought of it myself. The train station?''

''He might be leaving on the nightly express that just rolled in from Calgary.''

"Do you really think he'd put his horse in a boxcar and leave by train?"

"Highly unlikely. He doesn't strike me as having a whole lot of money. Do you want to go see anyway? He owes you the price of your bicycle."

"Sure," she answered, wiping her mouth, doubting that Lorne Wilson could afford to replace it.

As Tom signed his name to the bill, Amanda said goodbye to Ruby.

They left and headed to the train station, carrying nothing in their arms. Earlier in the day when they'd hunted for Wilson, she'd parked her kerosene jug at Tom's sawmill, along with her broken bicycle, which he said he'd get rid of for her.

The express train was already in the station, unloading cattle, two horses, dozens of trunks, townsfolk and brandnew tourists. People crowded the platform, but none who looked like the disheveled man they were searching for.

A Mountie stood nearby, on guard at the station house, and they gave him a description. "I'll look for Wilson," the Mountie responded. "I'll tell the conductor to search the train and if he's on it, we'll catch him."

Amanda and Tom turned back and began walking down the platform. "I nearly forgot with all the commotion today, but Quaid's arriving on this train. I told him I'd meet him here and help him with the luggage home. He'll be with Beth. He didn't want her traveling alone so he went to get her, all the way to Winnipeg and back. I'd...I'd like you to meet her."

Tom's nervousness filled Amanda with a fresh wave of sentiment. He could be so tender when he didn't want to be. And Quaid was awfully nice to his wife, going that distance for her.

"I'd like to meet her, too," replied Amanda, her curiosity growing. What was the rest of his family like? Amanda had a sudden urge to meet Gabe, too, as well as Beth.

Why was that?

Because, she admitted to herself, she wondered how and if *she'd* fit into his family.

A familiar brown bonnet caught Amanda's eye the same time it caught Tom's. Amanda's hopes unraveled.

Clarissa was mounting the train stairs, her luggage being handed through an open window on the car marked First Class. She was leaving.

With a nervous flutter, Amanda dared to peek at Tom to gauge his reaction.

Tom and Clarissa held each other's gaze for a long moment, then Tom slowly lifted his long arm in goodbye.

Clarissa gripped the railing, then lifted her well-manicured hand in a sad, silent salute. Then, catching Amanda's quiet, sympathetic expression, Clarissa didn't wait for more. She spun on her polished heels and up into the compartment.

Tom's veneer of self-command vanished. He tugged a hand through his black hair.

"Are you all right?" Amanda asked.

"At one time, I didn't think I would be, but yeah, I'm fine."

Amanda was glad to hear it. The heartache that was etched on his face left, and she hoped the pain of his loss wouldn't remain for long. Today in court was the first time she'd heard that Clarissa had left him for Finnigan, and Amanda staggered at how stoic he'd been for weeks, keeping that information to himself.

"Do you think Finnigan's back in the area?" she asked.

"He's got no ties to this town. If he came back, he'd

be walking right into the hands of the Mounties, so I can't see it. I hope he *is* back. I'd like to get my hands on him.''

When they swung around to walk down the other direction of the platform, they noticed Quaid standing in the crowd.

"Quaid!" Tom shouted, weaving his arm around Amanda's shoulders. "Quaid! Beth!"

The eagerness in Tom's voice rushed through Amanda. When Quaid turned around to them, his face was lined with worry. His mouth was set in a grim line as he helped his wife down the steps. What was wrong?

Then she saw Quaid's trouble.

His wife, Beth, was in the family way. Amanda stopped for a moment to catch her breath. No one had told her Beth was pregnant.

That's why Quaid had gone to get her. As an extra precaution in her pregnancy.

She was a heavy-set pretty woman, around twenty. By her engorged size, Amanda guessed her to be around eight months along, perhaps eight and a half. As Beth lifted her skirt to take the last two steps, she revealed slippers on her bare feet. No boots, no shoes, but wide, leather, men's slippers.

She was wearing house slippers! *And* bare feet. Why?

Amanda peered closer. Because her ankles were swollen like sacks of water. No wonder she couldn't fit into her shoes. Her wrists were also thick with excess water—edema. She looked pale from traveling. The woman needed bed rest.

When Quaid clenched his medical bag close to his side, looking as though he never wanted to let it go, Amanda realized he'd traveled all this way with his wife, alone and anxious. A first-time father.

Amanda knew all too well the anxiety he felt.

Tom burst through the crowd toward his brother and sister-in-law, happily dragging Amanda by the wrist. "Beth, how wonderful to see you. I'd like you to meet Amanda Ryan."

After a round of warm introductions, Amanda looked at Quaid and shared a private, mutual look of concern.

"She's been having contractions for the last three hours," he whispered to Amanda. "She was fine before she left two months ago to visit her mother, or I never would have allowed her to travel. It started halfway through our trip. I was stuck in the middle of nowhere, on the plains, and didn't know which way to turn."

"You did the right thing, bringing her home where you can care for her. Are they strong contractions?"

"No, thank God."

"How far apart?"

"Every thirty minutes or so."

"That's not too bad," said Amanda, feeling relieved, at the same time trying to encourage Quaid.

Amanda stepped up and tucked her arm under Beth's, falling naturally into place as a midwife. "I think you need to rest. It must have been a weary ride. Tom and I will walk you home."

Lorne Wilson obviously wasn't there, so there was no need to stay.

Beth was an affectionate woman, and readily took Amanda's hand.

Amanda knew the walk was only two blocks away. She debated whether to ask Tom to carry his sister-in-law home—seeing how much bigger and stronger he was than his brother—but on second thought, knew it might only frighten Beth, embarrass her and cause more anxiety than relief. Which might in turn, speed more contractions.

"It was such a long haul over the prairies," Beth responded. "Nothing but acres of grassland to see. And my dear Quaid, so concerned over a few small contractions."

"Mild contractions are normal for the most part, this far along in your term," Amanda reassured her. Tom looked over Beth's head to Amanda and she silently sent him confirmation of her own apprehension.

"Quaid told me you were a midwife," Beth said to her. The train roared around them and Beth's words were lost.

"Quaid also told me about Clarissa," Beth whispered to Tom above the screech of wheels, probably thinking Amanda couldn't hear it. "I think that's awful. You deserve someone a lot better than her. Quaid also told me about you know who—" she nodded toward Amanda, making Amanda like her all the more. "And personally, I think you should pick whoever makes you happy.

"Thank you for the cradle, too," Beth said a little louder, but the train had already stopped its rumbling so her words were clear again. "Quaid told me you finished it early." Beth patted Amanda's arm. "He's going to be the godfather, you know."

Amanda found herself enjoying the banter, despite her concerns for Beth's health. Tom had once told Amanda she'd enjoy the company of Quaid's wife, and Amanda could understand why. She was a natural talker, one who tried to make Amanda feel at ease.

"Some men are just happier being married." Beth squinted beneath the lamplight. "And I feel like Tom here is one of them, even though he might not know it."

Amanda warmed to her, smiling with renewed pleasure at Beth's gentle teasing of her brother-in-law.

"He'd like to have plenty of his own children one day," Beth added in Amanda's direction.

The cutting comment was quick to fade Amanda's smile. She picked up the pace, hoping the topic would change.

As far as she knew, neither Quaid nor his wife was aware of *her* medical problem, so she swallowed her distress, determined to take the comments of others in the way they were meant—a harmless attempt to be kind and friendly.

"Beth, please," said Tom, his step faltering as his quiet gaze sought Amanda's. "Don't say that. It's not…true."

Beth stopped to catch her breath. "Don't deny it," she insisted with a broad smile. "How many times have you told us you can't wait for children of your own?"

Amanda felt queasy.

"I don't recall ever saying that." Tom's eyes pleaded for understanding.

"Why, you said it just before I left. Five or six, you said to me."

"I was only teasing you," he said, his eyes still on Amanda.

"You were not."

"But that was two months ago," he whispered coarsely.

Beth peered at him with curiosity, but kept talking. "You'd make a mighty fine father. Wouldn't he, Amanda?"

The sting of the truth delivered a brutal blow. Amanda nodded softly in agreement, lowered her lashes, and kept walking.

Would she ever be able to make Tom happy?

Chapter Sixteen

"Beth didn't mean to, but she made Amanda feel awful yesterday. How can I fix that?"

Wolf whimpered.

"Don't know, huh?"

Carrying a basin of warm water, Tom stepped over the dog, who lay at his boots panting in contentment in the small room off the sawmill office. Wearing his rugged denims with the orange stitching, and stripped to the waist except for the sleeveless undershirt that clung to his skin, Tom prepared for his nightly scrub.

"I figure if I pay Quaid and Beth a call, I can see how Beth's feeling. If she's up to it, I'll explain to them about Amanda's condition, so that neither one of them will bring up the subject again."

Wolf headed to the far corner to lie on his sheepskin rug.

"Hey, are you listening to me? I need your advice. I have a feeling Amanda won't like me telling anyone about her private business. But they'll keep it quiet if I ask them to."

The husky barked in approval, then lowered his head.

"Okay, glad you agree."

With a quick yank, Tom peeled off his undershirt then splashed water over his face and chest. The sizzling heat from the nearby stove seeped into his skin, drying the water that drizzled down his muscles.

Two months ago he never would have thought he'd be able to say goodbye to Clarissa as he had yesterday.

At the train station, watching Amanda interact with his brother and sister-in-law, he realized if he had to do it all again, he'd make the same decisions. The very ones that seemed to irritate Clarissa most—taking care of his family, building his sawmill from scratch, sending Quaid and Gabe to their schooling while he worked outdoors at what he loved to do.

Amanda made him feel proud of his accomplishments, proud that he'd chosen the simpler things that matter in life, such as family and home, over money.

Could he convince her what he'd said to Beth about wanting children was something he'd worked through in his heart and felt at ease with? He wasn't sure he knew how. He was a lumberjack and a carpenter and big oaf who knew how to chop wood, but he didn't have the finesse of insightful words.

Well, tomorrow morning, he'd bring back the jug of kerosene she'd forgotten, and try to explain what he'd been unable to explain at the train station when he'd flubbed his words and could only stare at her shrinking face.

Lifting the sea sponge, he rubbed it against the cake of soap, then lathered the dark expanse of his chest and underarms. Another round of furniture was varnished, which meant three more dollars profit to buy back his house.

His men had been asking questions ever since Tom had moved into this room, so Tom had simply told them the truth. He was strapped for cash, but rather than letting go of any one of them, he let the bank rent his house for the summer.

Gazing into the square mirror, Tom rubbed his bearded jaw with satisfaction. And didn't his men surprise him? Instead of walking away, they'd dug their spurs in a bit harder, with Patrick suggesting they all stay an extra half hour in the evenings as free labor, which would contribute at least another thirteen dollars per month.

A far way off from two hundred and forty, but he was headed in that direction.

Dabbing his towel beneath his arms, Tom heard a faint rustling sound. Wolf jumped to attention, his ears pricked.

What was it? A pebble? The wind? A bird trapped in the rafters?

Tom went to check. Away from the stove's heat, the cool office air blasted his bare flesh, but he saw nothing. The windows above the saws and tables—and water pails that lined the ceiling—indicated a clear black night.

He locked the doors. Settling back into his bedroom, he slapped the towel on the dresser and prepared for shaving. It was nothing but his nerves.

The warm, evening air lapped against her cheeks. Amanda rode high in the saddle of Donald's mare, trotting through town. Since her bicycle was useless, and Tom had promised to dispose of it, the O'Haras in their kindness had insisted Amanda borrow what she need from them.

She needed to speak to Tom. Her thoughts turned to Margaux, the girl's anguish and turmoil of the day, and the incident that triggered Amanda's desire to speak to him tonight. She'd head to the sawmill right after she checked on Beth's condition and Quaid's fragile state of mind.

Earlier in the afternoon, Margaux had come running to Amanda in terror. After she calmed the panic from Margaux's face, Amanda explained that menstruation was normal. She'd already explained it a couple of weeks before, when she'd quietly asked about Margaux's personal history, but her first time still came as a surprise. Amanda repeated that it meant Margaux could now conceive and have babies of her own, that she'd someday cherish that and be very proud she was a woman.

Margaux thought about it carefully, and then asked in her gentle-hearted way, "Are you proud?"

Amanda had paused, so shocked by the question that seemed to be the key of what had been distressing Amanda for the last months, that she couldn't at first respond.

"Yes," she'd finally said. "I'm proud of being a woman—and a midwife—and being able to guide you through it, too." Margaux didn't need to know yet that Amanda lacked her monthly cycles, but it was important and necessary to explain her joy in this part of life.

Menstruation was a topic no one discussed, yet most men understood this about their women, if they were tenderly involved and cared about their wives. They knew what it meant when they saw the carefully hung white cloths drying on the lines; that the intimate bonding of marriage would be interrupted for a few short days. It was this intimacy, this quiet understanding of life, that Amanda felt with Tom.

He was a noble man, and she wanted to share what she'd learned about herself tonight. She wanted to be with him, she thought as she got off the mare and tied it up outside Quaid's office.

It was Tom who answered Quaid's door when Amanda knocked. His eyes flashed at her when he spotted her standing there. As he leaned back to stare at her startled expression, his limber stance emphasized the force of his thighs. All the way here she'd been practicing what she'd say to him, but now that she had the opportunity, all sensible thought escaped her.

"You look surprised to see me," he said with a dimpled grin, leaning against the door of the huge log house. He ran his gaze down her clenched shawl, then over her split skirt right down to her boots, making it clear how happy he was to see *her.* "Come on in. I came by to speak to Quaid and Beth, but as soon as I got here, Quaid got called away. Mr. Langston broke his wrist."

Amanda caught her breath as she squeezed past his lean body. "Is he all right?"

"I'm not sure. His wife came racing over from the mercantile." Tom nodded in that direction, just around the corner. "But I haven't heard how Mr. Langston is."

Tom stared down at her. He'd just shaven; she could smell the scent of mint. His presence always seemed to overpower her.

"How did he manage to break his wrist?"

"He fell off his stepladder."

"I hope it's minor." She gulped, peering down the bustling street. "Do you think Quaid needs my help?"

"I don't think so. Besides, I'm sure he'd rather you stay here."

"Why?"

Tom's shoulders moved beneath the cotton of his shirt. His tone turned rather serious. "Well, the housekeeper is tending to Beth at the moment, but she's looking a bit peculiar to me."

Amanda focused her concern. "Where is she?"

Frowning heavily at Amanda's sense of alarm, he motioned to the room behind him. "She's been in bed for two days. The spasms—"

"You mean, contractions?"

"Yeah. They're still coming at regular intervals, but she looks pale. Her eyes are sort of...big."

Apprehension took hold of her and began to gnaw. "Did Quaid say anything about her condition?"

Tom snorted and swung around, rubbing a hand along his belt. "He's paler than she is. I've never seen him so upset. He's lost his concentration. Lately, I have to nudge him to answer me when I say anything."

"He's probably worried sick."

"Could you come take a look at her? She took a sip of water from me just now, but told me she's got a headache."

Amanda's heart tripped and thudded. *Please don't let it be anything.*

"I'll follow you," she said. Last time she was here, she'd entered by the public door, around the side above the sign that read Dr. Quaid Murdock. This private area she walked through was filled with polished wood, ivory candleholders, English knickknacks and even a small piano pressed against the wall.

"She's back behind the parlor." Tom opened the makeshift curtains dividing the room in two, letting his hand linger over Amanda's back as she stepped in.

It was considerate of Quaid to put his wife in a large room off the main hall, where she wouldn't feel as cut off from the world as she might in a back bedroom, and therefore more likely to remain in bed.

When they entered, Beth called from the bed, propped up against several fluffy pillows. "How lovely to see you." She struggled to rise on an elbow. Her hair, done in two plaits, spilled over rounded shoulders.

Amanda nodded hello to the elderly housekeeper, Mrs. Garvey, who was preparing a hot tea by the window, then lowered herself to a stool beside Beth.

Tom was right. Beth's eyes were enlarged, almost bulging, with dark circles. Her face was puffier than before, and Amanda bet if she pressed her fingers into Beth's swollen wrists, she'd leave an indentation of pitting edema. An indicator of poor circulation.

"What brings you here?" Beth asked.

"I came to check up on you."

"That's kind of you. But you know, I'm getting the best care in the world from my husband."

Amanda nodded, knowing that sometimes doctors who cared for their own kin overlooked symptoms and problems because they were too emotionally involved to make a detached analysis. Quaid sounded like one of those people, and if there was anything Amanda could do to help the situation, she'd try.

"Would you mind, Beth, if I examine you? Tom told me you have a headache, and since Quaid's not here, I'd like to make certain we give you back to him in the same splendid condition he left you."

"You're fussing over me too much." Beth pressed her palm over her forehead, as if rubbing away an ache. "I told Quaid my mother gained a lot of weight with every child of hers, too…" Her voice began to fade. "But she never ran into any problems." Overcome with fatigue, she fell back into her pillows.

Amanda reached for the sleek medical equipment on the dresser. By the glass thermometer, Beth's temperature was slightly elevated. Using the brand-new experimental sphygmomanometer that Quaid had taught her how to use when she'd assisted in Josh's procedure, Amanda pressed the cup against Beth's radial pulse, while her other hand felt the diminishing pulse. Good Lord, her blood pressure was much too high! Amanda broke into a clammy sweat. Although the experimental equipment was the only method they had to gauge blood pressure and it wasn't entirely accurate, it gave Amanda an indication that something was terribly wrong.

By stethoscope, Amanda heard crackling rales in Beth's chest, another indication of too much water retention. Thank goodness the baby's heartbeat was strong and even, but Beth displayed hyperreflexia, jittery with every touch. With rising distress, Amanda returned the stethoscope to the dresser. When she turned around to face Beth again, Amanda stopped cold.

Beth was having a seizure! She rolled her eyes, stiffened, and seemed to lose consciousness.

Oh, no! Shock wedged in Amanda's throat. "Tom!"

Tom lurched to her side, complete horror on his face. "Beth…?"

Amanda knew what needed to be done. They only had a few minutes to do it or the baby would be damaged. "Run and get Quaid! I need you both back here in one minute flat!"

Tom dropped everything and ran.

She stayed with Beth, watching the seizure finish. It lasted roughly fifteen seconds. Amanda had heard of it, but never seen it. *Eclampsia.* High blood pressure and edema in pregnancy, culminating in seizures or coma. For some unknown reason, the baby caused a toxic condition. Once the baby was delivered, the eclampsia would disappear. The only thing that might save the lives of mother and child was immediate Cesarean delivery.

While Mrs. Garvey stayed with her, Amanda raced to Quaid's office to gather what she'd need. Scalpels, sutures, retractors, surgical scissors. *She'd* have to perform the surgery, and prayed Quaid would be coherent enough to keep his wife under choloroform.

Quaid and Tom burst into the bedroom as Amanda was dashing in with her second armload of supplies.

Quaid gently shook his wife, trying to get her out of her stupor. "What is it?"

There was no time for formalities. Amanda glared from Tom's stark face to his brother's. "Beth had a seizure."

"Oh, my God." Quaid's face darkened. As he looked down at his fragile wife, his eyes began to water with a faint touch of hysteria.

Amanda needed him calm. "Scrub your hands. You've got to assist me."

"We can't cut her open," Quaid sobbed.

Although Amanda was torn, as well, she took a deep breath and braced herself. "She won't feel it. You'll put her under and together we'll do this. Scrub *now*."

"It may be a death sentence."

"She'll die for sure if we don't do this. So will the baby."

"Come on, Quaid." Tom gently tugged his brother by the arm to the washstand. Amanda was grateful Tom was here.

Battling tears, Quaid scrubbed.

Would he be of any use, or better if he stepped aside?

"What can I do?" Tom asked her as she donned her surgical frock. He was equally pale, but more in control than Quaid.

"Stay beside your brother," Amanda said in a feverish whisper. "If he happens to collapse, you'll have to take over. I'll guide you."

"Oh, my God," blurted Tom, echoing his brother's words.

Beth was just coming out of her woozy trance when Amanda placed the cloth, soaked with chloroform, over her mouth and nose. There was no time to explain it to dear

Beth. She faded off into unconsciousness as Quaid whispered loving words.

Amanda hiked up the nightshirt to expose the rounded belly. She raised the scalpel.

"What are you doing?" Quaid hollered from beside Beth's head.

Amanda's hand trembled at his harsh rebuke. "A transverse lower incision."

"*No.* Go with the classical. A vertical midline, straight down the abdomen from the belly button."

"But some surgeons say there are fewer ruptures and infections with the transverse."

"Some?" Quaid asked, stumbling back.

Amanda held firm to her decision but was forced to wait, knowing that as Beth's husband, Quaid had the final, legal say. "We're running out of time, Quaid."

Tom patted Quaid's shoulders, again nudging his brother.

"My God, man," mumbled Quaid, almost incoherent. "I don't want to be the one to…"

Amanda steadied herself and tried again. "I know what I'm doing. I've done this once before with my grandpa."

"Let Amanda do her job," Tom urged.

Closing his eyes, Quaid nodded, and with a slackening in her tense shoulders, Amanda began.

Within two to three minutes, the healthy baby was out.

"Ah-hh…" Quaid said, openly weeping now at his beautiful baby boy.

Smiling in joyous wonder, Amanda handed him the crying baby—around seven pounds, Amanda guessed—a bit subdued from the morphine given to his mother. Quaid placed him in a towel and rubbed his back. Without benefit of being squeezed through the birth canal, Cesarean babies had more mucous left in the lungs, which needed to be drained.

With staggering relief that the worst was over, Amanda nodded to Tom to take over the anesthesia and hold the cloth over Beth's mouth, while she delivered the placenta, then began suturing the uterus.

Tom was looking ill.

She stared at his off-color face. "Are you going to be all right?"

"As long as I don't look."

Quaid bellowed from across the room where he was suctioning the baby's mouth with a bulb syringe. "What are you doing now?"

"I found these silver wire sutures in your office. I knew you'd have the latest, and the best."

Quaid's voice was low and gruff. "Another controversial decision that rests on my shoulders? If you stitch her up internally, we can't remove the stitching when it's healed. It may cause a heavy infection. The theory is you're supposed to let her uterus naturally contract—no sutures—and let her stop her own bleeding."

"She'll bleed to death," Amanda begged. "Max SaumInger's recent paper proved it. And besides, Quaid, how can this amount of bleeding stop on its own?"

Quaid was near collapse. "Did you suture the other woman?"

"Yes, but not with silver wire." She swallowed past her dry lips. "Silver wire has less chance of infection."

Quaid took a moment to decide, then slowly nodded his approval.

Thirty minutes later, with Amanda drenched in perspiration, it was over. The baby was fine and Beth was stable, still under the effects of chloroform and morphine. Quaid placed the wrapped newborn at her side, but Beth didn't stir.

They'd have to watch her carefully over the next few days, especially for postpartum fever, or any redness or oozing at the surgical site. Her blood pressure and edema should quickly return to normal. Amanda prayed she'd make it.

She watched the brothers coo over the infant, Quaid gently checking the baby's chest and mouth and limbs for anything unusual, and finding all clear. It was touching to see two grown men tending to a tiny infant that either could fit into their palm.

"You were born to do this," Quaid said softly in Amanda's direction.

It was the first time he'd acknowledged her skill, and she gloried briefly in the shared moment of pride. Her wistful gaze locked with Tom's. His warm look of respect sent tremors up her spine.

Amanda turned back to her task, seeing to it that Beth looked comfortable, giving her another dose of morphine. She'd be acutely sore for days.

When things were settled, and a nightly breeze hummed through the air from the opened window, Amanda watched Quaid and Tom with the newborn. It brought back aching memories of her own. She hadn't held this baby yet and she would have liked to, but deferred the honor to the father and equally proud new uncle.

From the corner of the room, Amanda straightened Beth's pillows and sheets around the sleeping woman, while trying to camouflage her own anguish. Looking on quietly, she wondered what a seven-pound newborn might feel like curled and sleeping in her arms.

Beth didn't stir for four hours as they sat by her side. Trying to stifle his fears, Tom watched his tormented brother with renewed concern.

Quaid mixed honey with boiled water and fed it to his son, clinging to the baby as if by holding and comforting him, he could hold and comfort Beth.

If anything should happen to her, Tom knew Quaid wouldn't want to go on. Quaid was the most emotional man Tom knew, and although he'd never say so, Tom's heart ached whenever one of his brother's did. This evening, he'd been privileged to witness the love Quaid felt for Beth, and he felt intrusive, observing their sacred vows of marriage.

Every time Tom looked at Amanda, he thought of marriage, too. How would *they* cope if faced with a similar tragedy? When he imagined Amanda lying there in bed, unresponsive and possibly near death...he wanted to lift her into his arms and never let her go....

His pulse took a trembling leap. He watched Amanda gently taking care of all three of them, silently tending to Beth's wound, counting the baby's soft respirations, making something for Quaid to eat and watching to make sure he drank his tea.

Finally, in the middle of the night, around three o'clock when another dose of morphine had knocked out Beth and Amanda declared she'd be out until morning, Tom urged Amanda to get some rest herself.

"I'll take you home," he whispered.

She blinked her tired eyes. "How can I leave them?"

"They'll be fine for four or five hours." He yawned. "You can come back and check on them as soon as you wake up. You need your rest, too. Won't your grandmother be worried?"

"You're right about that." Amanda brushed back her silky hair. Candlelight caught her smooth face and the upswing of her lashes, which fringed her weary eyes. "I told

Grandma I was coming to town to check on Beth, then I'd pick up the kerosene that I'd forgotten at your house. I sent her a message by Mrs. Garvey's grandson that Beth was in labor, but she'll still be concerned.''

"Let's go, then.''

Mrs. Garvey had a sister who lived nearby, and that sister came to sit with Beth, promising she and Mrs. Garvey would rotate in shifts. Quaid was content to remain at his wife's bedside, sleeping in a cot next to the baby's cradle, with instructions to be woken every hour to check on his wife.

As they left Quaid's home, the balmy night air lifted Tom's hat and rattled his shirt, taking some of the sting out of his eyes. During the past several hours, he'd tended to his horse and Amanda's, and they were now unsaddled in Quaid's small stable. He put an arm around Amanda's shoulders as they strolled over the beaten grass.

Would it be fair to open up the conversation now, when she was so tired? How should he begin to tell her how he felt?

She turned quiet at his touch. "The evening turned out so differently than how it started.''

"I don't know what we would have done without you.''

"I'm glad I was here to help.''

"Quaid is especially grateful.''

Amanda's lips curled into that soft, sensual smile he'd come to know intimately. She looked as though she wanted to say more, too, but then glanced at the quiet houses surrounding them, and seemed to change her mind. "I can ride myself home,'' she said. "You're too tired. You need your rest, too.''

"I'll ride with you,'' Tom insisted. "I can't let you ride alone.''

"Really, Tom. Banff is a safe place. Everyone's sleeping. Sometimes I get other medical calls in the middle of the night, and I go out alone for those."

"But whoever comes to get you rides back with you to wherever you're needed."

"But when I'm finished, I ride home alone. If I'm serious about my practice, then I've got to be able to do what the men doctors do. And that is, get myself to and from wherever I'm going. Alone."

Although he saw her point, his instinct was to protect her. When he brought their horses, saddled and ready to go, she was staring up at the half moon.

Maybe this wasn't the proper time or place to talk to her, and he could use some sleep himself, but he yearned for a quiet moment alone with her. "Can I show you something at the sawmill before you disappear?"

She rubbed her arms in the chill, shivering, but perking up from her fatigue. The cool air kicked up his energy, too. "Do you think it's proper?"

"No one in town is awake, so they won't know it. And I promise to keep my hands off you."

She stared up at the stars again, teasing him with that tantalizing expression. "Well, I still do need that kerosene," she said with exaggerated worry. "We're right out and we'll need it in the morning to light the lamps."

"Well, then you've got to come," he said with equal humor. "We can't have you stumbling around in the dark. You might stub your toe."

Her soft laughter filled the air and pleased him. They both knew what might happen when she reached the sawmill. He groaned with the thought of making love to her. Groaned louder still with the thought of not being able to.

"What's all the groaning?" she asked from atop her

mare, looking down at him with amusement as he marched to his own horse.

He choked back his real response and said casually, "I'm feeling sorry for myself, up till four in the morning."

"I could make it worth your while," she said boldly.

"Really?" His wayward eye traveled down her legs in the stirrups, playing to her innuendo. "What on earth do you think you could possibly do to make it worth my while?"

"Well, I could make you a cup of tea." She feigned innocence. "They say I have a special knack with tea leaves."

He shook his head. "Not worth my while."

Her eyes widened. "I could fry up some ham."

"Wouldn't satisfy me."

"Hmm. Let me see." Her lips grew rounded, her mouth slackened. "How about a long, soothing back rub?"

He cocked his brows. "Now you're getting warmer."

Her shoulders dipped with laughter. There was something enchanting about the way she moved on her horse. It was a slow, easy glide, and it made him think of another time, when he'd watched her, *felt her,* gliding on top of him. His muscles tensed with pleasure, thinking of it.

He wouldn't keep her, though, he promised himself. He wouldn't tarnish her reputation. His log cabin nearby had been rented to a couple from Scotland, and although they were strangers, they might spread rumors.

Wolf barked softly from the other side of the back door when Tom and Amanda reached it. It was dark inside. Tom lit the closest lantern, and it filled the sawmill with an orange glow.

"What is it you want to show me?"

In a burst of boyish enthusiasm, he motioned to the corner. "Your bicycle."

She looked to where he pointed, then let out a small scream of delight. "Ah-hh!"

It was standing upright, leaning against one of the saw tables, looking much different than the broken wreck they'd dragged here. "I wanted you to see it, but I can bring it 'round for you tomorrow."

"What did you do to it?" She was breathless as she walked to the newly repaired bicycle.

"I had it fixed."

Her blue eyes shimmered with glee. "How?"

"The blacksmith welded new tubes of metal for the shaft. He replaced the gripping bars. He also fixed the spokes, welding the top pieces together again. It doesn't look quite the same as it used to, but it's stable and it works."

She ran her fingers eagerly along the handles, then slid them down the sleek lines of the seat. "The crack in the seat is gone."

He backed against a worktable and sunk his palms into the rough wood. "The bootmaker stretched a new skin of leather over the old one. I should have fixed the crack a while ago."

She came back to face him. Her eyes misted. "You did this for me?"

He nodded.

"No one has ever done anything like this for me before."

"Then I'm glad I'm the first."

She furrowed the smooth bridge of her nose, staring at him with open admiration.

His voice was low and deep. "I'd like to be the first at a lot of things, Amanda."

The top of her unbuttoned blouse riveted his attention. God, if he touched her now, he'd never let her go. He couldn't let that happen. She needed sleep. She'd have to help Quaid in the morning. Beth would need her. Just four hours of sleep, he vowed, then he'd say everything he needed to say.

Amanda was too moved to speak. Her gaze dropped to the saw table, where his hand rested. She concentrated on the brown skin of his knuckles, as if trying to decide how to answer.

"I promised I wouldn't touch you," he said, "but I'm having a hard time keeping my hands off you."

She had no smile for him this time, just a somber look. Her eyes traveled from his gaze, over his nose, then settled on his lips. How could he control himself when she looked at him like this?

He fought his urges. "If we start something now, I won't be through with you till the morning, so you better get home while the gettin's good."

"It would be the sensible thing to do."

"Very sensible." He wanted to crush her against him, to feel her nakedness beneath the worn cloth of her blouse.

"Goodbye, then," she said, as light as a caress, not moving an inch to leave.

"Goodbye." He also stayed rooted where he was.

With a soft shuffle, Wolf made his way between them and whined.

Tom's rumble of laughter met with Amanda's. "I think we're confusing him."

With a sigh, she collected herself, brushed back her hair, and strode to the door.

Please stay, he silently begged.

She struggled with her decision. "If I don't leave now I won't be of any use to anyone in the morning."

"I know. You have to go. People depend on you."

With a grumbling look of determination, she wove her

slender hips past his side, then out the door to the black, crisp night. He watched her mount the mare, lifting her leg high over the saddle with ease.

With a murmured goodbye, she disappeared into the night.

It still bothered him that she was riding home alone, and his horse was still saddled, so he took the opportunity to follow behind her at a distance, making sure she made it home safely. When she reined her horse onto her dirt path, he pulled around and galloped back. She was one stubborn woman. There had to be a way for her to protect herself. If she were *his* wife, he'd make sure someone accompanied her on all her night calls.

"Wolf, come back inside," he said, after he'd slipped his horse back into the barn.

The dog obeyed. Tom closed the door, but Wolf began to bark.

"Shh," said Tom. "You'll wake the neighbors. I miss her, too. She'll be back."

Wolf pranced to the office, barking louder at the interior door this time.

"You better stop that," Tom reprimanded. Lifting his arm, he turned and leaned over to blow out the lantern.

"Hello, Tom," called a familiar voice from behind him.

Blazes, his heart jumped! Spinning around, instinctively ducking in self-defense, he recoiled at the sight of Zeb Finnigan, slowly stepping out of the office doorway.

Chapter Seventeen

Amanda was three minutes at her shack when she realized she'd forgotten the kerosene. Standing beside the horse, she stopped unbuckling the saddle, then remounted. The horse snorted in the stillness, its massive muscles flexing beneath her legs.

"We forgot something," she said, patting the sleek brown neck. "I got distracted by the bicycle."

Peering down the forested road, she gave the mare a nudge and headed back toward the sawmill. There'd been less than half a candle left last night when Amanda had gone to town. This morning when they arose, they wouldn't be able to see in the dark. They had chores to do inside, and people might drop by with unexpected medical calls. She had to be able to see!

It wasn't likely Tom was asleep already. Although she might catch him in bed.... The vision of Tom in bed held her captivated. She'd never tire of thinking about him. Never.

If he'd made one move toward her tonight, she might never have left. It was a good thing *he* had so much will-power, for it was almost impossible to keep her fingers from trailing his forehead, and lower down his body....

She approached the sawmill. It was nestled against the looming black wall that would turn into a mountain in the morning. The drone of the rushing water dam filled her ears. When she turned into the yard, she saw a horse she didn't recognize tied to a tree almost hidden in the corner. Was that horse there when she'd been here earlier? Did it belong to the tourists in Tom's cabin, or someone else? Why wasn't it unsaddled and resting in the barn? Sometimes city folks didn't know how to handle their animals, needing more than a bit of instruction.

A lantern glowed in the sawmill's back room. Wolf was barking. Why? A nervous flutter rose in her stomach. Sliding off her mount, she glanced into the darkened window and noticed the shadows of two men, facing each other in a threatening stance.

The hairs at the back of her neck bristled.

Who was that?

Her heart began to pump. With a mad whirl, she hit the dirt and ran. Dashing through the tall reeds to Tom's cabin, tripping over her skirts and legs, she banged on the neighbor's door as hard and loud as she could. "Help...! Please help, we need the Mounties!"

Zeb Finnigan didn't have a gun visible, but Tom knew he usually carried his favorite derringer, an ivory-and-silver one-of-a-kind inside his wool jacket, on the left side where Finnigan's hairy hand was trailing. In his other hand, the bastard was holding something much more threatening than a gun.

A burning cigar.

The threat of fire had Tom's stomach churning. If he lost this place, dammit, he'd bloody well lose it all. He cursed the fact that his guns were in the back room, hanging above his dresser. He'd never used a gun on anyone before, but as did most men in town, he kept them handy in case he needed them. Who would have thought he'd need one against his own business partner?

Finnigan used to be well-dressed and groomed. What had happened to him? Scruffy dark hair dangled in his eyes. He brushed it back with a sweep of pudgy fingers. His gray wool suit, well-worn in the shoulders and elbows, looked as if he'd been wearing it for days. Standing at the office door, stocky and pompous, he took a drag of his cigar and blew the smoke at Wolf's face. "Hi, boy. Remember me?"

Wolf barked in delight, and before Tom could stop him, Finnigan spun around and trapped Wolf inside the office, closing the solid wood door with a loud thump.

"What the hell are you doing?" Tom lunged forward, but Zeb motioned him to stop. If Tom could get close enough, he'd aim for the man's neck.

"Your dumb dog will be fine in there."

Jumping up on his hind legs, Wolf barked happily through the square panes of glass, in recognition of his supposed friend, Finnigan.

Tom remembered it was payday tomorrow, and the wad of cash he picked up from the bank was normally kept in the vault. Was that why Finnigan was here?

Well, wouldn't he be surprised? Tom had paid his men earlier today. With all the troubles he'd had lately, he didn't like leaving the money in his vault overnight.

Tom dropped his hands, trying not to threaten Finnigan. There was no telling how desperate he was. "Did you come for my last dollar?"

Finnigan sneered. "I don't need your lousy dollar."

Judging by his dirty appearance, he did. A man on the run with nowhere left to hide, he was like a cornered animal.

"I want you to clear my name."

"Huh!" Tom stumbled back and leaned against the counter. "You're worried about your reputation? That's laughable."

Finnigan took another drag and deliberately tapped the ashes over a stack of lumber, watching Tom's reaction.

Tom clenched his fingers into the counter behind him, holding back his desire to pummel the son of a bitch.

"If you burn down this place, I *will* kill you."

Finnigan chortled, then spotted the bicycle. He took a deliberate, slow stride toward it. "The crazy madman ranting again. First about his broken bicycle, now about his sawmill."

"How did you know that?"

"It doesn't matter."

To Tom, it meant Finnigan had been in town at least long enough to talk to someone. Who would he have talked to that wouldn't have turned him in? Tom couldn't think of a single name. Maybe Finnigan had witnessed the courthouse scene himself. "Were you there?"

"At the courthouse?"

Tom nodded.

"Hell, no! But I've still got friends in this town. One of the Coover brothers—Dean, the fur trader—we used to play a lot of cards together, and he knows I don't renege on my bets. He knows I'm going to replace your money."

Tom shook his head in disbelief.

The lantern flickered over Finnigan's brow as he patted the bicycle seat. Something felt different in the room. Tom looked around. Wolf had stopped barking. That was it. The dog was looking in another direction, toward Tom's bedroom. In a flash, Tom caught the edge of a green skirt moving behind his door.

Amanda! No!

Every fiber in Tom's body tightened in response. His pulse shot forward. What was she doing here? She was going to get hurt!

Tom's gaze whirled back to Finnigan, who didn't appear to noticed Amanda's presence.

The freckles deepened across Finnigan's wide brow. He scowled. "Why did you have to go to the Mounties? You should have known I'd be back to return that money. With twice as much."

"Why did you steal it?" Tom kept his face a mask of indifference, but he was bracing himself against the counter to keep from looking in Amanda's direction.

Hell. Had she seen the guns hanging over the dresser? Would she take them?

No, he commanded. She might get hurt.

"The money was half mine," Finnigan responded.

"Then where's the other half?"

Finnigan laughed, but the hollow ring contained no humor.

"Who are you? I thought I knew Zeb Finnigan. I thought he was a man of his word."

"I'm still a man of my word! And that's what I'm here for. You're going help me get my reputation back."

"Is that right? How am I supposed to do that?" Dammit, Tom had to make a move before Amanda did. He was willing to risk himself, but never her.

Finnigan's eyes narrowed. "If I give you back seven thousand, would you drop the charges?"

"What about all the other people you stole from?"

"Those are fabrications."

"How about the property you sold twice over? Amanda Ryan's?"

"I can't help it if people are stupid."

"What about your brother?"

Finnigan's jaw contorted.

"Do you consider your brother stupid for helping you out?"

"Shut up."

"How could you do that to Frank? He's got a wife and five kids, for cripe's sake."

"I'm not here to talk about that!"

"All right. Then tell me…why the hell did you get involved with Clarissa?"

The man circled the bicycle and took a puff on his cigar. "She wanted me to."

It wasn't what Tom wanted to hear. He could feel the blood rushing to his limbs, ready to punch anything within punching distance.

"She wanted me to kiss her. She wanted me to carry her off to a fancy place more exciting than this."

Tom's voice dropped to a threatening hush. "How could you hit a woman?"

"Last week, her complaints about the lack of fancy hotels we were staying at started getting on my nerves."

"You're a son of a bitch, you know that?"

"I'm here to persuade you to clear my name."

"You ruined it, you clear it."

From the corner of his eye, Tom saw Amanda inching toward the office. What was she doing?

Finnigan's nostrils flared at Tom's comment. With a simmering rage, he slid the derringer from his jacket and lifted it to Wolf's direction. "It'd be a shame if something happened to your dog."

"Don't!"

In one swift move Amanda pulled the door handle and Wolf came running out. He leaped at Finnigan, wagging his tail and jumping up on Finnigan's legs.

"Get the hell off me!" Finnigan shouted, spotting

Amanda at the same time. He bellowed a curse, swung the gun toward her and hurled the red-hot cigar into the air.

Tom jumped on the man, knocking them both to the floor. "This," he said, driving his fist into Finnigan's gut, "is for beating up on a woman."

Finnigan ground his fingernails into Tom's face. Tom felt his skin peel and shouted in agony. Finnigan slammed his knee into Tom's thigh.

Tom, unwilling to let go, punched again in Finnigan's chest. "And this is for everything else."

The cigar fell into a pile of splintered, dry pine. It ignited. Amanda yelled. Tom tried to punch him again, but didn't dislodge the gun.

It was pointed in Wolf's direction, and Finnigan pulled the trigger.

It missed and zinged by Wolf's ear.

Tom swore.

Amanda raced to Finnigan and banged him hard over the head with Tom's gun, which she'd obviously found.

"Get the hell away from me!" Finnigan yelled.

She banged again, with not quite so much strength, but it missed and hit his shoulder. With a mighty heave, Tom lifted the man by his collar, and drove his fist hard into the stubbly jaw. That knocked him out.

Drenched in sweat, Tom yanked himself off Finnigan's body. Catching his breath, he pulled Amanda toward him for a brief moment before they both looked to the burning pine. Two Mounties crashed through the door, but one stack of lumber was already shooting flames.

The policemen lifted Finnigan outside. Through a window, Tom saw them drag him to a spot two hundred feet away. They handcuffed him to a tree then raced back to help with the fire. The Scottish neighbors guarded Finnigan.

"Get out of here!" Tom yelled to Amanda.

"I can't find Wolf!"

"Leave! I'll find him!"

From across the room, Tom nearly cried out with relief to see the police beside her, coaxing her out the door. Dammit, he'd find Wolf, as long as he knew Amanda was safe.

Tom leaped to the tabletops, jumping across the aisles from one to the other to systematically turn over the water pails that hung below the rafters. He raced to catch up with the fire, but it was too fast. He held his sleeve to his nose to mask the smoke. Where was Wolf?

In roughly two minutes, with the room engulfed with soot and flame, Tom heard the blessed church bells clanging, calling the volunteer fire brigade.

Sirens screeched down the middle of town, two red fire carts pulled by six men.

One hour later, with half the town watching from outside, the last of the firemen pulled out the hose from the pond and coiled it back onto the fire cart. "If it weren't for those water pails you had hangin' on the ceilin', Tom, it would have spread a lot faster and I don't think we could'a stopped it."

Tom had lost one-quarter of his lumber, but it was hardly a loss considering the building was still intact.

Tom shook the man's hand, as well as those of the six other volunteers. He wished he could shake everyone's hand who'd helped tonight, but there were dozens of men who'd lined the pond to pass buckets and buckets of water. Exhausted from the ordeal, he turned to find Amanda.

Coming toward him in the crowd, her nose and face smudged with black soot, Amanda found his gaze.

Emerging from the fog, Wolf limped beside Amanda, his fur matted with dirt, and panting so hard his tongue hit the ground.

Sickened at the sight of a bloody paw, Tom dropped to his knees. "What is it, boy?"

Amanda crouched beside Tom and she began to sob, the first time he'd ever seen her cry. "I think he broke his foot. He must have tripped over something."

"How's Wolf doin'?" Margaux asked, peering over the breakfast table at Amanda, then Grandma. The kitten meowed behind Margaux's stool.

"He still has the splint on his paw, but he's fine," said Amanda. "It's only been three days, Margaux, and you already know it has to stay on for at least four weeks."

"I know, but I like hearing about it. Don't you, Josh?"

Josh nodded and Amanda smiled at her grandmother while the older woman scraped the last remnants of egg off her plate.

"Who put the splint on?"

"You already know that, too. Dr. Quaid did."

"Woof cwy?" asked Josh, struggling with the words, but already making noticeable strides in his speech.

"Dogs don't cry," his sister told him. "They bark, or they whimper. And Amanda already told us Dr. Quaid gave him medicine before he stitched up his paw, so he couldn't have cried. Medicine like you got for your stitches."

Josh kicked his feet beneath the table, apparently happy to be compared to the husky.

The ordeal was over, thought Amanda, clearing the table. Finnigan was behind bars and would remain so for five years. He was as broke as broke could be, and no one was getting back any of the money he'd taken from them.

At least Tom hadn't lost his mill. His men had already cleared out the burned lumber and were fast on track cutting more. Everything was working out.

Wasn't it?

She tried to rationalize the emptiness she felt. The only reason Tom hadn't been able to drop by to speak to her was that he was cleaning up the mess Finnigan had made. And the only reason she hadn't gone to him was that she was spending time with a new patient in town—Mr. and Mrs. Langston's married daughter, three months along— as well as visiting with Beth. Why, Amanda had spent twenty minutes with her yesterday as Quaid tended to the baby, listening to her lovely descriptions of Winnipeg and funny observations of Quaid and Tom.

Josh and Margaux finished with their plates and ran out the door, only to come running back in. "He's here!"

"Who's here?"

"Tom," Margaux cried. "And he brought Wolf!"

Amanda yanked her apron over her head and flung it on the table, dashing out to greet them.

She squinted in the sunlight, staring up at Tom's grinning face as he rolled onto the path, his wagon rumbling behind him. Wolf was lying on a large rectangle of sheepskin, peering over the wagon edge like a grand duke on tour.

The children jumped up beside the husky onto the wagon, unable to keep from hugging the jovial dog, and Amanda slipped in a pat or two of her own.

"Can he come with us to the river?" Margaux asked Tom.

"Sure," Tom said. "He can walk on his own, but you better watch that his sore foot doesn't get wet. Don't let him run in the water. Here, take his collar and leash to make sure."

"I'll go with them," Grandma declared.

That left Tom alone with Amanda.

"Lord help me," he said, "but I've been wishing everyone away for the last three days so I could come to see you.''

''You have?''

He nodded and slid off the wagon, his lean legs touching the ground, his heated look on her. She gulped at the sexual charge in the air.

She knew if she lived for a hundred years, it would always be the same between them.

''First of all,'' he said, taking her hand and leading her to the half-built log cabin. ''I need to do this.''

He twirled her around and kissed her, her muslin skirts swirling over his cowboy boots, the black ones with the shiny silver toes he'd worn on the first day they'd met.

Her mouth joined with his. He coaxed the pleasure from her, the tip of his tongue meeting hers and gently rolling over her lips, making her crave for more.

Rising on tiptoe, she pressed herself against his length, recognizing the need in him, hard and burning as her own. She pressed her breasts against his vested chest, enjoying the coolness of the leather as it seeped into her blouse.

He sucked in his breath, tearing himself away from her and staring down into her face. She slid her gaze over his firm, dark cheekbones, the straight eyebrows, the dark intense eyes.

His grasp was firm around her waist. ''Why didn't you tell me the bicycle was worth so much?''

Her lips opened slightly as she pulled back to stand at arm's length, watching the question drift across his face.

''You found out,'' she said quietly.

''You didn't expect it to be a secret for long, did you? You had to know the banker would come calling.''

''What did he say?'' She wanted to hear it word by word, from Tom's lips alone.

''He gave me the most surprising, wonderful news.''

Tom's obvious happiness weaved its way through her.

He grabbed her by the shoulders and tugged her closer. His grasp felt urgent. "Two hundred and eighty dollars. I didn't know your bicycle was worth that much. Why didn't you tell me?"

She shrugged and thought about it. "It's not something I wanted to broadcast. It wasn't a secret, but it…didn't seem important."

"But I asked you once, remember? Why didn't you tell me that day at Ruby's, the day it got smashed?"

"I thought you'd feel so sorry for me that you'd… overextend yourself."

He stared at her long and hard.

"You must admit, you do tend to overextend yourself."

He smiled and closed his eyes for a moment, crossing his arms over his ribs. "You gave almost all the money to the banker in exchange for my log cabin. Why?"

"Because what you and your sawmill do for this town is a lot more important than my bicycle."

"That's not why I had it fixed. I didn't want you to give it away."

"I know."

"I wanted you to have your freedom."

Emotion choked her words. "And you gave it to me." She wasn't talking about the bicycle, but the freedom to be herself, to accept herself the way she was with all her flaws and inabilities.

"I'll buy you another one."

She tilted her face in his direction and smiled. "I believe you will."

"Where did you find a buyer?"

"Remember that older couple from England who offered to buy it once before? The man with the checkered hat and big red feather?"

"You sold it to him?"

She nodded.

"How did you find him?"

"I asked at the big hotel and everyone knew him by his hat."

"What do you intend to do about a means of transportation?"

"With the money left over from the sale, I bought a second-hand wagon. Donald and Ellie are letting me keep it in their barn for now, until I build a barn for myself. Donald's letting me rent one of his mules anytime I need it. It's just a few hundred yards up the road, so it's very convenient. I need a bigger rig anyway, on account of the children. A bicycle would be useless, now that I have a bigger..."

"...a bigger family," he finished for her.

Her eyes watered in happy agreement.

"I'm still not sure I can accept your gift." He looked at the half-built walls around him, then began to walk slowly around the floor, stroking the logs with his hand, deep in thought. "Now you've got to come with me, and I'm not taking no for an answer. Hop into the wagon." With a firm arm between her shoulder blades, he shooed her out the door.

"I should run down to the river and let the others know."

"They'll be fine without you for a while. Miss Clementine will know you're with me."

She climbed up her side of the buckboard, leaning close to his warm body as he hiked up beside her. The springs of the seat rocked them.

"Where are you taking me?"

"Somewhere special." He flicked the reins and the horse pulled out.

"But where?"

He laughed. "You'll have to sit back and *trust* me."

Chapter Eighteen

"It's been a hectic three days," Tom said, halfway to town.

Feeling hot beneath her bonnet, Amanda watched the sunlight stream around his black Stetson. It created deep shadows across the front folds of his blue shirt. Her gaze lingered on his profile. "We need to talk about...about what's going on between us."

With one hand holding the reins, he pushed up one sleeve over his elbow, then the other. The light bounced around his wrists, the dark glistening hairs and the sinewy muscles of his forearms.

"There's so much I want to say to you, too, but if you'll just indulge me for another hour, I promise we'll find a quiet corner and talk then. There's someone...something... I want you to do first."

She looked straight ahead at the rutted, pebbled road, clasping her hands around her skirted knees. "All right." What was it he wanted her to do?

Tom brought her to the sawmill, and she was happy to see it. It looked different from the charring of three days ago. The sun was shining on the place, streaming down the plank walls. The two huge side doors, on sliding wheels, sat wide open, exposing the cleaned-out interior. Men were carrying several new planks of lumber inside. Outside in the yards, a dozen more men were sawing and chopping green lumber.

The place looked alive with growing business, new deals, and the simple jubilation of surviving the fire.

"It looks wonderful," Amanda breathed.

"It does, doesn't it?" Tom said with pride.

Looking up the hill, she noticed the two tourists from Scotland leaving Tom's cabin in their hats and jackets. They weren't carrying any bags. When they waved in their direction, Tom and Amanda waved back.

"They're going hiking," Tom said. "For the day."

"Aren't you going to make them leave your cabin, now that it's yours again?"

Tom stepped down from his side of the wagon and strode over to her. He held out his hand, and she gladly took it, reveling in the warm contact.

"Their original deal with the bank was that they could stay for two more weeks. I can wait it out till then. After all, during the fire, they were the ones who ran for the Mounties." He tugged her down. "After you knocked on their door."

She jumped to her feet beside him, but he didn't let go of her hand. He stroked his thumb across her knuckles. Of course Tom would let them stay. If there was one thing she was certain of, it was that he was a fair man.

"Howdy, Tom!" one of his men shouted.

Tom let go of Amanda and lifted his hat in salute.

His foreman, Patrick, walked by. "How ya doin' this mornin', Amanda?"

"Feeling pretty good," she answered.

Tom clamped his hand possessively across her back as he led her toward the building. "By the way, I spoke to

Graham. He says your legal deed should make its way here within two weeks.''

Her mouth opened in delight. ''Two weeks?''

Tom broke into a smile. It lit up his eyes. ''That's all.''

''Oh…'' She clasped her fingers together, eager to show him how she felt about that, but very aware that they weren't alone. When *would* they be alone?

''Is that why you brought me here?''

''Nope.''

She swirled around and lifted her arms to the sky. ''Did you bring me here to show me the mill?''

''Nope.''

''Then what?''

''I brought you here to meet someone.''

''Who?'' she asked, looking around.

''Come wait inside, and I'll be back in ten minutes.''

''More waiting?''

''It's the last time, I promise.''

Her curiosity was bounding, but she obeyed. He escorted her into the sawmill, told her to wait right there, then walked out the front door.

She peered out the window behind him, untying the ribbon that held her bonnet beneath her chin. He was walking somewhere. What on earth was he up to? Did he want her to meet another family member? Was Gabe in town?

Strolling down the room, she slid her fingers down the well-sanded curve of a worktable, enjoying the smooth feel of wood beneath her fingertips. Above her head, the rows of water pails were again in place; probably the first thing Tom had done after the fire.

She thought of the first day she'd arrived here, meeting Tom on that May morning in the rain. How preoccupied he'd been with his letter from Clarissa, how preoccupied she'd been with her problems with William. Tom had brought about a big change in her, and her life was moving in a wonderful direction.

The door clicked unexpectedly, breaking into her thoughts, giving her a little jolt. With a gentle laugh, she rushed to it to open it for Tom. Through the window, he looked as though he was alone, but when he stepped in past her, he was carrying a little reed basket.

There was a baby inside.

She stepped back in surprise.

Tom removed his Stetson. "Do you recognize this little tyke?"

She leaned over the bundled, sleeping baby and smiled. "I recognize the wide little nose. He's got Quaid's nose. And those tiny pointy lips, they're Beth's."

"Right again."

Her hands felt suddenly clammy. She wiped them down her skirt. "He's the person you wanted me to meet?"

Tom held the reed basket gently in his arms. "I was watching you the other night, during Beth's delivery. You looked like…I just thought you might like to…away from everyone's stare…"

If there was ever any doubt, she knew now that she loved this man. Her throat clamped with hot tears.

Tom spoke for her. "Quaid understands about your situation…and so does Beth. They're both so concerned about you, Amanda, I hope you don't mind that I told them."

She nodded softly. She didn't mind. Quaid and Beth were her beloved friends, and she knew they'd keep her private matters to themselves.

Her voice was raw. "Have they named him, yet?"

"Quaid's waiting until Beth gains some strength."

Tom peered from the baby's sleeping face to Amanda's. "When was the last time you held a baby?"

She blinked. She took a deep breath and watched the baby's mouth twitching in deep sleep. "Not for a long time," she whispered. She swallowed hard and took a moment to say it. "I never got to hold Sharon Rose."

She heard Tom's intake of breath.

He bundled the baby into one of his long arms, balancing the basket with the other. Directing Amanda to the back room, his bedroom, he left the door wide open for the sunshine and the breeze to wrap around them.

When she sank into a Windsor chair, Tom placed the baby in her arms.

It felt wonderful to hold the moving child, a warm bundle of firm legs and clear, pink skin. He smelled wonderful, too, a combination of soap and milk. She rocked him gently, humming softly in the fresh air. Holding him didn't sadden her, it lifted her spirits and made her happy. She thought of Sharon Rose, and where she was in heaven, and wondered when it was Amanda's time to leave the earth, if they'd ever meet again.

With a silent nod, Tom left, allowing her the privacy of her thoughts. She felt protected here in the cocoon of Tom's room, his belongings scattered in every corner. She was safe. She didn't need a large space with Tom, she realized, she'd be happy with a little corner they could call their own.

When Tom came back half an hour later, he asked, "Is it time to take him home?"

She sighed. "I think so. He's waking up. I think he's hungry. Look how he's stuffing his fist into his mouth." They both looked down, fascinated with everything the baby did.

Gazing up at Tom, Amanda added, "I don't know how it is, but you always seem to know what I need."

* * *

Mrs. Garvey answered the door when Tom and Amanda knocked, baby basket in hand. With a welcoming smile, she shooed them inside, trying to close the door behind them before the flies got in.

In the back room of the parlor, Beth was sitting up in bed, looking pink and rested. She smiled when she saw them, and by her relaxed state, Amanda deduced she must have just received her morphine. Although it made the baby drowsy after breastfeeding, Beth would be in severe pain without it.

Beth's braided hair fell across her plump shoulders. For the first time in days she was out of her nightclothes and wearing a daytime frock. She stretched her arms out for the basket when she spotted it. "There he is."

"Thank you for letting us borrow him," said Amanda, taking the bundle out of the basket from where Tom had placed it on the bed, and settling him into his mother's awaiting arms.

Beth cuddled him to her breast. "It's my pleasure."

The baby smacked his lips, more vigorous now that he'd been earlier, causing the women to laugh.

"Do you need help getting him to your breast?" asked Amanda, ignoring Tom's look of male discomfort.

"Nah, I'll be fine."

"We'll leave you then, and let you attend to him."

Beth reached out and grasped Amanda's hand. "How are you feelin'?"

Amanda gazed into the woman's soft features, knowing what Beth was asking. "Much better, now that I've held your baby. Thank you."

"It was Tom's idea," Beth answered.

Amanda looked at him, lean and tanned, standing tall at the foot of Beth's bed.

The baby whimpered. Beth rocked him, making an apologetic face to her guests. "We'll talk later."

Amanda nodded and she and Tom left the room, escaping outside to the boardwalk. "Where to?"

He took her hand and started walking. "Follow me."

He was holding her hand in public and not letting go. It was a strange sensation, walking down the street with Tom at her side, his hand a symbol of his claim. *On her.* She'd never had anyone display his affection in public before. It felt right. *He* felt right.

"Tom," yelled Ruby across the road. "I need to talk to you about where to set that load of lumber—"

"Later!" he shouted back with a grin.

"Tom," someone else hollered on the other side of the street. "I was out of town, but I heard what happened to your mill. If there's anything I can do—"

"Thanks, Mr. Abbott, I'll catch up with you tomorrow!"

The mercantile door swung open onto their path and Mr. Langston came walking out backward, holding a stack of rakes that he was adding to the ones already for sale by the door. His sprained wrist—not broken—was still bandaged. "Amanda, hello. I've got a payment to give you, on account of my daughter—"

She slowed down, but Tom gave her a friendly tug to speed her along.

"It'll have to wait till later, sir," she said, whizzing by. "We're just on our way…" To where? she wondered.

"For an important meeting," Tom finished for her.

They crossed the dry, cracked ground, leaving the buildings of town and heading up toward the big hotel.

"If we don't find a spot soon where we can be alone for a few minutes," Tom declared, "I think I'm going to walk into that saloon, drag out a table and two chairs and plunk them in the middle of the road. We'll sit there for as long as it takes for me to tell you what's on my mind. To hell with interruptions.''

She laughed in the warm sunshine, looking up the winding mountain road with its hues of green foliage, tiny yellow mountain flowers and chirping chickadees.

It dawned on her. ''I think I know where you're taking me.'' He was leading her to his favorite place.

''Well, don't say it out loud, or we'll have a hundred people following us with one more question they need answered.''

It took them another fifteen minutes to reach it, hidden in the mountainside, overlooking the town. All the way here, her stomach was turning in flip-flops, remembering the last time she was here with Tom. Making love in the wild open.

They stepped inside their hidden circle. It looked different in the sunshine compared to the evening, but as luscious and secluded. Raspberries grew in clumps on the south side of the hill, while pines pressed against each other on the north. The scent was heavenly.

Tom wheeled her around. She looked up, saw the sentiment in his eyes, and her heart lurched.

He took a moment to catch his breath and study her. ''How do you feel about me, Amanda?''

''I think it's time I showed you.''

She reached up on tiptoe, weaving her fingers through the back of his unruly hair, letting them slide over the dewy, soft skin she found there, and touched her lips to his.

He groaned with satisfaction and tugged her closer, wrapping his burly arms around her back and waist. He dragged his fingertips over her spine, setting her skin atingle.

Breaking free of his controlling mouth, she murmured, "I'm in love with you."

A corner of his lips tugged high and he gave her that dimpled grin she loved so much. "What did I just hear?"

She ducked out of his grasp and fled behind the trunk of a pine. "You heard me."

"Come here and say it to my face."

"I can't," she teased.

"Why not?"

"I'm afraid you might…bite me."

"I will," he promised with a flourish. "You know I will." He dashed around the tree, but she slipped out of reach behind another. "Rrrr…." he muttered in mock frustration.

She kept her eyes on him, knowing how quick he was, expecting him to leap at any moment like a tiger hunting his prey. *She* was his prey this time, and she delighted in that fact.

"You're provoking me, Amanda, and you're getting me hot and riled. When I catch you, you better watch out…"

She laughed with wild abandon. "Don't you find it hot up here?" She flung her shawl into the air. "I need to remove some of this."

"Huh?" he said, catching it.

Next came her bonnet. As she tossed it to the tree he stood behind, her hair tumbled down her shoulders. He leaped out, sliding into the grass to dive for it, but missed altogether and landed in a heap.

She stepped over him as she raced behind a bush. She cocked her eyebrow with amusement. "It's that darned hot sun, beating down on us, making me swelter. And these heavy clothes."

While he watched, she unbuttoned her blouse, knowing

full well that it exposed her corset and the top of her breasts.

"Dammit, Amanda, come here," he said, gulping from his corner.

"Oh-hh, I couldn't do that." She slid her blouse off her shoulders, languishing in the heat.

He dropped his chin with a contented sigh. Lying in the grass, he turned his body to face her, propping his head on his palm as he watched with heated rapture.

"Should I charge you admission for this performance?"

"I'll pay anything you ask."

"There you go, overextending yourself again."

He laughed, then grew thoughtful. "Do you know that I love you?"

She basked in the knowledge, letting her gaze mingle with his for a long, serious moment, letting herself marvel in the sheer joy the words brought.

"Well," she said, smiling again. "For that, I suppose I should reward you."

"Please do. Feel free to reward me in any way you feel is fair."

"Ah, I think at least one breast is in order."

His eyes widened in glorious shock.

Sliding out of her blouse, she unhooked the corset's laces until the corset was completely free down the middle. With no hesitation, she opened it to reveal her bare left side.

His eyes dropped from her face to her jiggling bosom. "Amanda, come here...."

"I'm not done yet," she said, revealing the other side. The heat on her bare nipples felt extraordinary.

Both of his brows shot up at what she was doing. His face flushed. He pressed his hands into the grass, but before he could run at her, she tossed the corset to him and jumped away.

"Now it's your turn," she instructed.

"What?"

"I'd like you to stand up and take off your clothes. One at a time."

His mouth dropped and he laughed. "It's one surprise after another with you. You want me to strip for you?"

"Just like you asked me the other night. I'd like nothing better."

He tossed off his Stetson.

"Hats don't count," she said.

"Do you want me to leave it on?"

She nodded and giggled. "I think I'd like to see you naked with nothing on but your hat."

Trying to stifle his laughter, he planted the hat back on his head, then began unbuttoning his shirt.

Her pulse began to hammer beneath her breast. She took a heady breath of air as he unpeeled his shirt, revealing acres of tanned skin and softly curled dark hair.

Fighting with his denim pants, his body twisted and turned, his biceps rippling with his graceful movements.

As soon as he unbuttoned the line of buttons at his crotch, she felt her muscles heat. A bead of perspiration drizzled down her temple, beneath her heavy hair, trailing down her throat and down between her jutting breasts.

Stepping out of his boots, then pants and underwear, he stood on the grassy hill across from her, naked and beautiful, with such yearning in his eyes she felt it in her heart.

When he came toward her, enveloping her in his arms, his bare flesh pressed against hers. His hard shaft met with the cloth on her hips. He swooped her up and pressed her to the ground beneath him, trapping each of her wrists against the grass.

Desire welled up inside of her, making her shiver, hardening her nipples and pooling the moisture between her thighs.

He kissed her eyelids, grazed her lips then worked down her throat to her breasts. He kissed one nipple, then the other.

"Is this what you want?"

"More," she answered.

He bracketed his palms against the sides of her breasts, letting his tongue trail a path over one circle, down beneath the undercurve of her creamy breast. His gentle probing tickled down her soft stomach till she nearly screamed.

Undoing the button at her waistline, he slid her skirt over her hips, then tugged off her bloomers.

"I want a life with you, Amanda. I want to wake up beside you every morning and know that you're my wife."

She listened to him say it.

He continued. "Do you believe me when I say I've thought about our future, and I've worked it out in my heart?"

She nodded. "I love you for telling me."

His voice grew husky. "I can live without children of my own, Amanda, but I can't live without you."

His mouth throbbed with passion; a knot rose in her throat. For the first time in a long, long time, she was happy to be who she was.

Grasping his fingers between her own, she lifted them up to her lips and kissed. "Not too long ago, I thought I'd be alone for the rest of my life. You don't make me feel alone anymore. Let me love you, Tom."

His look was so rooted in hers, a shudder passed through her. She felt his flesh shiver next to hers.

He surrendered to her seduction, and she to his. They

lost themselves in exploration, he still wearing his hat, she searing a path down his neck. Together, they culminated in the ultimate union, and the sweet, delicious promise of many years ahead.

Epilogue

Five years later

Tom sank himself into the comfortable chair on the porch, swung his booted feet over the cedar railing, took a sip of ice-cold lemonade and scrutinized his little slice of paradise.

Josh, now nine and tall for his age, joined the neighbors' children, who jumped and played among the trees, their delighted screeches echoing through the forest. The adults—a combination of family and neighbors—were fussing over the great meal they'd prepared for Canada's July First Dominion Day. Amanda would be back from her call at any minute to join them all for Saturday lunch.

Tom tugged his hat low over his brow and sipped again. Ice was a marvelous thing in this summer heat, and next to Amanda's original root cellar, they'd built their own ice shack.

It wasn't part of Amanda's original plan, but then neither was this cabin. After they were married, he'd had to double it in size to allow for all the spare rooms. One for their daughter Margaux—who was now living down the road with her husband, Pierce O'Hara—another for their son

Josh, Miss Clementine's in the back, Amanda and Tom's in the front side, and of course, the large spare room for taking in more children when the need arose. It was empty at the moment, but Amanda had placed six more children and three babies in the homes of loving families since Margaux and Josh had first stepped off the mud wagon.

Tom was mighty proud of her.

He swatted at a bee that hummed around his boots. Peering into the forest, he spotted Wolf doing what he loved most—chasing groundhogs and fetching sticks for the youngsters. Sunset, preening her orange fur, was lying in the sunshine, big and fat and content.

Strolling around the corner into his view, Margaux and her young husband walked hand in hand, he carrying a bowl of something to add to the bowls already there, and she, waddling alongside him, nine months along and due any day now.

Tom watched his family, gazing at his beautiful adopted children. Tom couldn't love Margaux and Josh more if they were his own blood. He couldn't imagine a life without them. Or Amanda.

He heard a bell tinkle on the road, looked that way, then watched Amanda ride her bicycle toward him, pretending as if she was aiming to mow him down. He gave her a lazy nod and smiled beneath his hat.

Riding her bicycle had kept her slender, and she wore her wavy black hair more down than up these days, but it was the familiar spark of humor that he loved so much.

No, sir, life didn't get any better than this.

"Well, don't you look comfortable," she said.

"That's my job in life. Come join me."

"I think I will." She propped her bicycle in the rack he'd built, trying to balance it between the half-dozen other bicycles their guests had already placed there.

This one was different than her first. This one had pneumatic tires filled with air, not solid rubber. Thank goodness bicycles were mass-produced in factories now, so less pricey. Tom was able to get it for less than a hundred bucks.

Giving him a kiss on the cheek, Amanda fell into the chair beside him.

"Hey, what kind of a kiss was that?"

She glanced to the crowd. "You know we're in public."

"I don't care." He leaned over and planted a full, rich kiss on her lips, and she responded with the sweet sensuality with which she always did.

"Happy anniversary," he whispered against her lips.

She kissed him back. "I love you."

Folks didn't normally celebrate their anniversaries, so it was only Amanda and Tom who remembered the significance of the date. They were celebrating their fifth wedding anniversary, but most of the other folks here were celebrating Canada's birthday.

"It's about time you got back," said Miss Clementine, walking past them, down the front stoop with a tray of roasted potatoes. She was a little heavier than she used to be, but with the same youthful braids rolling down her back. Tom noticed that lately she'd upgraded her wardrobe and wore only the finest dresses, likely due to her bout of good fortune with her new bicycle shop.

Pa and Miss Clementine had become business partners. Two years ago, Tom had funded the opening, and they'd already paid him back. As owners of the only bicycle shop in Banff, they were amassing a small fortune selling and renting bicycles to the folks in town, especially to the wealthy tourists. Much to James Jefferson's dismay, his daughter Fannie had been their first customer.

"I was hopin' you wouldn't miss the party," Miss Clementine said to her granddaughter. "Everything go okay?"

"Just a routine checkup on a new mother," Amanda answered. "They're all fine."

"That's good."

Tom's pa stepped up to the stairs to help the older woman with her tray of potatoes. Pa still occasionally had his forgetful spells, but Tom was grateful they weren't getting any worse.

Peering over the railing, lifting her long-sleeved arm, Amanda waved at Beth and Quaid.

"Glad you could make it," Quaid hollered, cupping his hands over his neatly trimmed, short mustache. Beth patted his shoulder as she fussed around the dishes. She enjoyed running in a hundred different directions, she'd told them, eager and begging to help organize the big party. Under the tree beside them, their young boy, Timothy, was playing with Ellie O'Hara's five-year-old son, who Amanda had also safely delivered that same year.

Tom leaned back into his seat. If all went well, he'd be lucky enough to have his youngest brother living in Banff soon, along with the rest of them. Just last week, Gabe had wired that he'd finished law school, soon to be joining them, bringing along his new bride. One from Nova Scotia, he'd written, as bonnie as they come. Everyone was eager to meet her.

Tom hadn't heard again from Zeb Finnigan. The Mounties had moved him to Toronto to serve his sentence, with the judge tacking on another eighteen months to his original five years for the three more men who'd arrived with an invalid deed. None of them had regained their money, but Frank Finnigan had at least received his brother's fine horse and saddle, and was able to buy back his small plot of farmland.

Tom felt great, seated here at Amanda's side. Too bad their secret place in the woods had been discovered by an enterprising fellow, who'd built a sprawling dining house and small hotel on it, but Tom and Amanda were having fun discovering new spots on the mountain. Ones where they could rest after a long day, share their private conversations and enjoy the spectacular view.

Josh came running over, interrupting Tom's train of thought. The boy's brown hair glistened with perspiration, his face red from running. "I'm hungry, Ma," he said. "Whaddya have that I can eat?"

"You're always hungry," said Amanda, playfully swatting him off the porch.

"Aw, come on," said Josh, pronouncing each word with perfection. "How about one radish?"

"Well, then, go ask your sister. I saw her by the vegetable platter. She'll sneak you one."

"I'll sneak him one what?" Margaux's head peered from above their heads. With Pierce attentive at her side, she sat beside Amanda on the porch, struggling to get into position with her huge belly. Tom saw a lovely young woman when he looked at his daughter, one still protective of her brother. The freckles on her skin faded into a tan above her nose, and the wire-rim spectacles framed her pretty brown eyes.

"Your brother's hungry," Amanda said to her, moving close to Margaux. "I thought you were over by the food, but I guess you aren't. You can get the radish yourself, Josh."

"All right." Josh turned and ran toward the table.

"My troops," Amanda said, sighing and looking over her clan.

Tom wrapped his arm around her.

Men from the sawmill, and their wives and children, began pouring into the yard. Twenty men in total.

"They're having fireworks tonight at the big hotel," one of them shouted.

Tom glanced at Amanda and winked. "You don't say. Amanda and I love fireworks. We'll have to go out for a stroll later, won't we, sweetheart?"

Amanda gave him a soft smile. "Whatever do you mean?"

He grinned at their private plan.

"Hey," said Quaid. "Let's play kick ball."

With lots of laughter, they divided into two teams. The men against the women.

Tom was convinced the men just enjoyed watching their wives running through the grass in their long skirts and full blouses. A few of the bravest were following the latest fashions and no longer wore corsets.

"Too restrictive," Amanda had told him when she'd tossed hers. "We can't breathe, how hard they're squeezed against our ribs. Especially riding a horse, or gardening."

"Well, by all means, take it off," he'd told her, which caused her to toss a shoe in his direction.

She'd replaced it by a looser-fitting garment, shaped like a corset but without the whalebone strips, and laces pulled not quite so tight. He was still as mesmerized by her today as he was that first day they'd met.

When Amanda finished playing ball, she fell into a heap beside him.

Margaux groaned from the picnic table. Amanda was by her side in a flash. "What is it?"

"I think the lemonade went down the wrong way."

"Are you sure that's all it is?"

Amanda exchanged a concerned look with Tom. Was it time? Tom walked over to Margaux's side, trying to be tender and concealing his own fears for her labor. He recalled the day when Amanda had explained to him about Margaux's first menstruation. It felt as if it had only been yesterday.

Quaid noticed them and appeared beside Tom. Ellie O'Hara, the soon-to-be grandmother, strolled casually to join them.

"Ow-ww, there it goes again."

Amanda placed her hand on Margaux's firm abdomen. "It's a contraction, Margaux, normal and nothing to be afraid of. We'll time this one," she said.

"What can I do?" asked Pierce.

Ellie smiled and placed her slender arm across her son's shoulders. "Amanda will take good care of your wife. And Quaid is here, too, promisin' he'll help if you need it."

Twenty hours later, with all of them standing outside the door, Amanda delivered a healthy newborn girl.

Margaux gave her a long name; much too long, the men teased, but the women adored it. Jillian Amanda Rose O'Hara. Jillian after Margaux's cherished natural mother, Amanda after the mother Margaux had grown to love and respect as her own, and Rose, named after the little baby Amanda occasionally spoke so fondly of, when it was just between the two of them.

It made Amanda's eyes shimmer with love, and Tom knew, all was right with the world.

* * * * *

Author's Note

Although the characters and events in this novel are fictional, the story takes place in the real town of Banff, Alberta, with the backdrop of the Banff Springs Hotel, completed in 1888.

In 1926, when the original structure burned to the ground, it was replaced by the current steel and stone hotel, even more massive and magnificent than the first. William Cornelius Van Horne, the president and visionary of the Canadian Pacific Railway and its hotels, was later knighted for his achievements.

The park reserve, which is now called Banff National Park, has grown to many times its original size.

As businesses changed hands throughout the years, property disputes persisted.

Banff continues to be a thriving tourist destination, and will always be one of my favorite places.

COMING NEXT MONTH FROM

HARLEQUIN HISTORICALS®

- **TEMPTING A TEXAN**
  by **Carolyn Davidson,** author of THE TEXAN
  When beautiful nanny Carlinda Donnelly suddenly shows up and
  tells the ambitious and wealthy Nicholas Garvey that he has custody
  of his five-year-old niece, he couldn't be more shocked. But before
  it's too late, will Nicholas realize that love and family are more
  important than financial success?
  HH #647 ISBN# 29247-3 $5.25 U.S./$6.25 CAN.

- **THE SILVER LORD**
  by **Miranda Jarrett,** book one in *The Lordly Claremonts* trilogy
  Behind a facade of propriety as a housekeeper, Fan Winslow leads
  an outlaw life as the leader of a notorious smuggling gang. Captain
  Lord George Claremont is an aristocratic navy hero who lives by his
  honor and loyalty to the king. Can love and passion join such dis-
  parate lovers?
  HH #648 ISBN# 29248-1 $5.25 U.S./$6.25 CAN.

- **THE ANGEL OF DEVIL'S CAMP**
  by **Lynna Banning,** author of THE COURTSHIP
  Southern belle Meggy Hampton goes to an Oregon logging camp
  to marry a man she has never met, but her future is turned upside
  down when her fiancé dies in an accident. Without enough money
  to travel home, Meggy has no choice but to stay in Devil's Camp,
  even if it means contending with Tom Randall—the stubborn and
  unwelcoming log camp boss who's too handsome for his own good!
  HH #649 ISBN# 29249-X $5.25 U.S./$6.25 CAN.

- **BRIDE OF THE TOWER**
  by **Sharon Schulze,** the latest in the *l'Eau Clair* series
  On his way to deliver a missive, Sir William Bowman is attacked by
  brigands. More warrior than woman, Lady Julianna d'Arcy rescues
  him and nurses him back to health. Julianna suspects the handsome
  knight may be allied with her enemy, but she can't deny the attraction between them....
  HH #650 ISBN# 29250-3 $5.25 U.S./$6.25 CAN.

KEEP AN EYE OUT FOR ALL FOUR
OF THESE TERRIFIC NEW TITLES

KATE BRIDGES

is fascinated by the romantic tales of the spirited men and women who tamed the West. She's thrilled to be writing for Harlequin Historicals.

Growing up in rural Canada, Kate developed a love of people watching and reading all types of fiction, although romance was her favorite. She embarked on a career as a neonatal intensive care nurse, then moved on to architecture. Later, working in television production, she began crafting novels of her own. Currently living in the bustling city of Toronto, she and her husband love to go to movies and travel.